BY MARY HIGGINS CLARK

The Magical Christmas Horse (Illustrated by Wendell Minor)
I'll Walk Alone
The Shadow of Your Smile
Just Take My Heart
Where Are You Now?
Ghost Ship (Illustrated by Wendell Minor)
I Heard That Song Before
Two Little Girls in Blue
No Place Like Home
Nighttime Is My Time
The Second Time Around
Kitchen Privileges
Mount Vernon Love Story
Silent Night / All Through the Night
Daddy's Little Girl
On the Street Where You Live
Before I Say Good-bye
We'll Meet Again
All Through the Night
You Belong to Me
Pretend You Don't See Her
My Gal Sunday
Moonlight Becomes You
Silent Night
Let Me Call You Sweetheart
The Lottery Winner
Remember Me
I'll Be Seeing You
All Around the Town
Loves Music, Loves to Dance
The Anastasia Syndrome and Other Stories
While My Pretty One Sleeps
Weep No More, My Lady

MARY
HIGGINS
CLARK

The
Lost Years

Simon & Schuster

New York   London   Toronto   Sydney   New Delhi

Simon & Schuster
1230 Avenue of the Americas
New York, NY 10020

First Simon & Schuster hardcover edition April 2012

For information about special discounts for bulk purchases, please contact Simon & Schuster Special Sales at 1-866-506-1949 or business@simonandschuster.com.

The Simon & Schuster Speakers Bureau can bring authors to your live event. For more information or to book an event, contact the Simon & Schuster Speakers Bureau at 1-866-248-3049 or visit our website at www.simonspeakers.com.

Designed by Jill Putorti

Manufactured in the United States of America

10 9 8 7 6 5 4 3 2 1

ISBN 978-1-4516-6886-5
ISBN 978-1-4516-8893-3 (ebook)

Acknowledgments

To say writing a book is a long journey is entirely true. To say that it would be a two-thousand-year trip is quite different. When Michael Korda, my editor, suggested that it would be interesting to have a biblical background to this story and that it should be about a letter written by Christ, I shook my head.

But the possibility kept nagging, and the words "suppose" and "what if?" kept jumping into my mind. I started writing and four months later realized I didn't like the way I was telling the tale.

No matter how experienced you are as a writer, it doesn't mean that the story always unfolds the way you had envisioned. I tossed those pages and began again.

My joyous thanks to Michael, my editor, mentor, and dear friend for all these years. We've already booked our celebration lunch. During it, I know what will happen. Over a glass of wine, his eyes will become speculative and he will say, "I was thinking . . ." Meaning here we go again.

My in-house editor, Kathy Sagan, is great. I knew she was busy with her own long list of authors, but having worked with her on our mystery magazine, I knew just how valuable she is and requested her. This is our second novel together. Thank you, Kathy.

Thanks to the team inside Simon & Schuster who turn a manuscript into a book: Production Manager John Wahler, Associate

Director of Copyediting Gypsy da Silva, Designer Jill Putorti, and Art Director Jackie Seow for her wonderful cover design.

My home team of rooters, Nadine Petry, Agnes Newton, and Irene Clark are always there. Cheers and thanks.

Love abiding to John Conheeney, spouse extraordinaire. Can't believe we just celebrated our fifteenth wedding anniversary. It does truly seem like yesterday. Here's to all our tomorrows sharing love and laughter with our children and grandchildren and friends.

To all of you my readers, I do hope you enjoy this new tale. As I've quoted before from that wonderful ancient parchment, "The book is finished. Let the writer rejoice!"

Cheers and Blessings,
Mary Higgins Clark

In memory of my dear brother-in-law and friend,
Kenneth John Clark
Beloved husband, father, grandfather, and great-grandfather
And
"The Unc"
To his devoted nieces and nephews
We loved you deeply
Rest in Peace

Prologue

1474 A.D.

In the hushed quiet as late shadows fell over the walls of the eternal city of Rome, an elderly monk, his shoulders bent, made his silent and unobtrusive way into the Biblioteca Secreta, one of the four rooms that comprised the Vatican Library. The Library contained a total of 2,527 manuscripts written in Latin, Greek, and Hebrew. Some were available under strict supervision to be read by outsiders. Others were not.

The most controversial of the manuscripts was the one known as both the Joseph of Arimathea parchment and the Vatican letter. Carried by Peter the Apostle to Rome, it was believed by many to be the only letter ever written by the Christ.

It was a simple letter thanking Joseph for the kindness he had extended from the time Joseph had first heard Him preaching at the Temple in Jerusalem when He was only twelve years old. Joseph had believed He was the long-awaited Messiah.

When King Herod's son had discovered that this profoundly wise and learned child had been born in Bethlehem, he'd ordered the young Christ's assassination. Hearing this, Joseph had rushed to Nazareth and received permission from the boy's parents to take

Him to Egypt so that He could be safe and could study at the temple of Leontopolis near the Nile Valley.

The next eighteen years of the life of Jesus Christ are lost to history. Nearing the end of His ministry, foreseeing that the last kindness Joseph would offer Him would be his own tomb for Him to rest in, Christ had written a letter expressing gratitude to His faithful friend.

Over the centuries some of the Popes had believed that it was genuine. Others had not. The Vatican librarian had learned that the current Pope, Sixtus IV, was contemplating having it destroyed.

The assistant librarian had been awaiting the arrival of the monk in the Biblioteca Secreta. His eyes deeply troubled, he handed him the parchment. "I do this under the direction of His Eminence Cardinal del Portego," he said. "The sacred parchment must not be destroyed. Hide it well in the monastery and do not let anyone know of its contents."

The monk took the parchment, reverently kissed it, and then enfolded it in the protection of the sleeves of his flowing robe.

The letter to Joseph of Arimathea did not appear again until over five hundred years later when this story begins.

1

Today is the day of my father's funeral. He was murdered.

That was the first thought twenty-eight-year-old Mariah Lyons had as she awoke from a fitful sleep in the home where she had been raised in Mahwah, a town bordering the Ramapo Mountains in northern New Jersey. Brushing back the tears that were welling in her eyes, she sat up slowly, slid her feet onto the floor, and looked around her room.

When she was sixteen, she had been allowed to redecorate it as a birthday present and had chosen to have the walls painted red. For the coverlet and pillows and valances she had decided on a cheery red-and-white flowered pattern. The big, comfortable chair in the corner was where she always did her homework, instead of at the desk. Her eyes fell upon the shelf that her father had built over the dresser to hold her trophies from her high school soccer and basketball championship teams. He was so proud of me, she thought sadly. He wanted to redecorate again when I finished college, but I never wanted it changed. I don't care if it still has the look of a teenager's room.

She tried to remind herself that until now she had been one of those fortunate people whose only experience with death in the family had been when she was fifteen and her eighty-six-year-old grandmother had passed away in her sleep. I really loved Gran, but I was so grateful that she had been spared a lot of indignity, she thought. Her strength was failing and she hated to be dependent on anyone.

Mariah stood up, reached for the robe at the foot of the bed, and slipped into it, tying the sash around her slender waist. But this is different, she thought. My father did not die a natural death. He was shot while he was reading at his desk in his study downstairs. Her mouth went dry as she asked herself again the same questions she had been asking over and over. Was Mom in the room when it happened? Or did she come in after she heard the sound of the shot? And is there any chance that Mom was the one who did it? Please, God, don't let it turn out to be that way.

She walked over to the vanity and looked into the mirror. I look so pale, she thought as she brushed back her shoulder-length black hair. Her eyes were swollen from all the tears of the last few days. An incongruous thought went through her mind: I'm glad I have Daddy's dark blue eyes. I'm glad I'm tall like him. It sure helped when I was playing basketball.

"I can't believe he is gone," she whispered, recalling his seventieth birthday party only three weeks earlier. The events of the past four days replayed in her mind. On Monday evening she had stayed at her office to work out an investment plan for a new client. When she got home to her Greenwich Village apartment at eight o'clock, she had made her usual evening call to her father. Daddy sounded very down, she remembered. He told me that Mom had had a terrible day, that it was clear the Alzheimer's was getting worse. Something made me phone back at ten thirty. I was worried about both of them.

When Daddy didn't answer, I knew that something was wrong. Mariah thought back to that seemingly endless drive from Greenwich Village as she had rushed to New Jersey that night. I called them again and again on the way over, she thought. She remembered how she had turned into the driveway at eleven twenty, fumbling for her house key in the dark as she ran from the car. All the downstairs lights were still on in the house, and once she was inside, she went straight to the study.

The horror of what she had found replayed in her mind as it had been doing incessantly. Her father was slumped across his desk, his head and shoulders bloodied. Her mother, soaked in blood, was cowering in the closet near the desk, clutching her father's pistol.

Mom saw me and started moaning, "So much noise . . . so much blood . . . "

I was frantic, Mariah remembered. When I called 911, all I could scream was "My father is dead! My father has been shot!"

The police arrived in minutes. I'll never forget how they looked at Mom and me. I had hugged Daddy, so I had blood all over me too. I overheard one of the cops say that by touching Daddy I had contaminated the crime scene.

Mariah realized she had been staring unseeingly into the mirror. Glancing down at the clock on the vanity she saw that it was already seven thirty. I have to get ready, she thought. We should be at the funeral parlor by nine. I hope Rory is getting Mom ready by now. Rory Steiger, a stocky sixty-two-year-old woman, had been her mother's caregiver for the past two years.

Twenty minutes later, showered and her hair blown dry, Mariah came back into the bedroom, opened the door of the closet, and took out the black-and-white jacket and black skirt she had chosen to wear to the funeral. People used to be draped in black when there was a death in the family, she thought. I remember seeing pictures of Jackie Kennedy in a long mourning veil. Oh God, why did this have to happen?

When she was finished dressing, she walked over to the window. She had left it open when she had gone to bed and the breeze was making the curtains ripple on the sill. She stood for a moment looking out over the backyard, which was shaded by the Japanese maple trees her father had planted years ago. The begonias and impatiens he had planted in the spring ringed the patio. The sun made the Ramapo Mountains in the distance shimmer with tones of green and gold. It was a perfect late August day.

I don't want it to be a beautiful day, Mariah thought. It's as if nothing terrible has happened. But it *has* happened. Daddy was murdered. I want it to be rainy and cold and wet. I want the rain to weep on his casket. I want the heavens to weep for him.

He is gone forever.

Guilt and sadness enveloped her. That gentle college professor who was so glad to retire three years ago and spend most of his time studying ancient manuscripts had been violently murdered. I loved him dearly, but it's so awful that for the last year and a half our relationship has been strained, all because of his affair with Lillian Stewart, the professor he met from Columbia University, whose very existence had changed all of our lives.

Mariah remembered her dismay when she came home a year and a half ago to find her mother holding pictures she had found of Lillian and her father with their arms around each other. I was so angry when I realized that this had probably been going on while Lily was with him on his archaeological digs to Egypt or Greece or Israel or God knows where, for the past five years. I was so furious that he actually had her in the house when we had his other friends, like Richard, Charles, Albert, and Greg, over for dinner.

I despise that woman, Mariah told herself.

The fact that my father was twenty years her senior apparently did not bother Lily, Mariah thought grimly. I've tried to be fair and understand.

Mom has been drifting away for years, and I know it was so tough on Dad to see her deteriorate. But she still has her somewhat good days. She still talks about those pictures so often. She was so hurt knowing that Dad had someone else in his life.

I don't want to be thinking like this, Mariah said to herself as she turned away from the window. I want my father to be alive. I want to tell him how sorry I am that I asked him only last week if Lily of the Nile Valley had been a good traveling companion on their latest jaunt to Greece.

Turning away from the window, she walked over to the desk and studied a picture of her mother and father taken ten years ago. I remember how loving they used to be with each other, Mariah thought. They were married when they were in graduate school.

I didn't make my appearance for fifteen years.

She smiled faintly as she remembered her mother telling her that as long as they had had to wait, God had given them the perfect child. Actually, Mom was being more than generous, she thought. Both of them were so strikingly handsome. And elegant. And charming. Growing up I certainly was no head-turner. A mop of long, straight black hair, so skinny that I looked undernourished, beanpole tall, and teeth that I grew into but were too big for my face when they first arrived. But I was lucky enough to end up being a decent composite of both of them.

Dad, Daddy, please don't be dead. Be at the breakfast table when I get there. Have your coffee cup in hand, and be reading the *Times* or the *Wall Street Journal*. I'll grab the *Post* and turn to "Page Six," and you'll look over your glasses and give me that look that means a mind is a dreadful thing to waste.

I don't want to eat anything, I'll just have coffee, Mariah decided as she opened the door of the bedroom and walked down the hall to the staircase. She paused on the top step but didn't hear any sound from the connecting bedrooms where her mother and Rory slept. I hope that means they're downstairs, she thought.

There was no sign of them in the breakfast room. She went into the kitchen. Betty Pierce, the housekeeper, was there. "Mariah, your mother wouldn't eat anything. She wanted to go into the study. I don't think you'll like what she's wearing but she's pretty insistent. It's that blue and green linen suit you bought her for Mother's Day."

Mariah considered protesting but then asked herself, What in the name of God is the difference? She took the coffee that Betty poured for her and carried it into the study. Rory was standing there looking distressed. At Mariah's unasked question she jerked her head toward the closet door. "She won't let me leave the door open," she said. "She won't let me stay in there with her."

Mariah tapped on the closet door and opened it slowly while murmuring her mother's name. Oddly sometimes her mother answered to it more easily than when Mariah called her "Mom." "Kathleen," she said softly. "Kathleen, it's time to have a cup of tea and a cinnamon bun."

The closet was large, with shelves on either side. Kathleen Lyons was sitting on the floor at the far end of it. Her arms were wrapped protectively around her body and her head was pressed against her chest as though she was bracing for a blow. Her eyes were shut tight and her silver hair was falling forward, covering most of her face. Mariah knelt down and embraced her, rocking her as if she was a child.

"So much noise . . . so much blood," her mother whispered, the same words she had been repeating since the murder. But then she did let Mariah help her up and smooth back the short, wavy hair from her pretty face. Again Mariah was reminded that her mother had been only a few months younger than her father and would not look her age if it weren't for the fearful way she moved, as though at any minute she could step into an abyss.

As Mariah led her mother out of the study she did not see the baleful expression on the face of Rory Steiger or the secret smile she permitted herself.

Now I won't be stuck with her much longer, Rory thought.

2

Detective Simon Benet of the Bergen County Prosecutor's office had the look of a man who spent a lot of time outdoors. He was in his midforties, with thinning sandy hair and a ruddy complexion. The jacket of his suit was always wrinkled because the minute he didn't have to wear it, he tossed it over a chair or in the backseat of the car.

His partner, Detective Rita Rodriguez, was a trim Hispanic woman in her late thirties with stylishly short brown hair. Always impeccably dressed, she made an incongruous counterpart to Benet. In fact they were a top-notch investigative team, and they had been assigned to the Jonathan Lyons murder case.

They were the first to arrive at the funeral parlor on Friday morning. On the theory that if an intruder had been responsible for the murder, he or she might come here to view the victim, they were on the watch for anyone whom they might recognize as a potential suspect. They had studied the pictures of convicted felons who were now on parole but had been involved in break-ins in the surrounding communities.

Anyone who has gone through this kind of day knows what it's all about, Rodriguez thought. There were flowers galore, even though she knew that in the obituary it had been requested that, in lieu of them, donations be made to the local hospital.

The funeral parlor began to fill up well before nine o'clock. The

detectives knew that some of the people there had come out of mor-
bid curiosity—Rodriguez could spot them in an instant. They stood
at the casket for an unnecessarily long time searching for any sign of
trauma on the face of the deceased. But Jonathan Lyons's expression
was peaceful and the artistry of the cosmetician at the funeral home
had successfully hidden any bruising that might have occurred.

For the past three days they had been ringing the doorbells of
the neighbors in the hope that someone might have heard the shot
or observed someone running from the house after the bullet was
fired. The investigation had come to nothing. The closest neighbors
were away on vacation, and no one else had heard or seen anything
unusual.

Mariah had given them the names of the people who were very
close to her father and in whom he might have confided if he had
been having any kind of problem.

"Richard Callahan, Charles Michaelson, Albert West, and Greg
Pearson have gone on all of Dad's annual archaeological trips for at
least six years," she had told them. "All of them come to our house
for dinner about once a month. Richard is a professor of Bible stud-
ies at Fordham University. Charles and Albert are also professors.
Greg is a successful businessman. His company has something to
do with computer software." And then, her anger clearly showing,
Mariah had also given them the name of Lillian Stewart, her father's
mistress.

These were the people the detectives wanted to meet and set up
appointments to interview. Benet had requested that the caregiver,
Rory Steiger, identify them when they arrived.

At twenty minutes of nine, Mariah, her mother, and Rory entered the funeral parlor. Even though the detectives had been in her
home twice in the past few days, Kathleen Lyons stared vacantly at
them. Mariah nodded to them and went to stand by the casket and
greet the visitors who were already passing by it.

The detectives chose a spot nearby where they could clearly see their faces and how they interacted with Mariah.

Rory got Kathleen settled on a seat in the front row, then joined them. Unobtrusive in her black-and-white print dress, her graying hair pulled back into a bun, Rory stood behind the detectives. She tried not to show that she was nervous about assisting them. She could not stop thinking that the only reason she had taken this job two years ago was because of Joe Peck, the sixty-five-year-old widower in the same apartment complex she lived in on the Upper West Side of Manhattan.

She had been going out for dinner regularly with Joe, a retired fireman who had a home in Florida. Joe had confided to her how lonely he had been since his wife died, and Rory had built up her hopes that he was going to ask her to marry him. Then one evening he told her that while he enjoyed their occasional dates, he had met someone else who was going to move in with him.

At dinner that night, angry and disappointed, Rory had told her best friend, Rose, that she would take the job she'd just been offered in New Jersey. "It pays well. It does mean I'll be stuck there from Monday to Friday, but no reason to come rushing home from a day job hoping Joe will call," Rory had said bitterly.

I never thought taking this job would lead to *this*, she thought. Then she spotted two men in their late sixties. "Just so you know," she whispered to Detectives Benet and Rodriguez, "those men are experts in Professor Lyons's field. They came to the house about once a month, and I know they used to talk on the phone a lot to Professor Lyons. The taller one is Professor Charles Michaelson. The other one is Dr. Albert West."

A minute later she tugged at Benet's sleeve. "Here are Callahan and Pearson," she said. "The girlfriend is with them."

Mariah's eyes widened when she saw who was coming. I didn't think that Lily of the Nile Valley would dare show up, she thought, even while unwillingly admitting to herself that Lillian Stewart was a very attractive woman, with chestnut hair and wide-set brown eyes. She was wearing a light gray linen suit with a white collar. I wonder how long she ransacked boutiques to find it, Mariah asked herself. It looks like the perfect mourning outfit for a mistress.

That's exactly the kind of crack I've been making to Dad about her, she thought remorsefully. And I asked him if she wears those high heels of hers when they're digging for ruins. Ignoring Stewart, Mariah reached out to clasp the hands of Greg Pearson and Richard Callahan. "Not the best day, is it?" she asked them.

The grief she saw in both their eyes was comforting. She knew how deeply these men had valued her father's friendship. Both in their midthirties and avid amateur archaeologists, they could not have been more different. Richard, a lean six feet four, with a full head of graying black hair, had a quick sense of humor. She knew that he had been in the seminary for one year and had not ruled out returning to it. He lived near Fordham University, where he taught.

Greg was exactly her height when she was wearing heels. His brown hair was close-cropped. His eyes, a light shade of gray-green, dominated his face. He always had a quiet deferential manner, and Mariah had wondered if despite his business success, Greg might be innately shy. Maybe that's one of the reasons he loved to be around Dad, she thought. Dad was truly a spellbinding raconteur.

She had gone on a few dates with Greg, but knowing she was not going to be interested in him in any romantic way and afraid he might be going in that direction, she hinted that she was seeing someone else and he never asked her out again.

The two men knelt by the casket for a moment. "No more long evenings with the storyteller," Mariah said as they stood up.

"It's so impossible to believe," Lily murmured.

Then Albert West and Charles Michaelson came over to where

she was standing. "Mariah, I'm so sorry. I can't believe it. It seems so sudden," Albert said.

"I know, I know," Mariah said as she looked at the four men, who had been so dear to her father. "Have the police talked to any of you yet? I had to give a list of close friends and of course that included all of you." Then she turned to Lily. "And needless to say I included your name."

Did I sense a sudden change in one of them in that instant? Mariah wondered. She couldn't be sure because at that moment the funeral director came in and asked people to walk past the casket for the last time, then go to their cars; it was time to leave for the church.

She waited with her mother till the others had left. She was relieved that Lily had had the decency not to touch her father's body. I think I would have tripped her if she had bent over to kiss him, she thought.

Her mother seemed totally unaware of what was going on. When Mariah led her over to the casket, she looked blankly down at the face of her dead husband and said, "I'm glad he washed his face. So much noise . . . so much blood."

Mariah turned her mother over to Rory, then stood by the casket herself. Daddy, you should have had another twenty years, she thought. Somebody is going to pay for doing this to you.

She leaned over and laid her cheek against his, then was sorry she had done so. That hard, cold flesh belonged to an object, not her father.

As she straightened up, she whispered, "I'll take good care of Mom, I promise you, I will."

3

Lillian Stewart had slipped into the back of the church after Jonathan's funeral Mass was under way. She left before the final prayers so there would be no chance of running into Mariah or her mother after the frosty reception she had just received at the funeral parlor. Then she drove to the cemetery, parked at a distance from the entrance, and waited until the funeral cortege had come and gone. It was only then that she drove along the road that led to Jonathan's grave site, got out of the car, and walked over to his freshly dug grave, carrying a dozen roses.

The grave diggers were about to lower the casket. They stood back respectfully as she knelt down, placed the roses on it, and whispered, "I love you, Jon." Then, pale but composed, she walked past the rows of tombstones to her car. Only when she was back inside the car did she let go and bury her face in her hands. The tears she had held back began to gush down her cheeks and her body shook with sobs.

A moment later, she heard the passenger door of her car open. Startled, she looked up, then made a futile attempt to wipe the tears from her face. Comforting arms went around her and held her until her sobs subsided. "I thought you might be here," Richard Callahan said. "I spotted you briefly in the back of the church."

Lily pulled away from him. "Dear God, is there any chance

Mariah or her mother saw me?" she asked, her voice husky and unsteady.

"I wouldn't think so. I was looking for you. I didn't know where you went after the funeral home. But you saw how packed the church was."

"Richard, it's awfully nice of you to think of me, but aren't you expected at that luncheon?"

"Yes, but I wanted to check on you first. I know how much Jonathan meant to you."

Lillian had originally met Richard Callahan on that first archaeological dig that she'd attended five years ago. A professor of biblical history at Fordham University, he had told her then that he'd studied to be a Jesuit but had withdrawn from the priesthood before taking his final vows. Now with a rangy body and easygoing manner, he had become a good friend, which somewhat surprised her. She knew it would be natural for him to be judgmental of her relationship with Jonathan, but if he was, he had never shown it. It was on that first dig that she and Jonathan had fallen desperately in love.

Lily managed a weak smile. "Richard, I'm so grateful to you, but you'd better get to that luncheon. Jonathan told me many times that Mariah's mother is very fond of you. I'm sure it will be a help if you're around for her now."

"I'm going," Richard said, "but, Lily, I have to ask you. Did Jonathan tell you that he believed he had found an incredibly valuable manuscript among the ones he was translating that were found in an old church?"

Lillian Stewart looked straight into Richard Callahan's eyes. "An old manuscript that was valuable? Absolutely not," she lied. "He never said anything about it to me."

4

❦

The rest of the day passed for Mariah in the merciful and pre-
dictable pattern of funerals. Now poised and beyond tears, Mariah
listened attentively as her family's longtime friend Father Aiden
O'Brien, a friar from Saint Francis of Assisi in Manhattan, celebrated
the Mass, eulogized her father, and conducted the graveside prayers
at nearby Maryrest Cemetery. After that they went to the Ridgewood
Country Club, where a luncheon had been laid out for those who
had attended the Mass and funeral.

There were over two hundred people there. The mood was som-
ber, but a Bloody Mary or two cheered everyone up and the atmosphere took on a more festive note. Mariah was glad because the
stories she was hearing from people were about what a great guy
her father was. Brilliant. Witty. Handsome. Charming. Yes, yes, she
thought.

It was when the luncheon was over and Rory had started home
with her mother that Father Aiden pulled her aside. His tone low,
even though there was no one near them, he asked, "Mariah, did
your father confide in you that he had a premonition he was going
to die?"

The look on her face was obviously answer enough for him.
"Your dad came to see me last Wednesday. He told me he had that
premonition. I invited him into the friary for coffee. Then he shared

a secret with me. As you may know, he has been translating some ancient parchments that were found in a hidden safe in a church that has been closed for years and is about to be torn down."

"Yes, I knew that. He mentioned something about their being remarkably well preserved."

"There is one that is of extraordinary value if your father was right. More than just value in terms of money," he added.

Shocked, Mariah stared at the seventy-eight-year-old priest. At Mass she had noticed that his arthritis was causing him to limp badly. Now his thick white hair accentuated the deep creases in his forehead. It was impossible to miss the concern in his voice.

"Did he tell you what was in the manuscript?" she asked.

Father Aiden looked around. Most people were standing up and saying their good-byes to their friends. It was obvious that they'd be making their way to Mariah to offer their final condolences, accompanied by a squeeze of the hand and the inevitable words, "Be sure to call us if you need anything."

"Mariah," he asked, his tone urgent. "Did your father ever talk about a letter it is believed that Christ wrote to Joseph of Arimathea?"

"Yes, a number of times over the years. He told me it had been in the Vatican Library, but little was known of it because several Popes, including Sixtus IV, refused to believe it was genuine. It was stolen during his reign in the fifteenth century, supposedly by someone who believed Pope Sixtus was planning to burn it." Astonished, she asked, "Father Aiden, are you telling me that my father thought he had found that letter?"

"Yes, I am."

"Then he must have had his findings verified by at least one other expert whose opinion is beyond reproach."

"He told me that he did exactly that."

"Did he name the person who saw it?"

"No. But there must have been several, because he said he regretted his choice of one of them. He intended of course to return the parchment to the Vatican Library, but that person told him they could get an enormous amount of money for it from a private collector."

In the pre-Lily days, I would have been the first one Dad told about his find, Mariah thought, and he would have told me who else he was going to share it with. A fresh wave of bitterness and regret washed over her as she looked from table to table. Many of the people here were my father's colleagues, she thought. Dad might have consulted a couple of them, like Charles and Albert, about an ancient parchment like that. If, pray God, Mom isn't responsible, is it possible that his death was something other than a random burglary gone wrong? Is someone in this very room the person who took his life?

Before she could voice that thought to Father Aiden, she saw her mother rushing back into the room, Rory a step behind her. Her mother headed straight to where Mariah and Father Aiden were sitting. "She won't leave without you!" Rory explained, her tone annoyed and impatient.

Kathleen Lyons smiled vacantly at Father Aiden. "Did you hear all that noise?" she asked him. "And see all that blood?"

Then she added, "The woman in the pictures with Jonathan was standing next to him today. Her name is Lily. Why did she come? Wasn't going to Venice with him enough for her?"

5

Alvirah and Willy Meehan were on their annual trip on board the *Queen Mary 2* when they heard that their good friend Professor Jonathan Lyons was shot to death. Shocked beyond words to express how terrible she felt, her voice shaking, Alvirah conveyed the news to Willy. But she realized that apart from leaving a message of condolence on an answering machine, they could do nothing else at this time. They would not be getting home until the day of the funeral.

The ship had just sailed from Southampton and the only way to get off would be by medical helicopter. Besides, Alvirah was a guest lecturer who was booked as a celebrity author to tell stories about lottery winners she knew and how some of them had lost every nickel in harebrained schemes. She talked about people who had worked two jobs most of their lives, won millions, then were conned into buying white elephant hotels or chains of knickknack stores that couldn't pay the rent selling cutesy items like cocktail napkins, sparkling key rings, and embroidered pillows.

She always explained that she had been a cleaning woman and Willy a plumber when they won forty million dollars in the lottery. They had elected to take the money in annual payments for twenty years. Every year they paid their taxes first and lived on half of what was left. The rest they invested wisely.

The passengers loved Alvirah's stories and snapped up copies of her bestselling book, *From Pots to Plots*. And though Alvirah was truly heartsick about Jonathan's death, being a trouper she did not show it. Even when people animatedly discussed theories of why the prominent scholar might have been murdered, neither she nor Willy ever mentioned that they had known Professor Lyons well.

Actually they had met Jonathan when Alvirah was lecturing on a cruise from Venice to Istanbul, two years ago. She and Professor Lyons had attended each other's lectures, and she had been so fascinated by his spellbinding tales of ancient Egypt, Greece, and Israel that, in her usual forthcoming way, she had invited him to have dinner with them. The professor accepted readily, but then added that he was traveling with his companion so it would be a foursome.

And that's when we met Lily, was the refrain that ran through Alvirah's head during the days of the crossing. I really liked her. She's smart, attractive in that way that lets you know she was always attractive; as a six-year-old I bet she knew what looked good on her. She's as passionate about archaeology as Professor Jon was and has just as many degrees. She doesn't have any airs about her, and no two ways about it, she was madly in love with Jonathan Lyons even though she's a lot younger.

Alvirah, of course, had Googled Professor Jonathan Lyons and knew he was married and had a daughter named Mariah. "But, Willy, I guess he and his wife grew apart," Alvirah had said to her husband. "It happens, you know. And sometimes, they stick it out together."

Willy had his own system of agreeing with Alvirah when she came to definite conclusions. "As usual, you hit the nail on the head, honey," he told her, although for the life of him he could not imagine even glancing at another woman when he was lucky enough to have his beloved Alvirah.

On the last day of that crossing, when they disembarked in Istanbul, there had been the usual flurry of people who had really enjoyed their time together and began to pass out hurried invitations, telling their new friends that they must come visit them in Hot Springs or Hong Kong or on their dear little island just a boat ride from St. John. Alvirah said, "Willy, can't you just see the look on their faces if we arrived bag and baggage? You know it's just a nice way of saying that they really enjoyed our company."

That was why six months after they got back to Central Park South from their Venice-to-Istanbul trip, they were astonished to receive a phone call from Professor Jonathan Lyons. Even if he hadn't started by introducing himself, there was no mistaking that warm, resonant voice. "This is Jon Lyons. I've told my wife and daughter so much about you that they want to meet you. If Tuesday works for you, my daughter, Mariah, who lives in Manhattan, will pick you up, drive you out to our home in the Garden State, and at the end of the evening drive you back home."

Alvirah was thrilled at the invitation, but when she hung up the phone, she said, "Willy, I wonder if his wife knows about Lily. Remember, keep a guard on your tongue."

Promptly at six thirty P.M. the following Tuesday evening, the doorman buzzed the intercom in the Meehan apartment on Central Park South to announce that Ms. Lyons had arrived to pick them up.

If Alvirah had taken a liking to Jonathan Lyons, her reaction to his daughter was equally strong. Mariah was friendly and warm, and had not only gone to the trouble of reading Alvirah's book but had the common ground of being in the business of trying to help people invest sensibly and with minimum risk. By the time they got to Mahwah, New Jersey, Alvirah had already decided that Mariah was the kind of person she wanted to steer some of her lottery winners to, especially the ones who had already lost too much of their winnings in crazy schemes.

It was only when they pulled into the driveway that, her voice hesitant, Mariah asked, "Did my father tell you that my mother has dementia? She's aware of it and tries hard to cover it up, but if she asks you the same question two or three times, you'll understand."

They had cocktails in Jonathan's study because he was sure Alvirah would be interested in seeing some of the artifacts he'd collected over the years. Betty, the housekeeper, had cooked a delicious meal, and between them, Mariah and her father successfully covered for the lapses in conversation of the delicately pretty, if aging, Kathleen Lyons. It was a stimulating and enjoyable evening that Alvirah was sure would be one of many more to come.

As they were saying good-bye Kathleen suddenly asked how Willy and Alvirah had met Jonathan. When they told her it was on a recent sailing they made from Venice to Istanbul, she became upset. "I wanted so much to go on that trip," she said. "We honeymooned in Venice, did Jonathan tell you that?"

"Sweetheart, I've told you how I met the Meehans and remember, the doctor warned you that it wouldn't be wise to make that trip," Jonathan Lyons said gently.

When they were driving home, Mariah abruptly asked, "Was Lillian Stewart on that trip when you met my father?"

Alvirah hesitated, trying to decide what to say. I'm certainly not going to lie, she thought, and I suspect that Mariah has already guessed that Lily was there. "Mariah, isn't that a question you should ask your father?" she suggested.

"I already have. He refused to answer, but you've as much as confirmed it by being evasive."

Alvirah was sitting in the front with Mariah. Willy was contentedly settled in the backseat, and Alvirah was sure that if he could hear what they were saying, he was happy to be out of the conversation. From the break in Mariah's voice, she knew she was on the verge of tears. "Mariah," she said, "your father is very loving with your mother and very attentive to her. Some things are better left alone, especially with your mother's mind beginning to fail."

"It hasn't failed so badly that she doesn't remember how much she wanted to go on that trip," Mariah said. "She told you they honeymooned in Venice. Mom knows she's sick. She wanted to go while she's still functioning pretty well. But my guess is that with Lillian in the picture, Dad got a specialist to convince Mom it would be too much for her. She gets really upset about it sometimes."

"Does she know about Lily?" Alvirah asked bluntly.

"Can you believe that Dad used to have her out to the house for dinner with some of the others who go on the annual dig? I never guessed that they were involved, but then Mom found a couple of pictures of the two of them in Dad's study. She showed them to me, and I told Dad to keep that woman out of the house, but sometimes my mother still asks about her, and when Mom does, she gets angry."

In the past year or so they had regularly driven out with Mariah to visit Jonathan and Kathleen, and Mariah was right. Kathleen, even with her ongoing memory loss, would often bring up the trip to Venice.

All of this was on Alvirah's mind when the *Queen Mary* 2 pulled into New York Harbor. By now Jonathan is in his grave, she thought. May he rest in peace.

Then with her infallible sense for coming trouble, she added, "And please help Kathleen and Mariah.

"And please, God, let them find that Jonathan was killed by an intruder," she added fervently.

6

All day Greg Pearson was burning to tell Mariah how he could understand her pain and wanted to share it with her. He wanted to be able to say how much he would miss her father. He wanted to tell her how grateful he was to Jonathan, who had taught him so much, not only about archaeology, but about life.

When Jon's colleagues and friends were telling stories about him, about how helpful he had been in personal ways, he wanted to share his own story that he had confided to Jon, about what an insecure kid he had been. I told Jon that I was the guy in high school who stopped growing at five feet six when the other guys soared up to six feet two and six feet three, he wanted to say. I was a skinny weakling, the poster boy for nerd of the year. There wasn't a team I tried out for that I made. I finally got to be five feet ten inches when I was in college, but it was too late.

I guess I was looking for sympathy but I didn't get any. Jonathan had just laughed.

"So you spent your time studying instead of throwing basketballs in the net," he said. "You've built a successful company. Get out your high school yearbook and look up the guys who were the hotshots in school. I'll bet you find that most of them are scraping along."

I told Jon that I'd looked up a few of them, especially the ones who gave me a hard time, and he was right. Of course some of the guys are doing fine, but the ones who were the bullies haven't amounted to a hill of beans so far.

He made me feel good about myself, Greg wanted to say. Besides sharing his incredible knowledge about ancient times and archaeology, he made me feel good.

Greg would have stopped there. It wouldn't have been necessary to add that he'd told Jonathan that despite his success, he was still painfully shy, an outsider at parties, lacking the most basic skill at small talk, or that Jonathan's suggestion had been to find a vivacious, talkative woman. "She'll never notice that you're quiet, and she'll do all the talking at parties. I know at least three guys with wives like that, and it's a great match."

All this Greg was thinking as he followed Mariah out of the country club. He held back until a valet brought Father Aiden's car and the caregiver was helping Mariah's mother into the black limousine that the funeral director had provided.

Then he went up to her. "Mariah, it's been a terrible day for you. I hope you understand how much we'll all miss him."

Mariah nodded. "I do know, Greg. Thanks."

He wanted to add, "Let's have dinner soon," but the words froze on his lips. They had started dating a few years ago, but then when he persisted in calling her, she had hinted that she was seeing someone else. He had realized she was only trying to warn him away.

Now, looking at the pain in her deep blue eyes and the way the afternoon sun was picking up the highlights in her shoulder-length hair, Greg wanted to tell her that he was still in love with her and would go to hell and back for her. Instead he said, "I'll give you a call next week to see how your mother is doing."

"That would be nice."

He held the door for her as she stepped into the limo, then reluctantly closed it behind her. He watched, not knowing that he was also being observed, as the car slowly made its way around the circular driveway.

Richard Callahan was in the group of departing guests who had formed a line to retrieve their cars. He had seen the expression on Greg's face brighten whenever Mariah came home for one of Jonathan's dinners, but he also sensed that she had no interest in Greg. Of course things could change now with her father gone, he thought. She might be more receptive to a guy who could, and would, do anything for her.

Especially, Richard thought as the valet brought his eight-year-old Volkswagen to the curb, if any of that gossip I heard at the table is true. From what I gathered, that caregiver has had too much to say to the neighbors about how angry Kathleen becomes when she gets on the subject of Jon's relationship with Lily. There was no need for Rory to tell them about Lily. It was none of their—or Rory's—business.

Kathleen was alone with Jonathan the night he was shot. Mariah has to know that her mother may be a suspect in his death, he thought. Those detectives are going to call Lily and Greg and Albert and Charles and me and arrange private meetings with all of us. What are we supposed to tell them? They certainly must know by now that Lily and Jonathan were involved with each other, and that Kathleen was terribly upset about it.

Richard tipped the valet and got into his car. For a moment he was tempted to stop and see how Kathleen and Mariah were doing, but then he reasoned that they both might be better off left alone for a while. As he started to drive home, his thoughts were of the shocked expression he had seen on Mariah's face when Father Aiden was talking to her just before the luncheon ended.

What did Father Aiden tell her? he wondered. And now that the funeral's over, will those detectives be zeroing in on the fact that there is no explanation for Jonathan's death other than that Kathleen pulled that trigger Monday night?

7

Charles Michaelson and Albert West had driven together from Manhattan to pay their respects to their old friend and colleague Jonathan Lyons. Both men were experts in the study of ancient parchments. But the resemblance between them ended there. Michaelson, impatient by nature, had a permanent frown in the creases of his forehead. Added to that, his imposing girth was enough to strike fear in the hearts of unprepared students. Sarcastic to the point of cruelty, he had reduced many PhD candidates to tears during their defense of doctoral theses they had submitted to him.

Albert West was small and thin. His students joked that his tie brushed against his shoelaces. His voice, surprisingly strong and always passionate, captivated his listeners when, in his lectures, he introduced them to the wonders of ancient history.

Michaelson had long been divorced. After twenty years his irascible temper became too much for his wife and she left him. If that event caused him any heartache, he never showed it.

West was a lifelong bachelor. An avid sportsman, he enjoyed hiking in the spring and summer and skiing in the late fall and winter. As often as possible he spent his weekends on one of those activities.

The relationship between the two men was the same one they had shared with Jonathan Lyons—it was based on their passion for ancient manuscripts.

Albert West had been trying to decide if he should share with Michaelson the call he had received from Jonathan Lyons a week and a half ago. He knew that Michaelson considered him a competitor and would be offended if he learned that Jonathan had consulted Albert first about a two-thousand-year-old parchment.

On the way back from the luncheon, West decided he had to ask the question. He waited until Michaelson had turned onto West 56th Street from the West Side Highway. In a few minutes Michaelson would be dropping him off at his apartment near Eighth Avenue and then driving across town to Sutton Place, where he lived.

He decided to be direct. "Did Jonathan talk to you about the possibility that he had found the Arimathea letter, Charles?" he asked.

Michaelson glanced at him for a split second before stopping the car as the light changed from yellow to red. "The Arimathea letter! My God, Jonathan left a message on my cell phone that he thought he had found something of tremendous importance and would like to have my opinion on it. He never said what it was. I called back later the same day and left word that of course I'd be interested in seeing whatever he had. But he didn't get back to me. Did you *see* the letter? Did he show it to you? Is there any chance that it's authentic?"

"I wish I had seen it, but the answer is no. Jon called to tell me about it two weeks ago. He did say he was convinced that it was the Arimathea letter. You know how calm Jonathan usually was, but this time he was excited, sure that he was right. I warned him how often these so-called finds turn out to be fakes and he calmed down and admitted that he might be rushing to judgment. He said he was showing it to someone else and would get back to me, but he never did."

For the next few minutes the men were silent until they reached Albert West's apartment building. "Well, let's hope to God that if it was authentic, and he had it in his home, his crazy wife doesn't come across it," Michaelson said bitterly. "If she did, it would be just like her to tear it up if she thought it was important to him."

As Albert West opened the car door, he said, "I couldn't agree with you more. I wonder if Mariah knows about the letter. If not, we'd better alert her to look for it. It's beyond priceless. Thanks for the ride, Charles."

Charles Michaelson nodded. As he steered the car away from the curb, he said aloud, "Nothing, not even a letter written by Christ to Joseph of Arimathea, is priceless if the right bidder can be found."

8

At the church Detectives Benet and Rodriguez had observed Lillian Stewart slipping into the Mass late and leaving early. They followed her to the cemetery and, using binoculars, observed her going to the grave, then Richard Callahan joining her in her car and putting his arms around her.

"And what do we make of *that*?" Detective Rodriguez asked as they drove back to the prosecutor's office in Hackensack, stopping only to pick up coffee. Finally they were in their office reviewing their notes on the case.

Simon Benet's forehead was drenched in perspiration. "Wouldn't it be nice if the air-conditioning worked in this place?" he complained. "And will you tell me why I didn't get iced coffee?"

"Because you don't like iced coffee," Rodriguez said calmly. "Neither do I."

They exchanged a brief smile. Simon Benet thought again that he always admired Rita's ability to deftly ferret out discrepancies in anyone's account so that it seemed she was only anxious to help the witness, rather than to catch that person in a lie.

Together they made a good team.

Benet started the conversation. "That caregiver, Rory, sure likes to talk. She was a fountain of information about what was going on in the house Monday night. Let's go over what we have." He began to read from his notes. "Rory has weekends off, but the weekend caregiver asked her to switch because she had a family wedding. Rory agreed, but then the caretaker couldn't make it back by Monday evening, and Professor Lyons told Rory to go home anyhow, that he could take care of his wife by himself for one night."

Benet continued. "She said that Professor Lyons had been in New York that day and seemed tired, and even depressed, when he got home at five o'clock. He asked how his wife had been, and Rory had to tell him that she had been very agitated. The housekeeper, Betty Pierce, served dinner at six o'clock. Rory was planning to meet a friend for a late dinner in Manhattan but sat with them at the table. Mrs. Lyons kept talking about wanting to go to Venice again. Finally, to appease her, the professor promised they would go back there soon and have a second honeymoon."

"Which was obviously the wrong thing to say," Rodriguez commented. "Because according to Rory, Mrs. Lyons got upset and said something like, 'You mean you'll take me instead of Lily? I don't believe you.' After that she wouldn't look at him again, closed her eyes, and refused to eat anything. Rory took her upstairs, got her into bed, and she fell asleep immediately."

The detectives looked at each other. "I don't remember whether or not Rory said anything about what medication she gave Mrs. Lyons that night," Benet admitted.

Rodriguez answered. "She said Mrs. Lyons was so tired that it wasn't necessary, that when she came downstairs, Betty Pierce was just leaving, and the professor had carried his second cup of coffee into his office. Rory looked in on him to let him know that she was on her way out."

"That's pretty much it," Rita concluded. "Rory checked the front door on her way out to be sure it was locked. She and Betty Pierce always left by the kitchen door because their cars were parked in the back. She swears that door was locked too. She never knew Professor Lyons kept a gun in a drawer in his desk."

They both closed their notebooks. "So what we have is a house that normally would have a caregiver in it, no sign of a break-in, a woman suffering from dementia who had been angry at her husband and was found hiding in a closet holding the gun that killed him. But she was very consistent in saying, 'So much noise . . . so much blood.' That could mean the shot woke her up, and she'd be an easy person to set up if she *didn't* do it." Benet tapped his fingers on the arm of the chair, a habit when he was thinking aloud. "And we couldn't talk to her immediately in the house or in the hospital because she was so hysterical, and afterward she was heavily medicated."

"We also have a daughter who's angry about her father's relationship with his mistress and who probably has the guardianship of her mother in case of her father's death," Rita said. "And here's another angle. If Jonathan Lyons had ever decided to divorce his wife, Kathleen, and marry Lillian Stewart, their assets would be split, and Mariah Lyons would have ended up with full responsibility for her mother."

Simon Benet leaned back in his chair, pulled out his handkerchief, and mopped his brow. "Tomorrow morning, we'll try to talk to the mother and to Mariah again. As we both know, most cases of this kind turn out to be family affairs." He paused. "And let's talk to somebody about getting the air-conditioning fixed!"

9

It was three o'clock when the funeral car deposited Mariah; her mother, Kathleen; and Rory back home after the luncheon at the Ridgewood Country Club.

As soon as they were inside the house, Rory said soothingly, "Now, Kathleen, you didn't sleep well last night and you were up very early. Why don't you get into something comfortable, then you can take a nap or watch television?"

Mariah realized she was holding her breath. Dear God, please don't let Mom insist on going into the closet in Dad's study, she thought. But to her relief, her mother willingly accompanied Rory up the stairs to her bedroom.

I honestly don't know how I could have dealt with another scene right now, Mariah thought. I need some quiet time. I need to think. She waited until she was sure her mother and Rory would be in her mother's bedroom with the door closed, then she hurried upstairs to her own room. She changed from her skirt and jacket into a cotton sweater, slacks, and sandals, and went back downstairs. She went into the kitchen, made a cup of tea, and carried it into the breakfast room. There she settled into one of the comfortable padded chairs and leaned back with a sigh.

Every bone in my body is aching, she thought as she took a sip of tea and tried to focus on the events of the week. I feel as if everything that happened since I arrived here Monday evening is a blur.

Trying to think unemotionally, she began to relive that evening, starting with the arrival of the police. Mom was in such a state that they sent for an ambulance, she remembered. In the hospital I sat beside her bed all night. She was moaning and crying. I had blood all over my blouse from where I leaned over Dad and put my arms around him. The nurse was good enough to give me one of those cotton jackets the patients wear.

I wonder what happened to my blouse? Usually they hand your clothes back to you in a plastic bag when you leave a hospital, even if they're soiled. I'm sure that the police kept it as evidence because it had blood on it.

It was just as well Mom wasn't released until Tuesday evening because that way she didn't see all of the police activity in the house. It had been declared a crime scene. They took Dad's study apart. Betty told me that they were dusting everywhere for fingerprints. She said they were dusting all the downstairs windows as well as the doors. The bottom drawer of Dad's desk, where he kept his gun, was open when I got home Monday night. But that drawer was always locked.

Mariah shook her head at the unwelcome memory that her mother was incredibly skilled at finding keys no matter where they had been hidden. Unwillingly, she thought of the incident last year when her mother had sneaked out of the house stark naked in the middle of the night. It was when the previous weekend caregiver was supposed to be taking care of her but had forgotten to put the alarm on in her mother's room. It was small consolation to remind herself that the new weekend caregiver was excellent.

But Mom could never have walked into Dad's study and used the key to open his desk drawer with him sitting there that evening, she thought.

That gun could have been somewhere else for months or even

years. I'm sure, or I think I'm sure, that Dad lost interest in going to the shooting range ages ago.

Even the warm cup she was cradling in her fingers could not prevent the chill that washed over Mariah's body. He used to take Mom to the range with him, she thought. She wanted to see if she'd be any good. That was about ten years ago. He said she was a pretty good shot back then.

Trying to avoid the terrible implication of where that train of thought was going, Mariah forced herself to think about the conversation she'd had with Father Aiden just before they left the club. Dad went to see Father Aiden nine days ago and told him that he thought he had found the letter Jesus may have written to Joseph of Arimathea. Dad claimed he had confirmed the fact that it was the parchment stolen from the Vatican Library in the fourteen hundreds. Who was that expert who saw it? But wait a minute. Father Aiden said that Dad was troubled because *one* of the experts had been interested only in its financial value. If Father Aiden got it straight, that would mean that Dad showed it to more than one person.

Where is the parchment now? My God, is it here, in Dad's files? I'll have to look for it, but what good would that do? I wouldn't recognize it among all the other parchments he was studying. But if Dad did have it and if Dad intended to return it to the Vatican Library, was it stolen after Dad was shot?

The ringing of the telephone in the kitchen made Mariah jump up and run to answer it. It was Detective Benet. He asked if he and Detective Rodriguez could drop over in the morning at about eleven o'clock and have a talk with Mariah and her mother.

"Of course," she said.

Mariah realized that the reason she was whispering was because her throat had tightened so much that she could hardly speak the words.

10

❧❧❧

Lloyd and Lisa Scott, a couple in their late fifties, had been next-door neighbors of Jonathan and Kathleen Lyons for twenty-five years. Lloyd was a successful criminal defense attorney, and Lisa, a former model, had turned her love for jewelry into a business. She made her own designs in crystal and semiprecious stones for a long list of private clients. Some of her designs were the products of her imagination. Others were inspired by the beautiful gems she had collected from all over the world. Her personal collection was now worth more than three million dollars.

With his balding head, prodigious girth, and pale blue eyes, Lloyd seemed an unlikely match for his beautiful wife. After thirty years of marital bliss he sometimes still woke up at night and wondered what she saw in him. His great pleasure was to indulge her love for what he jokingly called her trinkets.

Agreeing that it was a nuisance to keep going back and forth to the safety-deposit box at the bank, they had recently installed a supposedly burglar-proof safe bolted to the floor of Lisa's dressing-room closet, as well as a state-of-the-art alarm system.

The Scotts kept a pied-à-terre in Manhattan for their occasional overnights in New York for business or social events. But as Lloyd's reputation and income had continued to grow, neither one of them had any real interest in leaving the handsome brick and stucco

Tudor-style house that Lloyd had inherited from his mother. They liked their neighbors and the neighborhood. They had a view of the Ramapo Mountains from their back porch. They both were passionate travelers and preferred to spend their money on first-class accommodations all over the world, rather than on "McMansions or an oceanfront home in the Hamptons," as Lloyd put it.

They were in Japan when they heard about Jonathan's death and did not arrive home until the morning after the funeral. Knowing Kathleen's condition so well, they both had been concerned that she might be involved in the tragedy.

As soon as they set down their bags in Mahwah that Saturday morning, they rushed next door. The bell was answered by a visibly distressed Mariah. She broke in on their attempts to offer condolences. "Two detectives are here," she said. "They're talking to Mom now. They called last night and asked to come and speak to us."

"I don't like that," Lloyd snapped.

"It's because she was alone with Dad that night . . ." Mariah's voice trailed off as she tried to stay composed, but then she burst out, "Lloyd, it's meaningless. Mom doesn't even get it. She asked me why Dad didn't come to breakfast this morning."

Lisa looked at her husband. As she had expected, his face was settling into what she called his "take no prisoners" expression. Frowning slightly, his brow creased, his eyes narrowed behind his glasses, he said, "Mariah, this is my territory. I don't want to butt in, but whether your mother understands what's going on or not, she should not be answering questions from the police without legal counsel. Let me sit in with you and be sure we keep her protected."

Lisa cupped Mariah's face in her hands. "I'll see you later," she promised as she turned to go.

It was a hot day even for August. Back in the house Lisa lowered the temperature on the air conditioner and walked to the kitchen, glancing into the living room as she passed it. It was in perfect order and the warm feeling that inevitably followed a vacation enveloped her. No matter how nice the trip was, and how much we enjoyed it, it's always great to get home, she thought.

She made a decision not to nibble on anything. She'd skipped the breakfast snack on the plane, but she figured that when Lloyd got back they could have an early lunch. He'd be hungry too. Without looking, she knew the refrigerator had been stocked by their trusted housekeeper of twenty-five years. Again pushing back the urge to treat herself to something like a cracker and cheese, she retraced her steps to the foyer, picked up the carry-on bag that contained the jewelry she had traveled with, and went upstairs to the master bedroom.

She laid the bag on the bed, opened it, and removed the leather pouches containing the jewelry. At least this time I listened to Lloyd and didn't bring as much as usual, she thought. But I sure wish I'd had the emeralds with me for the captain's dinner on the ship.

Oh well.

She removed the rings and bracelets and earrings and necklaces from the pouches, spread them on the coverlet of the bed, and looked over them carefully, checking once again to be sure that everything she had taken with her had come back in the carry-on bag.

Then she transferred them to the tray on her vanity table, carried it into her dressing room, and opened the door of the closet. The steel safe, dark and formidable, was there. She tapped in the combination to unlock it and tugged at the door.

There were ten rows of drawers with various-shaped velvet-lined compartments. Lisa pulled out the top one, gasped, then frantically yanked out drawer after drawer. Instead of her beautiful and valuable jewelry sparkling up at her, she was staring at a sea of black velvet.

The safe was empty.

11

Alvirah decided she would wait until the next morning to phone Mariah. "Willy, you know how it is after a funeral. There's such a letdown. I'll bet anything that when Mariah got home, all she wanted to do was be quiet. And God only knows what's running through poor Kathleen's mind."

Six of Willy's sisters had entered the convent. The seventh, the oldest and the only one who had married, had died fifteen years earlier. Willy still remembered how glad he had been to get back home to their apartment in Jackson Heights after the funeral in Nebraska and the long flight home. Alvirah had fixed him a sandwich and a cold beer and let him sit and think about Madeline, who had been his favorite sister. Madeline had been quiet and unassuming, so unlike the wonderful but bossy Sister Cordelia, his next-oldest sibling.

"When was the last time we were out to Jonathan's house in Mahwah for dinner?" he asked Alvirah. "Am I right that it was about two months ago, in late June?"

Alvirah had finished unpacking and sorting clothes for the laundry and cleaners. Now happily comfortable in her favorite stretch slacks and a cotton T-shirt, she settled into a chair opposite Willy in their Central Park South apartment.

"Yes," she agreed. "Jonathan invited us over, and Mariah and Richard and Greg were there. And so were those other two who always go on the trips. You know who. What were their names?" Alvirah frowned in concentration as she went through the tricks for memory retention that she had learned at the Dale Carnegie course she had taken after they won the money in the lottery. "One of them is a direction. North . . . no. South, no. West. That's it. Albert West. He's a little guy with a deep voice. The other one was Michaelson. He's easy to remember. Michael is one of my favorite names. Just add the '-son' and you have it."

"His first name is Charles," Willy volunteered. "And you can bet nobody ever called that guy 'Charlie.' Do you remember how he cut down West when West misidentified one of the ruins they had on the pictures they showed us?"

Alvirah nodded. "But I remember Kathleen was pretty good that night. She seemed to enjoy seeing the pictures, and she didn't say a word about Lily."

"I suppose Lily was on that trip too, even though they didn't show any photos with her in them."

"Sure she was." Alvirah sighed. "And, Willy, if it turns out that Kathleen pulled that trigger, you can bet it was because of Lily. I just don't know how Mariah will be able to handle it."

"They certainly wouldn't put Kathleen in prison," Willy protested. "It's obvious the woman has Alzheimer's and isn't responsible for what she does."

"That's up to the courts," Alvirah said soberly. "But a psychiatric prison hospital wouldn't be much better. Oh, Willy, pray God it doesn't turn out that way."

The thought of that possibility did not improve Alvirah's chances of a good night's rest, even though she was grateful that she would be back in her own bed, comfortably spooning against the sleeping Willy. The beds on those ships are so big, you can hardly see each other, she thought. Poor Kathleen. Mariah told me how happy her parents had been together before the dementia set in. But Kathleen never did go on the archaeological trips with him. From what Mariah said, that was *his* thing and her mother couldn't take the summer heat in the places he went. Maybe that's one of the reasons that Jonathan got involved with Lily. From what I could see, she sure shared his passion for digging through old ruins.

Reluctantly, Alvirah thought of that first trip two years ago from Venice to Istanbul where they had met her fellow lecturer Jonathan Lyons and his companion, Lily Stewart. No question they were in love, she thought. They were crazy about each other.

Alvirah remembered how after Jonathan had invited Willy and her to dinner that first time, and they had met Mariah and Kathleen, she and Mariah had lunch the next week. "You're the right fit for some of my lottery winners," she had told Mariah. "I can tell you're the kind of conservative investment advisor they need to make sure they don't squander their money or put it in high-risk stocks."

A month or so after that, Jonathan had been lecturing at the 92nd Street Y and invited Alvirah and Willy to attend and have dinner with him afterward. What he did not tell them was that Lily would be there.

Lily had sensed Alvirah's discomfort and addressed it. "Alvirah, I told Jonathan that you and Mariah have become very friendly and that she would resent it bitterly if she thought that you were seeing her father with me socially."

"Yes, I think she would," Alvirah had answered frankly.

Jonathan had tried to dismiss that possibility. "Mariah knows that Richard and Greg, to name just a few, see Lily and me together. What's the difference?"

Alvirah remembered how Lily had smiled sadly. "Jonathan," Lily said, "it's different for Alvirah, and I do understand. She would feel two-faced about seeing us socially outside your home."

I like Lily, Alvirah thought. I can only imagine what she's feeling right now. And if it turns out that Kathleen killed Jonathan, I'll bet

Lily will be blaming herself for being the cause of the problem. I should at least call her and tell her how sorry I am.

But I won't meet with her, she decided as she happily accepted Willy's offer of a glass of wine.

"It's the witching hour, honey," he said. "Five P.M. on the dot."

In the morning, she waited until eleven o'clock to call Mariah. "Alvirah, I can't talk," Mariah said quickly, her voice strained and tremulous. "The detectives are here to talk to Mom and me again. Are you home? I'll call you back."

Alvirah did not have time to say more than, "Yes, I'm home," before the click in her ear told her that the connection was broken.

Less than five minutes later, her phone rang. It was Lily Stewart. It was obvious that she was crying. "Alvirah, you probably don't want to hear from me, but I need your advice. I don't know what to do. I just don't know what to do. How soon can we get together?"

12

Mariah admitted to herself that she liked her mother's weekend caregiver Delia Jackson, a handsome black woman in her late forties, better than she liked Rory Steiger. Delia was always cheerful. The only drawback was that her mother would sometimes absolutely refuse to get dressed or eat when Delia was with her.

"Mom's intimidated by Rory," Mariah and her father had agreed, "but she's more relaxed with Delia."

On Saturday morning when the detectives arrived, despite Mariah and Delia's entreaties, Kathleen was still in her nightgown and robe, sitting in the wing chair in the living room, her eyes half-closed. At breakfast she had asked Mariah where her father was. Now she had ignored the detectives' attempt to open a conversation with her, except to say that her husband would be down shortly to speak with them. But at the sound of Lloyd Scott's voice, Kathleen sprang up and rushed across the room to throw her arms around him. "Lloyd, I'm so glad you're back," she cried. "Did you hear that Jonathan is dead, that someone shot him?"

Mariah's heart sank as she caught the look the detectives exchanged. They believe Mom has been putting on an act, she thought. They don't realize how she goes in and out of reality.

Lloyd Scott led Kathleen over to the couch and sat beside her, holding her hand. Looking directly at Simon Benet, he asked, "Is Mrs. Lyons a person of interest in this investigation?"

"Mrs. Lyons was apparently alone with her husband when he was shot," Benet answered. "There is no sign of forced entry. However, we are aware that in her condition, Mrs. Lyons could be vulnerable to a setup. We're simply here to try to get a complete picture of what happened last Monday evening, as much as she can tell us."

"I understand. Then you do realize that Mrs. Lyons is in an advanced state of dementia and not capable of comprehending either your questions or her responses?"

"The gun was found in the closet with Mrs. Lyons," Rita Rodriguez explained quietly. "Three discernible fingerprints were on it. Professor Lyons, of course, had handled it at some point. It was his gun. We have his prints from the medical examiner. Mariah Lyons found her mother in the closet holding the gun and took it from her. Mariah's fingerprints are on the barrel. The fingerprints of Kathleen Lyons are on the trigger. Of course at the hospital we took their fingerprints for comparison purposes. From what Kathleen has said to her daughter and caretaker, she picked up the gun and hid it in the closet. According to the caregiver Rory Steiger, and this was verified by the housekeeper Betty Pierce, Mrs. Lyons was quite agitated at dinner on the night of the murder about her husband's involvement with another woman, Lillian Stewart. Both Mrs. Lyons and Mariah Lyons said they embraced the body, which is consistent with the bloodstains on both their upper bodies."

Appalled, Mariah realized that even though the detectives knew of her mother's dementia, it was clear that they thought her mother had pulled the trigger. And as far as Mariah knew, they weren't even aware yet that Kathleen had been taught how to fire a gun. When Lloyd asked his next question, it was as if he was reading her mind. "Was there any presence of blood or brain matter on the clothing of Mrs. Lyons?"

"Yes. Although whoever fired the bullet was at least ten feet from Professor Lyons, both the mother and daughter hugged him and got blood all over themselves."

Mariah exchanged glances with Lloyd Scott. Lloyd remembers that Mom used to go to the shooting range with Dad, she thought. He knows that will come up. They'll find out about it.

"Detective Benet," Lloyd began. "I am going on record as being the attorney for Mrs. Kathleen Lyons. I—"

He was interrupted by the frantic chiming of the doorbell. Mariah rushed to answer it, but Delia, who had left the living room when the detectives arrived, was there ahead of her. It was Lisa Scott. Shaking, she rushed into the house. "We've been robbed!" she shrieked. "All my jewelry is gone."

In the living room, Lloyd Scott and the detectives could hear what his wife was saying. Lloyd let go of Kathleen's hand and sprang up from the couch. The detectives exchanged startled glances and followed him, leaving Kathleen alone.

In an instant Delia was beside her charge. "Now, Kathleen, why don't we get dressed while the men who were talking to you are busy?" she asked gently, even as she hooked Kathleen's arm in hers, forcing her to get up.

A clear flash of memory came and went through Kathleen's failing brain. "Was there dirt on the gun?" she asked. "It was muddy in the flower bed along the walk."

"Oh, sweetheart, don't you even think about that kind of thing," Delia said soothingly. "It just gets you upset. I think you should wear your pretty white blouse today. Is that a good idea?"

13

Lillian Stewart lived in an apartment building opposite Lincoln Center on Manhattan's West Side. She had moved there after an amicable divorce from Arthur Ambruster, the husband she had met when they both were students at Georgetown University in Washington, DC. They had decided to put off having children until they earned their PhDs, hers in English, his in sociology. They then had both secured teaching jobs in New York, at Columbia University.

The children they were then ready to have had never arrived, and when they were both thirty-five they agreed that their interests and outlook on life were radically different. Now, fifteen years later, Arthur was the father of three sons and active in New York politics. Lillian's avocation had become archaeology, and every summer she had happily joined an archaeological dig. Five years ago, at age forty-five, she had gone on a dig headed by Professor Jonathan Lyons and that had changed both their lives.

I am the reason Kathleen killed Jonathan, was the thought that had haunted Lillian's dreams at night since his death. *And it wasn't necessary. Jonathan was going to give me up. He came to me last week and said that he couldn't live this way any longer, that it was making Kathleen's condition worse, and that his relationship with Mariah had become unbearably strained.*

The memory of that meeting was like a recording that played in

Lillian's mind over and over again on Saturday morning. She could still see the pain in Jonathan's eyes and hear the tremor in his voice. "Lily, I think you know how much I love you, and I did honestly think that when Kathleen was no longer aware, it would be all right to put her in a nursing home and divorce her. But I know now that I can't do that. And I can't spoil your life any longer. You're only fifty years old. You should meet someone your own age. If Kathleen lives another ten years, and I do as well, I'll be eighty. What life would you have with me then?"

Then Jonathan had added, "Some people have a premonition of their impending death. My father did. They say Abraham Lincoln, the week before he was shot, had a dream of his body lying in a casket in the White House. I know this may sound silly but I have a premonition that I am going to die soon."

I talked him into seeing me one more time, Lillian thought. It would have been Tuesday morning. But then Kathleen shot him on Monday night.

Oh, God, what shall I do?

Alvirah had agreed to meet Lillian for lunch at one o'clock. I like her so much, Lillian thought. But I already know what she will tell me to do. I already know what the right thing to do is.

But am I going to do it? Maybe it's too soon to decide. I'm not thinking straight.

Restlessly she walked around the apartment, making the bed, straightening up the bathroom, putting her few breakfast dishes in the dishwasher. The living room, restful with its earth-toned carpet and furniture, and the paintings of ancient sites on the walls, had always been Jonathan's favorite room. Lillian thought of the evenings when Jonathan and she would come back and have a nightcap after dinner. She could see him sitting with his long legs stretched out on the hassock of the roomy leather chair she had bought him for his birthday. "It's your home-away-from-home perch," she had told him.

"How can you love someone so much, then turn your back on her?" she had cried angrily when Jonathan told her that he was ending their relationship.

"It's *because* of love that I'm doing it," he had answered. "Love of you, love of Kathleen, and love of Mariah."

Alvirah had suggested that they meet at the relatively new restaurant down the block from her on Central Park South, then she had immediately changed her mind. "Make it the Russian Tea Room," she said.

Lillian knew why Alvirah had switched. The name of the restaurant on Central Park South was Marea's. Too close to "Mariah," she thought.

Lillian had gone for an early jog that morning in Central Park, then showered and slipped on a robe while she had breakfast. Now she went to the closet and selected white summer slacks and a blue linen blazer, an outfit Jonathan had particularly liked.

As always, she wore high heels. Jonathan had joked about that. Only a few weeks ago he had told her that Mariah had sarcastically asked if she wore high heels on the digs. I flared up at him and he was sorry, Lillian thought as she brushed her cheeks with blush and gave a final pat to the short dark hair that framed her face.

But it was that kind of remark that Mariah was always making that wore him down, Lillian thought as resentment and bitterness splashed over her.

The phone rang as she was ready to leave. "Lily, why don't I come around and take you to lunch?" the voice said. "Today has to be a terrible letdown for you."

"It is. But I was talking to Alvirah Meehan. She's back from her trip. We're having lunch together."

She felt, rather than heard, the pause that followed. "I hope you don't intend to say a word to her about certain matters."

"I haven't decided," she said.

"Then don't. Will you promise me that? Because once you do, it's all over. You've got to give yourself time to think calmly and practically. You owe Jonathan nothing. And beyond that, if it comes out that he broke up with you and you may have something he wanted, you could be suspect number two after his wife. Trust me, the wife's lawyer could claim you went there knowing the caretaker was gone. Jonathan left the door open for you. They could say that you went in with your face covered, shot him, then put the gun in his crazy wife's hand and got out of there. It would create doubt about his wife."

Lillian had answered the phone on the extension in the living room. She stared at the chair where Jonathan had so often sat, thinking of the times she had curled up with him in it. She looked at the door and could again see him walking out and saying, "I'm sorry. I'm truly sorry, Lily."

"That's absolutely ridiculous," she said heatedly into the receiver. "Kathleen killed Jonathan because she was jealous of me. It's bad enough without your dreaming up that scenario. But I will tell you this. I'm not saying one word to Alvirah or anyone else right now. For my own reasons. That's a promise."

14

In the thirty seconds following Lisa Scott's outburst, Simon Benet put in a call to the Mahwah police department to report the theft of her jewelry. Lloyd Scott snapped, "I'll be back," and rushed next door to wait with his wife for a squad car to arrive.

Mariah looked from one detective to the other. "I can't believe the Scotts were burglarized," she said. "I can't believe it. Just before they went on that trip last month, Lloyd was talking about the new security system and the cameras and God knows what-all he put in and around the house."

"Today, unfortunately, there are few systems that can't be penetrated by experts," Benet told her. "Was it generally known that Mrs. Scott kept a lot of valuable jewelry in her home?"

"I don't know. She talked about it to us, but certainly everyone knew she had a business creating her own designs and always wore beautiful jewelry."

As she was speaking, Mariah felt as though she was an observer of what was going on in this room. She looked past the detectives to the portrait of her father hanging over the piano. It was a wonderful likeness that captured the intelligence in his expression and the hint of a smile that was never far from his lips.

The sun was streaming through the windows on the back wall, creating patterns of light on the geometric design of the creamy carpet. Feeling somehow detached, Mariah realized how much cleaning Betty must have done to restore the shining orderliness of the spacious living room after the investigators had dusted for fingerprints. It seemed incredible to her that the room was now again so cheerful and welcoming, with its matching floral-patterned couches and wing chairs at the fireplace and occasional tables that could be moved so easily. When her father's friends had visited they would always pull the chairs up to the couch to form a semicircle where they would have coffee and a nightcap after dinner.

Greg, Richard, Albert, Charles.

How often had she sat here with them over the years since her father had retired from teaching? Some nights Betty would cook, but other nights, her father would take over the kitchen. Cooking had become a hobby for him, and he had not only enjoyed it but had been naturally good at it. Three weeks ago he made a big green salad, a Virginia ham, baked macaroni, and garlic bread, she thought. That was the last dinner we all had together . . .

The last dinner. The last supper. Dad's seventieth birthday.

She had to tell the detectives about the parchment her father may have found.

With a start, she realized that both detectives had been observing her. "I'm sorry," she said. "You asked about Lisa's jewelry."

"From what you said, she was known to have it, and maybe some people knew she kept it at home. But frankly, Ms. Lyons, that isn't our focus. We came here to speak with you and your mother. Since Mr. Scott has said he is now representing your mother, perhaps we can sit down now and talk to you."

"Yes, of course," Mariah said, trying to keep her voice steady. Suppose it comes up about the gun? she thought. How much should I tell them if they ask? Stalling for time, she said, "Please let me first check on my mother. There are some medications she has to take now."

Without waiting for a reply, she went into the foyer and saw Kathleen, followed by Delia, coming down the stairs. With a determined expression, Kathleen walked rapidly through the foyer into her husband's study, opened the door of the closet, and pushed Delia away. "You can't come in here!" she shouted.

"Mom, please . . ." Mariah's pleading voice could be heard in the living room.

Benet and Rodriguez looked at each other. "I want to see this," Benet said quietly. Together they went into the study. Kathleen Lyons was sitting at the far end of the closet, hunched against the wall. In an anguished voice she kept repeating, "So much noise . . . so much blood."

"Shall I try moving her?" Delia asked Mariah uncertainly.

"No, it's useless," Mariah said. "Just stay in the room. I'll sit in there with her for a while."

Delia nodded and stood at the place where Jonathan's leather chair had been. Seeing her in that exact spot brought back to Mariah the vivid memory of her father sprawled on that chair, blood dripping from his head. The police had removed the chair as evidence on the night of the murder. Will they give it back to me? she wondered. Do I *want* it back?

"Ms. Lyons," Benet said quietly, "we really need to speak with you."

"Now?" she asked. "You can see how my mother is. She needs me to be with her."

"I won't keep you long," he promised. "Perhaps the caretaker can stay with your mother while you're with us."

Mariah looked uncertainly from him to her mother. "All right. Delia, bring in a chair from the dining room. Don't go in the closet, just be here for her." She looked apologetically at Detective Benet. "I'm afraid to leave her alone. If she gets a crying spell she can lose her breath."

Rita Rodriguez heard the break in Mariah's voice and knew Mariah was aware of the skepticism in Simon Benet's face. Knowing him as well as she did, she was sure that Simon thought Kathleen Lyons was putting on an act for them.

When Delia returned carrying the dining room chair, she placed it just outside the closet and sat down.

Kathleen looked up. "Close the door," she demanded. "Close the door. I don't want any more blood on me."

"Mom, it's all right," Mariah said soothingly. "I'll just leave it open a tiny bit so you have some light. I'll be back in a couple of minutes."

Biting her lips to keep them from quivering, she led the detectives into the living room. Simon Benet was direct. "Ms. Lyons, this burglary is of course very unfortunate and we can understand that Mr. Scott is terribly upset about it. We also understand that he will be representing your mother and wants an opportunity to speak with her. However we are in the midst of investigating a homicide and must proceed without delay. Let me put it to you bluntly: We need to speak with both you and your mother and get answers to some important questions."

The doorbell rang, and this time without waiting for an answer, Lloyd Scott opened the door and came in. His face ashen, he said, "The Mahwah cops are in our house. My God, someone got in without tripping the house alarm or the alarm on the safe. I thought we had a foolproof system installed."

"As I just told Ms. Lyons, there's no such thing anymore," Benet told him. "It's obvious you had a pro in there." Then his tone changed. "Mr. Scott, we understand you're very involved in your own situation, but as I was just telling Ms. Lyons, it is imperative we speak to her mother and her."

"My mother is in no condition to talk with you," Mariah said, interrupting. "You should be able to see that for yourself." She realized she had raised her voice and had done it because now she could hear her mother wailing. "I said that I'll talk with you," she reminded Benet, "but could we do it when my mother is calmer?" Helplessly, she added, "I've got to go to her," and hurried back to the study.

Simon Benet looked straight at Lloyd Scott. "Mr. Scott, I can tell you that right now we have probable cause to arrest Kathleen Lyons for the murder of her husband. She was alone in the house with him. She was holding the gun and her fingerprints are on it. There is no sign of forced entry nor evidence of anything missing in the house. We have held off so far because we want to make sure that she hasn't been set up. If you won't allow us to speak to her in the next couple of days, we'll have no choice but to arrest her."

"There is no sign of forced entry into my house either, but some-one did get in and make off with some three million dollars' worth of jewelry," Lloyd Scott replied.

"But nobody was found in your house clutching a gun," Benet said.

Ignoring the remark, Lloyd Scott continued. "Obviously, I'm needed in my own home now. I will talk to Kathleen. But clearly she is in no condition to speak to even me right now. Give me until tomorrow. If I do allow her to talk to you at all, it will be tomorrow afternoon. If you decide to arrest her, contact me. I'll surrender her. As you can see, she is a very, very sick woman." Then he added, "I'm also advising Mariah to wait and talk to me before she answers your questions."

"Sorry," Benet said curtly. "This is a homicide investigation. We insist on talking to Mariah as soon as her mother quiets down. You don't represent her."

"Mr. Scott, you just heard Mariah say that she is willing to talk with us," Rodriguez said firmly.

Lloyd Scott's normally florid complexion was recovering from the paleness that had come over it when he had learned of the bur-glary in his home. "All right. It's up to Mariah, but you must under-stand that you cannot speak to Kathleen now or at any time without my permission."

"Yes, we understand. But if you try to put us off again tomorrow and she is not immediately arrested, your client will end up with a subpoena to appear before the grand jury, and there's no question she would be a target of that grand jury. If she takes the Fifth and won't testify after that, so be it," Benet told him. "But that would pretty much be telling us that she did it, wouldn't it?" he asked sarcastically.

"Given her illness, I can assure you that she has no idea what tak-ing the Fifth Amendment would even mean, and if she did, drawing that conclusion would be absurd." Lloyd Scott then looked in the direction of the study. "I have to get back to my wife. When Mariah comes out, I would appreciate it if you would tell her that I will call her later."

"Of course." Benet and Rodriguez waited until they heard the front door close behind the lawyer, then Benet said flatly, "I think the mother is putting on an act for our benefit."

"It's too hard to tell," Rita replied, shaking her head. "But I do know one thing. Mariah Lyons is sad about her father and also obvi-ously nervous. I don't think she has anything to do with this. Ten to one she's terrified her mother is guilty but will try to point us in other directions. It will be interesting to see what she comes up with."

It was twenty minutes before Mariah came back into the living room. "My mother is asleep in the closet," she said, her voice flat. "All this has been . . . " Feeling herself start to choke up, she stopped and began again. "All this has been overwhelming."

They spoke for over an hour. They were experienced detectives and they questioned her intently. She did not deny that she was in-tensely resentful about Lily or that she had been very disappointed in her father.

She answered all of their questions about the gun truthfully. Ten years ago her mother had enjoyed going to the shooting range with her father, but certainly she had not been there since the dementia had started. She was startled to hear that the gun showed no sign of rust. She told them that if her father had gone to the range himself since then, he had never mentioned it to her. "I know he used to keep it in his desk drawer," she said, "and I know what you may be thinking now. But do you seriously believe that if my father was sitting at his desk and my mother came down and reached into that drawer and took out the gun, he wouldn't have stopped her? I mean, my God, for all I know that gun may have been out of this house for years."

Then she added, "But I just learned yesterday that my father had a premonition of death, and that he may have revealed to someone that he had come across a priceless ancient parchment and was concerned about one of the experts he had consulted."

Mariah was intensely relieved when the detectives finally left. She watched their car pull out of the driveway and permitted herself a glimmer of hope. The detectives had phoned Father Aiden and were now headed to New York to speak with him about the parchment that may have been written by Christ to Joseph of Arimathea.

15

As the computer software company he had started began to grow, Greg Pearson had been definite in his plan that it would never go public. He had no desire to be splashed on the business pages of the *Wall Street Journal* or the *Times* or to have breathless speculation on the possible value of an initial public offering of Pearson Enterprises.

He was a low-key chairman and chief executive officer of the company while always totally aware of every detail. He was respected by his associates, but his painful shyness, which came across to many as aloofness, made it impossible for him to form close friendships. Over the years he had joined a few golf clubs and the Racquet and Tennis Club in New York. Never a good athlete, he didn't much enjoy golf. But then he had realized that a relatively high handicap made it possible for him to compete, and he made himself try to participate in the enthusiasm that his golfing companions shared.

His tennis game was not bad at all now and he was a welcome partner at the Racquet and Tennis Club.

Everything Greg did had one object only, and that was to make Mariah fall in love with him. He often wondered if Jonathan had understood how Greg felt about her. Jonathan had joked that he should find a girl who talked a lot. That thought always made Greg smile. It wasn't that Mariah was talkative. It was that she was sharp and funny and good company.

And beautiful.

When they were all at Jonathan's dinners, it was hard for him not to follow her every move. He had loved observing the warmth between her and Jonathan. "Oh, God help us, Betty isn't here and Dad's the chef," she would joke if she saw Jonathan in his chef's apron. She was always so thoughtful of her mother, and when, in her dementia, Kathleen would pick up the knife instead of the fork and put it in her mouth, Mariah would lean over in an instant and make the substitution.

Greg treasured the evenings when the group would linger over espresso in the living room and he would happen to sit next to Mariah on the couch. Feeling her nearness, watching the expression on her face, looking into the magnificent deep sapphire-blue eyes that were so like Jonathan's, was both thrilling and heartbreaking for him.

It's such a damn shame that Kathleen came across those pictures a year and a half ago of Jonathan with Lily, Greg thought. When that happened, Mariah put her foot down and banished Lily from the dinners.

Before that, Lily had always driven back and forth to Mahwah with Charles, and Greg knew that Mariah had thought Lily and Charles were involved with each other. It had been better that way. Jonathan's relationship with Mariah had suffered once she became aware of Lily, and it hurt both of them.

On Saturday morning, Greg played tennis, then went back to his apartment in the Time Warner Center on Columbus Circle. He had been in it for four years and still was not sure if its ultramodern décor had not been overdone by the interior designer.

It was a thought he dismissed as unimportant.

His avocation was his work, and he had brought home plenty of high-tech material, which he studied for a while before he finally gave up and realized he absolutely had to talk to Mariah.

When she answered the phone, her voice was strained but warm. "Greg, how nice of you to call. You won't believe what's going on around here."

He listened. "You mean someone broke into your neighbors' house in the past three weeks and cleaned out the jewelry? Do they know when it happened?"

"No, I don't know whether they can pin the time down," Mariah said. "And Lloyd Scott—that's our neighbor—is a criminal defense attorney. He's going to represent Mother. Greg, I think they're going to charge her with Dad's murder."

"Mariah, let me help. Please. I don't know how good a lawyer your neighbor is, but your mother needs top-notch representation and maybe you do, too. I'm afraid that it's pretty common knowledge that you and your father had serious problems." Then, while his courage lasted, Greg added, "Mariah, I'm coming over at six o'clock. I know you said your mother's weekend caregiver is very trustworthy. You and I are going out for dinner. Please don't say no. I want to see you and I'm worried about you."

When Greg put the phone down, he stood for a moment wondering if he could believe his ears.

Mariah had agreed to have dinner with him, and even said she was looking forward to it.

16

Professor Albert West knew he had taken a calculated risk on the drive home from the funeral on Friday afternoon by telling his fellow professor Charles Michaelson that Jonathan believed he had found the Joseph of Arimathea parchment. His eyes had narrowed behind his glasses as he had intently studied Charles's face for his reaction.

Charles's expression of shock may have been genuine, or it may have been a good act. Albert simply couldn't be sure. But Charles's immediate reference to the possibility that if Kathleen came across the parchment she might destroy it led to other possibilities. Would the same thought have occurred to Jonathan? And if so, would he have kept it someplace other than his home, perhaps even given it to someone he trusted to hold it for him?

Someone like Charles?

A lifelong insomniac, during most of Friday night Albert wrestled with that thought.

On Saturday morning, after a light breakfast, he went to his home office in what would have been the second bedroom in his modest apartment, settled at his desk, and spent the morning going over lesson plans. He was glad that the fall semester would be starting next week. He had not taught during the summer, and while he was never lonely, he did heartily enjoy interaction with his students.

He knew that because of his slight stature and deep voice their nickname for him was "Bellows." He thought it not only appropriate but actually quite clever.

At noon Albert made a sandwich to eat in the car, collected his camping gear, and went down to the garage in his building. As he waited for his SUV, he realized that his favorite word, "suppose," was running through his mind. Suppose Charles was lying? Suppose Charles had seen the parchment? Suppose he had told Jonathan that he, too, believed it was genuine?

Suppose Charles had warned Jonathan not to bring the parchment home? He might very well have reminded Jonathan that Kathleen had found the pictures of him and Lily that he thought were well hidden.

It was possible.

It made sense.

Jonathan respected Charles as a knowledgeable biblical expert and as a friend. He might easily have left the parchment with him. As Albert got in his car, he thought of the shocking incident fifteen years ago when Charles had accepted a bribe to authenticate a parchment that he knew to be fraudulent.

It happened when Charles was in the middle of his divorce and desperately needed money, he recalled. Fortunately for Charles, Desmond Rogers, the collector who had bought the parchment, was very wealthy and prided himself on his own expertise. When Rogers realized he had been duped, he had phoned Charles and threatened to call the police. Albert had then gone to him and pleaded with him not to turn this into a criminal case. He managed to convince Rogers that he would only embarrass himself if the matter became public, since he had openly scoffed at other experts who advised him that the parchment was a fake. "Desmond, you would ruin Charles, who over the years has helped you acquire some magnificent and valuable antiques," Albert told him. "I beg you to understand that he was in an emotional and financial tailspin and did not act rationally."

Desmond Rogers eventually decided to accept the two-million-dollar loss and, at least as far as Albert knew, had never told anyone else about it. He *did* express his utter contempt for Charles Michaelson. "I'm a self-made man, and I know many people who have been in a terrible financial bind. Not one of them would have accepted a bribe to cheat a friend. Tell Charles for me that no one will ever know of this incident, but also tell him I never want to see his face again. He's nothing but a crook."

If Charles has Jonathan's parchment in his possession, he'll probably sell it, Albert decided. He'll find a hidden buyer for it.

How much did Charles resent Jonathan? It was clear to Albert that on that first archaeological trip six years ago, Charles had been deeply interested in Lillian Stewart, only to find that door closed in his face as he watched Lily and Jonathan fall into each other's arms practically overnight.

That Charles had willingly allowed everyone else to believe that he and Lily were involved with each other when they attended dinners at Jonathan's home had been absolutely out of character for him. He must have done it at Lily's request.

What else might he do for her?

I wonder what will happen now? Albert thought as he started the drive to the campsite he had been frequenting of late, the one in the Ramapo Mountains just minutes away from the scene of Jonathan's murder.

17

Father Aiden O'Brien escorted Detectives Simon Benet and Rita Rodriguez to his office in the building connected to the Church of Saint Francis of Assisi on West 31st Street in Manhattan. They had called and asked if they could come in and talk to him, and he had willingly agreed, even though he immediately began to review in his mind exactly what he could tell them and the best way to word it.

It was his own grave fear that Kathleen had pulled the trigger that caused Jonathan's death. Her personality had changed so radically in the last few years, since the onset of her dementia. It was several years ago now that he had first noticed the telltale signs that her mind was beginning to fail. He had read that less than 1 percent of the population showed signs of dementia in their sixties.

Father Aiden had met Jonathan and Kathleen when they were newlyweds and he was a young priest. Jonathan, only twenty-six years old, already had his doctorate in biblical history and was on the faculty of New York University. Kathleen's master's degree was in social work, and she had a job with the city. They lived in a tiny apartment on West 28th Street and would come to Mass at Saint Francis of Assisi. They began chatting with Father Aiden one day on their way out, and before long he was frequently going to their apartment for dinner.

The friendship continued after their move to New Jersey, and he had been the one to baptize Mariah when, in her early forties, Kathleen had at last given birth to the child they had given up hope of having.

For over forty years they had what I would call a perfect marriage, Father Aiden recalled. He could understand Jonathan's emotions as Kathleen's condition increasingly worsened. Lord knows I see enough of it every day in my own parish as sons or daughters, or wives or husbands, struggle with the care of an Alzheimer's patient, he thought.

"I don't mean to get angry at him, but some days I feel as if Sam asks me that same question over and over again . . ."

"I left her for just a minute and she had thrown all the wash I'd just folded into the laundry sink and had water running on it . . . "

"Five minutes after we finished dinner, Dad told me he was starving and started pulling everything out of the refrigerator and dropping it on the floor. God forgive me, Father, I gave him a shove and he fell. I thought, Please, God, don't let him have a broken hip. Then he looked up at me and said, 'I'm sorry I'm so much trouble to you.' He had that moment of total clarity. He was crying, and I was crying . . ."

All this was running through Father Aiden's mind as he went behind his desk and invited Simon Benet and Rita Rodriguez to take the two visitor's chairs.

Jonathan was unfailingly patient and loving to Kathleen until he met Lillian, Father Aiden thought. And now, has Kathleen's twisted mind pushed her into committing an act she would never have committed if she was the Kathleen he had known for so many years?

"Father, thank you for seeing us on such short notice," Simon began. "As I explained on the phone, we are homicide detectives from the Bergen County Prosecutor's Office, and we are assigned to investigate the murder of Professor Jonathan Lyons."

"I do understand that," Father Aiden said mildly.

The kind of questions he had been expecting followed in close sequence. How long had he known the Lyonses? How often did he see them? Was he aware of Professor Lyons's friendship with Lillian Stewart?

Here starts the dangerous ground, Father Aiden thought as he reached into the pocket of his robe, took out his handkerchief, took off his glasses, polished them, and returned the cloth to his pocket before answering carefully.

"I have met Professor Stewart two or three times," he said. "The latest was over three years ago, although from the altar at the funeral Mass yesterday, I observed her come into the church late. I do not know when she left."

"Has she ever reached out to you for counseling, Father?" Rita Rodriguez asked.

"Many people who seek counseling do so with the understanding that their privacy will be respected. You are not to infer anything by my answer when I tell you I do not think it appropriate to reply to that question." That attractive young detective with the deferential expression already knows that I would be the last person Lillian Stewart would come to for advice, Father Aiden thought. The question is a setup.

"Father Aiden, we understand that Jonathan Lyons's daughter, Mariah, has been extremely upset by the fact that her father was involved with Lillian Stewart. Has she ever discussed that with you?"

"Again—"

Simon interrupted. "Father, we were speaking to Mariah Lyons an hour ago. She freely and openly told us that she had complained to you about Lillian Stewart and that she felt her father's relationship with Lillian Stewart was harming her mother's condition."

"Then you know what Mariah and I discussed," Father Aiden said quietly.

"Father, yesterday you told Mariah that her father, Jonathan

Lyons, had visited you ten days ago—on Wednesday, August fifteenth, to be precise," Simon said.

"Yes, I told Mariah, over a cup of coffee in the friary, that Jonathan Lyons believed he had found an object of immeasurable value that is referred to as either 'the Joseph of Arimathea parchment' or 'the Vatican letter.'"

"Did Jonathan Lyons visit you specifically to tell you about the parchment?" Rita asked.

"Jonathan, as we have established, was a longtime friend," Father Aiden said. "It would not have been unusual for him, if he was nearby, to drop in on me for a visit in the friary. That Wednesday afternoon he told me that he was in the process of reviewing ancient parchments that had been discovered in a church that had been long closed and was about to be razed. A safe was found buried in the wall there. Within it were some ancient parchments and he was asked to translate them." Father Aiden leaned back in his chair. "You may have heard of the Shroud of Turin?"

Both detectives nodded.

"Many believe that it is the burial cloth Jesus was wrapped in after the Crucifixion. Even our present Pope, Benedict, has been quoted as saying he believes it may be authentic. Will we ever really know that as a certainty? I doubt it, although the proofs are very strong. The Vatican letter, or, as it is known, the Joseph of Arimathea parchment, is of the same beyond-price value. If it is genuine, it is the only example of a letter written by Christ."

"Wasn't Joseph of Arimathea the man who asked Pontius Pilate for permission to take the body of Christ and bury it in his own tomb?" Rita Rodriguez asked.

"Yes. Joseph was a longtime secret disciple of Christ. As you may remember from your catechism lesson, when Christ was twelve years old he went with his parents to the temple in Jerusalem for Passover, but when it ended he did not leave with the others. He stayed behind in the temple and spent three days confounding the chief priests and the elders with his knowledge of the Scriptures.

"Joseph of Arimathea was an elder of the temple at that time. When he heard Christ speak and then learned he had been born in Bethlehem, he believed that Christ was the promised Messiah."

Warming to his subject, Father Aiden continued. "We do not know anything about Christ from the time he was twelve and discussed the Scriptures with the chief priests in the Temple until the wedding feast at Cana. Those years of his life are lost to us—the lost years. However, many scholars believe that some of that time was spent studying in Egypt because of the intervention of Joseph of Arimathea.

"The letter, if it is authentic, was written to Joseph by Christ shortly before the Crucifixion. In it he thanks Joseph for the kindness and protection he had offered him from the time he was a child.

"The authenticity of the letter has been disputed since Peter the Apostle carried it to Rome. Some of the Popes believed it was genuine, others did not.

"It was in the Vatican Library and word got out that Pope Sixtus IV was planning to destroy it to end the controversy. Then it disappeared.

"Now, some five hundred plus years later, it may have been found among these ancient parchments Jonathan was studying."

"A letter written by Christ. I can't imagine." Rita Rodriguez's voice was incredulous.

"What did Professor Lyons tell you about the parchment?" Benet asked.

"That he believed it was authentic, and that he was troubled that one of the experts he showed it to was concerned only about its monetary value."

"Do you know where the parchment is now, Father?" Benet asked.

"No, I do not. Jonathan gave no hint of where he was keeping it."

"Father, you said you had coffee in the friary. Before that, did you meet Jonathan Lyons in the church?" Rodriguez asked.

"We met in the church. The entrance to the friary is in the atrium."

"Did Jonathan Lyons also visit you in the reconciliation room?" Rita asked, her voice now innocent.

"If he did, I would not be at liberty to tell you," Father Aiden replied, his tone now severe. "Which I suspect you already know, Detective Rodriguez. I see you are wearing a small cross. Are you a practicing Catholic?"

"Not perfect, but yes, I am."

It was Simon Benet's turn. "Father, Jonathan Lyons was involved in a long affair with a woman who was not his wife. If he did go into the reconciliation room and confess his sins, could you have given him absolution if he intended to continue his affair with Lillian Stewart?" Benet smiled apologetically. "I was raised Catholic too."

"I thought I had made it clear that any references to Jonathan Lyons other than what he told me about the parchment are off the table. That includes your speculation, Detective Benet. However, I will add this. I have known Kathleen Lyons since she was a young bride in her early twenties. I do not believe, no matter how sadly twisted and lost her mind has become, that she would be capable of killing the husband she loved."

As he emphatically made that statement, Father Aiden realized that within the core of his heart, he believed what he had just said. Despite his early fears, he knew that Kathleen simply could not be guilty of Jonathan's murder. Then he looked from one detective to the other and knew he was wasting his breath defending Kathleen to them.

He wondered what they would think if he told them that Jonathan had a premonition of his impending death. Jonathan had said it openly at the table, but there was an inherent danger to mentioning it. They might think that he was in essence saying that he had come to fear Kathleen's increasingly violent outbursts. The last thing Father Aiden intended to do was to make things any worse for her.

Simon Benet did not apologize for asking an inappropriate question. "Father Aiden, did Jonathan Lyons give you the names of the expert or experts he consulted to authenticate the Joseph of Arimathea parchment?"

"No, he did not, but I can specifically say that he mentioned 'one of the experts,' so, of course, he showed it to more than one person."

"Do you know any biblical experts, Father Aiden?" Rita asked.

"The three I know best are Jonathan's friends, Professors West, Michaelson, and Callahan. They are all biblical scholars."

"What about Greg Pearson? Mariah Lyons said her father was his good friend and always included Pearson in that dinner group," Rita continued.

"Maybe as a friend Jonathan would have shown it to Greg, or told him about it, but I don't think he would have any reason to consult Greg as an expert."

"Why do you think he didn't tell his own daughter about his supposed discovery?"

"I don't know, except that sadly the closeness between Mariah and her father was strained by his relationship with Lillian Stewart."

"Would you consider Professor Lillian Stewart an expert on an ancient parchment?"

"I can't answer that, either. Lillian Stewart is a professor of English, but whether that extends to judging ancient parchments, I don't know."

The discussion with the detectives lasted about an hour, and when they got up to go, Father Aiden O'Brien was certain that they would be back. And when they do come back, he thought matter-of-factly, they'll be focusing on Jonathan's relationship with Lillian and whether he might have entrusted the priceless parchment to her.

After they left, feeling drained and weary, he sat down again at his desk. Before he had become aware of Jonathan's involvement with Lillian Stewart, he had occasionally been at Jonathan's dinners for his colleagues. He liked Lily and had gotten the impression that she and Charles Michaelson were a couple. She had a flirtatious manner when she spoke to Charles and would refer to a play they had gone to or a movie they'd seen. It was all a cover-up for the fact that she and Jonathan were involved.

And Jonathan went along with it, Father Aiden thought sadly. No wonder Mariah feels so betrayed.

Would Jonathan have kept the Vatican letter in Lily's apartment for safekeeping? he wondered. And if so, would she admit to having it now? Especially since Jonathan told me he was planning to give her up?

Father Aiden leaned on both arms of the chair as he rose painfully to his feet.

The terrible irony is, he thought sadly, if Kathleen killed Jonathan, it was just after he had decided to dedicate the rest of his life to taking care of her and to mending his relationship with Mariah.

God works in mysterious ways, he thought with a sigh.

18

Richard Callahan taught biblical history at the Rose Hill campus of Fordham University in the Bronx. After college, he had entered the Jesuit community but stayed only a year before realizing that he was not ready to make the commitment to the priestly life. At age thirty-four, he still had not come to a final decision.

He lived in an apartment near the campus. Raised on Park Avenue by his parents, two prominent cardiologists, it was convenient to be able to walk to work, but there was also something else. The beautiful campus with its Gothic buildings and tree-lined paths could have been set in the English countryside. When he walked outside the gates, he enjoyed stepping into the diversity of the crowded neighborhood and the abundance of splendid Italian restaurants on nearby Arthur Avenue.

He had intended to meet friends for dinner at one of those restaurants, but on his way home from the funeral, he canceled the date. The sadness of the loss of his good friend and mentor Jonathan Lyons would be a constant for a long time. But the question of who had taken his life was paramount in Richard's mind. If it was proved that Kathleen in her dementia had committed the crime, he knew it would mean she would be confined to a psychiatric hospital, probably for the rest of her life.

But if she was found to be innocent, who else would the detectives start looking at as someone who had a reason to kill Jonathan?

The first thing Richard did when he stepped into his cheerful three-room apartment was take off his jacket, tie, and long-sleeved shirt and put on a sport shirt. Next he went into the kitchen and got out a beer. I'll be glad when the cool weather comes, he thought as he stretched his long legs out and leaned back in the aging fake-leather reclining chair that he refused to allow his mother to replace. "Richard, you haven't taken the vow of poverty yet," she said, "and you may never take it. You certainly don't have to live it now." Richard smiled affectionately, remembering the exchange, then turned his mind back to Jonathan Lyons.

He knew that Jonathan had been translating ancient parchments that had been discovered in the safe of a long-closed church.

Had Jonathan found the Joseph of Arimathea parchment among them? If only I hadn't been away, Richard thought. If only he had told me exactly what he found. It was possible that by accident he had stumbled across it. Richard remembered that a Beethoven symphony had been discovered on the shelf in a library in Pennsylvania not that many years ago.

There was a nagging thought in the back of his mind that refused to surface as he later fixed pasta and a salad for himself. It was still there when he selected a movie on demand on his television set and watched it.

It was also there when he went to bed, and it slipped in and out of his dreams during the night.

It was midmorning on Saturday when it finally surfaced. Lily had been lying when she said she didn't know anything about the parchment. Richard was sure of it. Of course Jonathan would have shared that discovery with her. Maybe he might even have left it with her.

And, if so, now that he was dead, would she quietly find a buyer for it and pocket what could be an enormous sum of money?

It was a scenario he wanted to discuss with Mariah. Maybe it would do her good if I asked her out for dinner tonight, he thought.

But when he phoned her, it was to learn that Greg had already called and she was having dinner with him. Richard realized how deeply disappointed he was to hear that.

Had the decision he had finally made come too late?

19

That was a good night's work," the pawnbroker told Wally Gruber when Wally brought in his haul from the Scott home burglary. "You sure know how to pick them."

Wally beamed in agreement. Forty years old, short of stature, balding, with a somewhat bulky frame and an engaging smile that warmed the unsuspecting recipient, he had a long list of unsolved burglaries to his credit. Only one time had he been caught, and he had served a year in prison. Now he was employed as an attendant in a parking garage on West 52nd Street in Manhattan.

My day job, he would think sardonically—Wally had found a new and much safer way to engage in criminal activity without attracting the attention of the police.

The scheme he had dreamed up was to place tracking devices under the cars of people whose homes he might consider burglarizing, then follow the movements of those cars on his laptop computer.

He never did it to a regular patron of the garage, only the occasional customers who would come in just for an evening. The way he chose his victims was often by the jewelry the wife was wearing. In late July he had put a tracer on the Mercedes-Benz of a guy who was dressed for a black-tie dinner. The wife was a knockout even though she was fiftyish, but the emeralds she was wearing caught

Wally's eye. Dangling emerald-and-diamond earrings, a diamond-and-emerald necklace, a bracelet that jumped out at you, a ring that must have been seven carats. Willy had to force his eyes from feasting on the sight.

Surprise, surprise, he thought when Lloyd Scott handed him a five-dollar tip at the end of the evening. You don't know what a gift you just gave me.

He had driven out to Mahwah, New Jersey, the next night and passed by the Scott home. It had been well lighted both inside and out and he had been able to read the name of the security system. A pretty good one, he thought admiringly. Hard to get around for most people, but not me.

The Mercedes had gone back and forth to the city for the next week. Wally bided his time. Then one week passed and the car had not moved. Wally drove out again to check the site. The house was lit up in one downstairs room and in an upstairs bedroom.

The usual, he thought. Lights on timers, make people believe you're home. Then last Monday evening he'd made his move. Using stolen plates on his own car and with a "borrowed" E-ZPass from one of the cars in the garage, he had driven to Mahwah and parked down the block, where the neighbors were obviously having a gathering. Six or seven cars were lining the street. Wally easily bypassed the alarm, got into the house, and had just finished cleaning out the safe when he heard a shot and rushed to the window, getting there in time to see someone running from the house next door.

He watched as a hand reached up and pulled down a scarf or handkerchief just as the figure passed the overhead light on the cobblestone path to the sidewalk, then turned and disappeared down the block.

Wally saw the face clearly and in that instant it seared into his mind. Maybe someday he would find that memory useful.

He'd wondered if anyone else had heard the shot and if there might be someone in the house who was calling the police now. Grabbing his booty, Wally rushed from the house, but even in his haste he did not forget to lock the safe and reset the alarm. He got to his car and drove away, his heart pounding. It was only when he was safely back in Manhattan that he realized he had forgotten one very important detail. He had left the tracking device on the Mercedes-Benz, which was parked in the garage of the house he had burglarized.

Would it be found? *When* would it be found? He had been careful, but could he have left a fingerprint on it? Because if he had, his fingerprints were on file with the cops. It was a disquieting thought. Wally did not want to go back to prison. He had read with avid interest about the murder of Dr. Jonathan Lyons and could tell that the cops thought his wife, who suffered from Alzheimer's, was the one who had done it.

I know better, Willy thought. The one comfort he hugged to himself was that now if the cops *did* trace the tracking device back to him, he could trade his description of the killer for a light sentence on the jewelry heist, or maybe even immunity.

Or maybe I'll really get lucky. They'll go to some fancy party around here and park in my garage again.

As worried as he was, he realized it was too dangerous now to try to sneak back into that garage and try to get the tracker off the Mercedes.

20

Busy with their own thoughts, Detectives Simon Benet and Rita Rodriguez were silent for the first fifteen minutes after they got in their car and started to drive back to New Jersey.

When they reached the West Side Highway, Rita looked pensively out at the boats on the Hudson, remembering how only a few weeks before 9/11, she had met her husband, Carlos, at five o'clock at a café on the waterfront for cocktails and dinner. Some of the tall ships had been back and she and Carlos had gloried in the warmth of the late afternoon, the beauty of the nearby ships, and the feeling that New York was special, so terribly special.

He had worked in the World Trade Center, and the ultimate tragedy had occurred. It was the same sort of late-summer day as this that we were here, she thought. And once again she asked herself who could have predicted that disaster could ever have happened.

I never imagined I would lose him, she thought. Never.

But then, a week ago at this time, who could have predicted that Professor Jonathan Lyons would be a murder victim? He was killed on Monday, she mused. I wonder what he was doing last Saturday. He had a full-time caregiver for his wife. Did he slip over to New York to visit his girlfriend, Lillian Stewart?

It would be interesting to trace Professor Lyons's movements over last weekend. And what about the Vatican parchment, the letter to

Joseph of Arimathea that may have been written by Christ? Did Jonathan Lyons *really* find it? Its value would be incalculable. Would someone kill for it?

Of course we'll follow up on it, but I don't believe it has anything to do with this homicide, Rita thought. That gun was fired by a jealous and demented wife, and her name is Kathleen Lyons.

"Rita, my guess is that our professor went to confession, or should I say the reconciliation room, with Father Aiden." Simon Benet's matter-of-fact voice broke into her reverie. "I know I hit home when I asked the good father that question."

"Do you think Lyons might have been planning to give up his girlfriend?" Rita's voice was incredulous.

"Maybe, maybe not. You've seen how his wife acts. Maybe he was just saying, 'Father, I can't deal with it anymore. Right or wrong, I have to get out.' He wouldn't have been the first to say that."

"What about the parchment? Who do you think has it?"

"We'll check on the people whose names Father Aiden gave us. The professors and the other guy who hung out with them, Greg Pearson. And I want to talk to Lillian Stewart, too. If there is a valuable parchment and she has it, who knows how honest she'll be about it? She may have gone to Professor Lyons's grave, but just two minutes later she was in the car with Richard Callahan."

Simon Benet steered around a slow-moving driver. "Right now my money is still on Kathleen Lyons, and our next step is to get a search warrant. I want to go through every inch of that house. I have a hunch we'll find something more tying Kathleen Lyons to the murder.

"But whether we find anything else or not, I'm recommending to the prosecutor that we make the arrest."

21

❦✿❦

Willy was comfortably settled in his overstuffed chair, his feet on a hassock, watching the Yankees–Red Sox game. It was the bottom of the ninth inning. The score was tied. Willy, a lifelong Yankees fan, was holding his breath.

He heard the turn of the key in the lock and knew that Alvirah was returning from her lunch with Lillian Stewart.

"Willy, I can't wait to tell you."

Alvirah sat down on the couch, forcing Willy to mute the television and swivel in his chair to talk to her.

"Willy," Alvirah said emphatically. "I got the impression on the phone that Lillian wanted to get my advice on something, but when I met her she was downright evasive. I asked her when the last time she saw Jonathan was, and she said last Wednesday evening. He was shot five nights later on Monday, so that sounded really strange to me."

"So you turned on your pin." Willy knew that whenever Alvirah got even a sniff of something being wrong, she automatically turned on the recording device in her gold sunburst pin.

"Yes, because Mariah has said in the past that she knew for sure that Lily and her father got together at least two or three times a week, and they always saw each other at least one evening on the weekend. Jonathan would stay at home during the day. The weekend caregiver is really trustworthy, and if he and Lily went out for dinner, he'd stay at her apartment overnight."

"Uh-huh."

"But the point is, why didn't Lily see him that last weekend before he was shot? There's something fishy there. I mean, had they quarreled?" Alvirah continued. "Anyhow, Lily talked, of course, about how much she already missed Jonathan and how sad she was that he hadn't put Kathleen in a nursing home, if only to protect her from herself, that kind of thing.

"Then she got teary and said that Jonathan would tell her how much he and Kathleen had been in love and what a wonderful life they'd had together before the Alzheimer's set in. Jonathan told her that if Kathleen had a choice, which of course she didn't, she'd rather have died than be in this condition."

"I would too, honey," Willy said, "but if you catch me putting the key in the refrigerator, just pack me off to a good nursing home."

He permitted himself a brief glance at the television, in time to see the first Yankee up hit a pop fly ball for an out.

Alvirah, who missed nothing, had caught the side glance. "Oh, Willy, it's all right. You go ahead and watch the rest of the game."

"No, honey, keep thinking. I can tell you're onto something."

"You see what I mean, Willy?" Alvirah's voice became faster with every word. "Suppose Jonathan and Lily had quarreled?"

"Alvirah, you're not suggesting that Lillian Stewart shot Jonathan, are you?"

"I don't know what I'm suggesting. But I do know this. I'm going to call Mariah right now and ask if we can drop in for a visit tomorrow afternoon. I need to know more about what's been going on." As she finished speaking Alvirah stood up. "I'm going to change into something comfortable. Why don't you just finish watching your game?"

As Willy swiveled in his chair, he pushed the mute button on the remote control, this time to turn the volume back on. He looked at the screen. The Yankees were on the field jumping up and down and hugging each other.

The announcer was shouting breathlessly, "The Yankees win! The Yankees win! Two outs, bottom of the ninth, two strikes, and Derek Jeter hits a home run!"

I can't believe it, Willy thought sadly. I've been watching this game for three hours, and the minute I turn my back Jeter puts one in the seats.

22

On Sunday morning Mariah went to Mass, then stopped at her father's grave. He had bought the burial plot ten years ago in a beautiful area that had once been the grounds of a seminary. The headstone was engraved with the family name, LYONS. I have to call and get Dad's name put on it, she thought as she looked at the fresh dirt over the area where her father's casket had been lowered.

Phrases from the prayer she had chosen for the memorial cards at the funeral parlor came back to her. "When the fever of life is over and our work is done . . . may He give us a safe lodging and a holy rest and peace at the last."

I hope you're at peace, Daddy, Mariah thought as she fought back tears. But I have to say you've left us with a pretty awful problem. I know those detectives believe Mom did this to you. Dad, I just don't know what to believe. But I *do* know that if they arrest Mom and she ends up in a psychiatric hospital, she will be destroyed, and then I will have lost both of you.

She started to leave but turned back. "I love you," she whispered. "I should have tried to be more understanding about Lily. I know how hard everything was on you."

On the fifteen-minute drive home she began to brace herself for the day. At breakfast her mother had pushed back her chair and said, "I'll go get your father." Delia had jumped up to stop her from going upstairs, but Mariah had shaken her head. She knew her mother would resist any effort to stop her.

"Jonathan . . . Jonathan . . . "

Her mother's voice rose and fell as she went from bedroom to bedroom looking for her husband. Then she slowly came downstairs again. "He's hiding," she had said, her expression bewildered. "But he was upstairs just a few minutes ago."

I'm glad Alvirah and Willy are coming this afternoon, Mariah thought. Mom likes them so much. And she always recognizes them immediately. But as she turned down her parents' street, she was alarmed to see police cars in their driveway. Sure that something had happened to her mother, she parked on the street, ran along the walk, threw open the front door, and stepped inside to the sound of voices.

Detectives Benet and Rodriguez were in the living room. Three of the drawers of the antique secretary were on the floor. They were going through a fourth that they had placed on the cocktail table. Overhead she could hear the sound of footsteps in the hallway.

"What . . . ," she began.

Benet looked up. "The chief detective is upstairs, if you want to talk to him. We have a search warrant for these premises, Ms. Lyons," he said crisply. "Here is a copy of it."

Mariah ignored the document. "Where is my mother?" she demanded.

"She's in your father's study with the caregiver."

Mariah's feet felt leaden as she rushed down the hallway. A man who had to be one of the search team was sitting at her father's desk going through the drawers. As she had feared, her mother was in the closet again, hovering against the back wall, Delia beside her. Her mother's head was bowed but when she heard Mariah call her, she looked up.

She had a silk scarf tied around her face so that only her blue eyes and forehead showed.

"She won't let me take it off her," Delia said apologetically.

Mariah went into the closet. She could feel the eyes of the detective following her. "Mom . . . Kathleen, it's too hot to wear that scarf," she said soothingly. "Whatever made you put it on?"

She knelt down and helped her mother up. "Come on; let's get rid of that thing." Her mother let her untie the scarf and lead her from the closet. It was only then that Mariah realized Detectives Benet and Rodriguez had followed her into the study, and from the cynical expression on Benet's face, she was sure he still believed that her mother was putting on an act.

"Is there any reason why I cannot take my mother and Delia out while the search is going on?" she asked Benet curtly. "We often used to go to brunch at Esty Street in Park Ridge on Sunday mornings."

"Of course. Just one question: Are these your mother's sketches? We found them in her room." He was holding up a sketchbook.

"Yes. It's one of her few pleasures. She used to be an ardent amateur painter."

"I see."

When they got to the restaurant and the waiter began to remove the table setting for a fourth person, her mother stopped him. "My husband is coming," she said. "Don't take his plate away."

The waiter looked at Mariah, knowing she had requested a table for three.

"Just leave it, please," Mariah said.

For the next hour she tried to take consolation in the fact that her mother ate one of the poached eggs she had ordered for her and even remembered that she loved a Bloody Mary at Sunday brunch. Mariah ordered one for her, mouthing the words "without the vodka" to the waiter.

The waiter, a man in his sixties, nodded. "My mother too," he said quietly.

She deliberately lingered over coffee, hoping against hope that the detectives would have cleared out before they got back home an hour and a half later. The squad cars in the driveway told her that they were still there, but when she went inside, she could see that they were about to leave. Detective Benet handed her an inventory of what they were taking with them. She glanced at it. Papers from her father's desk. A box of documents that included a file of parchments. And her mother's sketchbook.

She looked at Benet. "Is that necessary?" she demanded, pointing to the sketchbook. "If my mother looks for this, she'll be upset that it's gone."

"Sorry, Ms. Lyons, we need to take it."

"I warn you that the parchment file may contain something of indescribable value."

"We know about the Joseph of Arimathea letter from Christ. I assure you we will find an expert to go through this file very, very carefully."

Then they were gone.

"Let's take a nice walk, Kathleen," Delia suggested. "It's so beautiful out."

Kathleen shook her head obstinately.

"Well, then, we'll just sit on the patio," Delia said.

"Mom, why don't you sit outside for a little while?" Mariah suggested. "Alvirah and Willy are coming, and I need to get ready for them."

"Alvirah and Willy?" Kathleen smiled. "I'll go outside and wait for them."

Alone, Mariah began to tidy up the living room where the detectives had not completely closed the drawers of the secretary and had pushed aside the vase and candles on the cocktail table. The dining room chairs they had drawn up to it were still there. Next she went into her father's study. The top of the big antique desk that had been his pride and joy was now littered with some of the contents of the drawers. I guess what they left here wasn't evidence, she thought angrily. It seemed to her that the essence of her father had been taken from the room. The bright afternoon sun revealed the worn spots on the carpet. The books that he had kept in meticulous order were piled haphazardly on the shelves. The pictures of her mother and father, and herself with both of them, had been turned down as though they had been a nuisance to the prying eyes of the detective she had seen here.

She straightened out the study, then went upstairs, where it was obvious that all the rooms had been thoroughly searched. It was five o'clock when the house was finally put back together, and from the window of her bedroom she saw Willy and Alvirah's Buick parking in the driveway.

She was at the front door opening it before they reached the front steps. "I'm so glad to see you two," she said fervently as Alvirah's comforting arms went around her.

"I'm so sorry we were away this week of all weeks, Mariah," Alvirah said. "I was wringing my hands that I was in the middle of the ocean and couldn't be with you."

"Well, you're here now and that's what counts," Mariah replied as they went inside the house. "Mother and Delia are on the patio. I heard them talking a minute ago, so Mother's awake. She fell asleep on the couch out there, which is good because she hasn't been sleeping much at all since Dad was—" Mariah stopped, her lips unable to form the word she had planned to say, "murdered."

Willy hurried to fill in the void. "Nobody gets much sleep when there's a death in the family," he said heartily. He hurried ahead and opened the sliding glass door that led from the living room to the patio. "Hello, Kathleen, hello, Delia. You girls getting the sun?"

Kathleen's delighted laugh was enough reassurance for Mariah that Willy would keep her mother occupied for at least a few minutes. "Alvirah, before we go out, I have to tell you. The police were here this morning with a search warrant. I think they've gone through every piece of paper in this house. They took the parchments my father was translating. I warned them that one of them might be an invaluable antiquity, a letter Christ wrote to Joseph of Arimathea. My father may have found it among that batch and believed it to be authentic."

Alvirah's eyes widened. "Mariah, are you serious?"

"Yes. Father Aiden told me about it at the funeral on Friday. Dad saw him the Wednesday before he died."

"Did Lillian Stewart know about this parchment?" Alvirah demanded.

"I don't know. I suspect he would have told her about it. For all I know she has it."

Alvirah brushed her hand against her shoulder, turning on her hidden microphone. I can't miss or misunderstand a word, she thought. Already her mind was awhirl.

Jonathan saw Father Aiden on Wednesday afternoon. Suppose Jonathan told him that he had decided to end the relationship with Lillian? Lillian saw Jonathan Wednesday night. Did he go straight up there, and if he did, what did he say to her? According to Lily, they never saw each other again and did not speak to each other in those five days.

Was she lying? Alvirah wondered. As I told Willy yesterday, somebody's got to get the phone records of any calls from Jonathan to Lillian and from her to him between Wednesday and Monday night. If there aren't any, it says to me that Jonathan told her it was quits . . .

It was too soon to suggest all this to Mariah. Instead, Alvirah said, "Mariah, let's make a cup of tea and you try to catch me up on everything."

"'Everything' is that I know the detectives believe my mother killed my father. 'Everything' is that I wouldn't be surprised if they arrested her," Mariah said, trying to keep her voice steady.

As she spoke, the doorbell rang. "Pray God those detectives aren't back," she murmured as she went to answer it.

It was Lloyd Scott. He did not mince words. "Mariah, I just got a call from Detective Benet. Your mother is being charged as we speak. He is allowing me to take her down to the prosecutor's office in Hackensack to surrender her, but we have to go now. She'll be fingerprinted and photographed there and then they will admit her to the jail. I am so sorry."

"But they *can't* put her in jail now," Mariah protested. "My God, Lloyd, can't they understand her condition?"

"My guess is that, in addition to setting the amount of bail, the judge will order that she have a psychiatric evaluation before releasing her so that he can set appropriate conditions of bail. That means that by tonight or tomorrow, she'll be in a psychiatric hospital. She won't be coming home, at least not for a while."

At the back of the house, Willy, Kathleen, and Delia were coming in from the patio. "So much noise . . . so much blood," Kathleen was telling Willy, this time in a lighthearted singsong voice.

23

His secret retreat was in a seemingly vacant warehouse on the far eastern side of lower Manhattan. The upper-level windows of the warehouse were boarded. The metal front door was padlocked. In order to enter and exit, he had to drive around to the back, past an old loading dock, to a set of double-wide rusted metal garage doors that to anyone passing would look sagging and broken. But when the doors were opened with a remote he kept in his car, he could drive straight forward into the cavernous cement first floor.

He had gotten out of his car and was standing there now in that vast, dust-filled, empty space. If by any horrible mishap someone else ever managed to get in there, that person would find nothing.

He walked over to the back wall, the sound of his heels echoing in the stillness. He leaned down, pushed aside a grimy electrical outlet cover, and touched a hidden button. A lift slowly descended from the ceiling. When it reached the ground, he stepped onto it, then pushed another button. Slowly as the lift rose up, he closed his eyes briefly and readied himself to return to the past. When it stopped, he took a long breath in anticipation and crossed over the threshold. He switched on the light and once again was with his treasures, the antiquities he had stolen or purchased clandestinely.

The windowless room was as vast as the one below. But that was the only similarity. In the center of the space was a carpet gloriously bright with intricate figures and designs. A couch, chairs, lamps, and end tables were grouped on it, a mini–living room amid a treasure-filled museum. Statues, paintings, wall hangings, and cabinets containing pottery and jewelry and table settings crowded every inch of space.

Immediately he began to feel the calmness that being surrounded by the past always brought to him. He was desperate to linger there but it was not possible. He could not even visit the upper two floors now.

He did allow himself to sit on the couch for just a few minutes. His glance darted from one object in his collection to the next as he feasted his eyes on the extraordinary beauty around him.

But none of it meant anything if he did not own the Joseph of Arimathea letter. Jonathan had shown it to him. He knew instantly that it was genuine. There was no possibility that it was a forgery. A letter written two thousand years ago by the Christ. It made the Magna Carta, the Constitution, and the Declaration of Independence worthless in comparison. Nothing, nothing, would or could ever be more valuable. He had to have it.

His cell phone rang. It was the prepaid kind and could not be traced to him. He only gave the number to one person, then discarded it and bought a new one as needed. "Why are you calling me?" he asked.

"It just came over the news. Kathleen has been arrested and charged with Jonathan's murder. Isn't that a good break for you?"

"It was utterly unnecessary for you to contact me about something I would have learned myself in a short time." His voice was cold, but he also recognized that it showed a measure of alarm. She could not be trusted. Worse, it was clear that she had a growing sense of power over him.

He terminated the call. Then for long minutes that he could not afford to take, he considered the best way to handle the situation.

When he had thought it all through, he called her back and made an appointment to meet with her again.

Soon.

24

On Sunday evening Lillian Stewart reflected with great relief on her decision not to admit to the police that Jonathan had given her the parchment for safekeeping. She had already been contacted separately by two members of the dinner group. Each had told her flatly that if she had the parchment, he could quietly find her a buyer—and for a lot of money.

Her first instinct had been to tell the police that she had the parchment. She knew that if it was what Jonathan thought it was, it belonged in the Vatican Library. But then she thought of the five years she had given to Jonathan with nothing to show for it now except a lot of heartache. I'm entitled to whatever I can get for it, she thought bitterly. When I sell it to one of them, I want the money in cash, she decided. No wire transfer. If two million dollars suddenly shows up in my savings account, I know that the bank has to report that to the government. I'll just put the cash in my safe-deposit box and take it out gradually, so that if they do check me out, I won't be raising any red flags.

What would it be like to have two million dollars at my disposal? I still would rather have Jonathan, she thought sadly, but since I don't, I'm going to do it this way.

Lillian looked at the clock. It was five of six. She went into the kitchen, poured a glass of wine, and carried it into the den. She curled up on the sofa and clicked on the television. The six o'clock news would be coming on in a couple of minutes.

If Mom were alive, I know what she would think of all of this, she told herself. Mom was the smart one. Dad was such a loser. He did have an impressive name, Prescott Stewart. I guess by giving him a name like that, Granny thought that he might make something of himself.

Lillian's father had been twenty-one and her mother had just turned eighteen when they eloped. Her mother had been desperate to get out of the house—her own father was a hopeless alcoholic who had physically and emotionally abused both her and her mother.

Mom leapt from the frying pan into the fire, Lillian thought. Dad was a compulsive gambler. They never had two nickels to rub together, but Mom stuck with him until I was eighteen because she was afraid he would fight her for custody of me. I know if she were here she would tell me firmly that the parchment belongs in the Vatican Library. The fact that I would even *think* of keeping it would infuriate her. I guess I have more of my father in me than I realized.

It's kind of crazy, she thought. The main reason that Jonathan wouldn't divorce Kathleen was because he knew Mariah would never speak to him again if he did. Mom would never speak to me again if she knew I was doing this, but unfortunately I don't have to worry about her reaction. I still do miss her so much.

The pain of that afternoon when Jonathan had phoned to say he was coming to speak to her washed over her again.

"Lily, there's no easy way to say this, but I have to stop seeing you."

He sounded as if he had been crying, but his voice had been resolute, Lillian thought angrily. He loved me so much that he dumped me, and then got shot despite all his noble intentions to repair his relationship with Mariah and dedicate himself to taking care of Kathleen.

He and his wife had had forty good years together before Kathleen got sick. Wasn't that enough for her? For the last few years, she didn't even know who he was most of the time. What was Jonathan staying for? Why couldn't he understand that he owed *me* something too? And eventually it would have been okay with Mariah—she knew how bad her mother had been and what her father was going through. Even she must be honest enough to realize that she didn't have to deal with it every minute, day in and day out, like he did.

The six o'clock news was coming on. Lillian looked up to see that the lead story was about Jonathan's death. The area around the courthouse was filled with media. The CBS on-scene reporter said, "I am standing on the steps of the Bergen County courthouse in Hackensack, New Jersey. As you can see from the video, and this was taken just about an hour ago, seventy-year-old Kathleen Lyons, accompanied by prominent defense counsel Lloyd Scott, and her daughter, Mariah Lyons, walked into the courthouse and up to the second floor, where she surrendered in the office of the Bergen County prosecutor. After an almost weeklong investigation, she has been charged with the murder of her husband, retired NYU professor Jonathan Lyons, who was found dead in his home in Mahwah last week. It has been reported that Kathleen Lyons, whom sources say has advanced Alzheimer's disease, was found crouched in a closet, clutching the gun that killed him."

The tape showed Kathleen walking slowly into the courthouse, between her lawyer and her daughter, each supporting one of her arms. For once, Rory the caregiver isn't on the scene, Lillian thought. I never did like her. She always had that expression that meant, "I know your secret," when she looked at me. I swear I blame her for all the problems. Jonathan told me he had hidden the pictures of us in a fake book in his study. How did Kathleen ever manage to find that one book, with all of the others that he had in his study? I can guess what happened. Good old Rory nosed around, and when she found the photos, she showed them to Kathleen. She's a born troublemaker.

As the clip ended, the reporter excitedly indicated that Lloyd Scott and Mariah Lyons were now leaving the courthouse. Mariah looks devastated, Lillian thought. Well, that makes two of us. As microphones were shoved in Mariah's face, Lloyd Scott protectively pushed them away. "I just have a few words to say and that will be it," he said tersely. "Kathleen Lyons will be in court at nine o'clock tomorrow morning before Judge Kenneth Brown. She will plead not guilty to the charges. The judge will also be addressing the subject of bail at that time." His arm around Mariah, Lloyd hurried her down the steps and into a waiting car.

I wish I could be a fly on the wall in that car, Lillian thought. What's Mariah going to do now? Cry? Scream? Kind of like I felt when Jonathan so nobly decided that I was expendable. I felt like a beggar, crying and screaming, "This is it? What about *me*? What about *me*?"

She thought about the parchment. It was hidden in her safe-deposit box in the bank, just two blocks away. There were people who wanted it desperately.

How much would they pay, she wondered, if she did a sort of silent auction for it?

When Jonathan showed it to her three weeks ago, she had seen the awe and reverence in his face. Then he asked her if she had a safe-deposit box where she could keep it until he made the arrangements to have it returned to the Vatican.

"Lily, it's the simplest of letters. Christ knew what was going to happen. He knew that Joseph of Arimathea would ask for His body after the Crucifixion. He is thanking Joseph for all the kindness he has given Him all of His life.

"Of course the Vatican will want to have their own biblical scholars authenticate the letter. I want to meet with them, hand it over personally, and discuss my reasons for believing it is the document I think it is."

When he was here for the last time, Jonathan wanted me to meet him at my bank the next morning so that I could get the parchment and give it to him. I stalled him, Lillian thought. I was desperate to give him a chance to see how much he'd miss me. I told him I'd give it to him in a week if he still felt the same way. And then he was dead.

A commercial was coming on. She turned off the television and looked at the prepaid cell phone Jonathan had given her. It was on the coffee table. I'd use up the minutes and then buy more, she thought. I'd call him on his own prepaid phone. Anything to prove I didn't exist.

And now I have three of them, she thought drearily.

The third prepaid phone had been given to her by one of the bidders for the parchment. "We don't want to leave any trail," he warned her. "The cops are going to be looking for that parchment. You have to know they suspect you have it or you know where it is. Too many phone calls between us would get their attention."

Whenever she touched it, it felt cold in her hand.

25

Professor Richard Callahan frequently had dinner on Sunday evenings with his parents in the Park Avenue apartment where he had been raised. They were cardiologists who shared a practice and whose names regularly appeared on those "Best Doctors" lists.

Both were sixty years old, but physically they could not have been more different.

His mother, Jessica, was small and slender, with chin-length dark blond hair, which she pushed back with the glasses that usually rested on the top of her head.

His father, Sean, had a mass of curly salt-and-pepper hair, a trim beard, and a tall, muscular frame that was a tribute both to his days of being a star defensive end on the Notre Dame football team and the discipline of his daily workouts.

Richard did not realize how quiet he had been until he and his father finished watching the Mets-Phillies game. When his mother went into the kitchen to check on dinner, his father got up, poured two glasses of sherry, lowered the volume on the television, and bluntly said, "Richard, it's obvious you're worried about something. That game went down to the last minute. Yet you sat there like a bump on a log. Now, what is bothering you?"

Richard attempted a smile. "No, Dad, it's not that I'm actually worried. I've been thinking a lot about the trust fund that my grandfather set up for me when I was born. Since four years ago, when I turned thirty, I've been free to use the money whatever way I want."

"That's right, Richard. It's too bad you never got to know your grandfather. You were just a baby when he died. He was one of those guys who started out with nothing but had an instinct for the market. He bought stocks of new companies he believed in for twenty-five thousand dollars when you were born, and what are they worth now, two million something?"

"Two million, three hundred and fifty thousand, twenty-two dollars and eighty-five cents according to the latest statement."

"There you are. Not bad for an Irish immigrant who arrived here with five pounds in his pocket."

"He must have been quite a guy. I've always regretted I never got to know him."

"Richard, it seems to me that you're thinking about doing something with that money."

"I may be. We'll see. I'd rather not go into it now, but I assure you it's nothing for you and Mom to worry about." Richard glanced at the television, then sprang up from his chair as he saw the promo for the ten o'clock news. "Kathleen Lyons has been arrested for the murder of her husband," the reporter was saying. A snapshot of Kathleen with Mariah and Lloyd Scott flashed on the screen.

Richard was so focused on the television that he did not notice that his father, deeply troubled by the conversation, was studying him intently and trying to figure out what was going on.

26

On Sunday evening, Alvirah and Willy waited at Mariah's until she returned with Lloyd Scott from the courthouse. Betty had left an assortment of sandwiches and fruit on the table for them before she and Delia left for the night. Alvirah said, "I know that Mariah won't have much of an appetite, but maybe she'll eat something when she gets home."

It was clear that when Mariah arrived, she was grateful to find them waiting for her. Lloyd Scott walked with her into the living room. Alvirah and Willy had never met him, but they had watched him on the news and both sensed immediately that he was the right person to defend Kathleen and to protect Mariah.

Lloyd had not planned to stay, but Alvirah told him that she needed to talk to him about her meeting with Lillian. "I was just about to tell Mariah about it earlier, but then you came in and said that Kathleen had to surrender," she explained. Then she added, "But let's do it over a bite to eat."

They sat around the dining table. Mariah, feeling as though a tsunami had engulfed her, realized that she had eaten almost nothing at the brunch and that she was hungry now. She even managed a smile when Willy placed a glass of red wine in front of her.

"After what you've been through the last week, you need it," he said firmly.

"Thanks, Willy. And thank both of you for waiting here, and for all of this," she said, gesturing to the food on the table.

Lloyd Scott helped himself to a sandwich and the glass of wine Willy was now pouring for him. "Mrs. Meehan," he began.

"Please, we're Alvirah and Willy," Alvirah said, interrupting.

"And I'm Lloyd. As you may know I'm Kathleen and Mariah's next-door neighbor. I knew Jonathan very well. He was a fine man. For his sake as well as Kathleen's and Mariah's, I am going to do my utmost to help Kathleen. I know it is what he would want."

Alvirah hesitated briefly and then began. "I think I'm going to say it straight out. We all know that Kathleen may have shot Jonathan. On the other hand it wouldn't be hard to set her up as the fall guy. She can't defend herself. So let's look at another angle. I had lunch with Lillian Stewart yesterday."

"You did?" Mariah asked, shocked.

"Yes. She called me. She was really distraught. Don't forget, Mariah, I met her on that cruise when she was with your father. After that I only saw her one other time, when your father invited us to his lecture at the 92nd Street Y. We had dinner but by then we had met you and she certainly sensed that I was uncomfortable being with her. That's the last time I saw or heard from her until she called me out of the blue yesterday. She said she wanted to talk to me about something, so of course I said okay."

"What did she tell you?" Lloyd Scott asked.

"That's just it. Nothing. Between the time she called me sounding very anxious to talk and a few hours later when we actually met for lunch at the restaurant, it was obvious she had changed her mind about confiding in me. All she did basically was go on about how much she missed Jonathan and how he should have put your mother in a nursing home a long time ago." Alvirah leaned back in her chair. "But without knowing it, she may have told me something very important."

"What, Alvirah, what is it?" Lloyd Scott and Mariah asked the same question.

"I asked Lillian when was the last time she spoke to Jonathan and she told me it was the Wednesday evening before the Monday evening that he died."

"But that's impossible!" Mariah exclaimed. "I know that he always went to see Lillian over the weekend. Delia—who, as you know, is always here on the weekends when Rory is off—has told me about that. He'd spend part of Saturday with Mom, then take off. He often didn't come back until Sunday afternoon, unless he knew I was coming over in the morning."

"Think about this," Alvirah said, allowing herself a degree of excitement. "Perhaps they weren't speaking for those last five days. What if something big happened between them? And, Mariah, we haven't had much time to talk, but I've read in the paper that your father may have come into possession of a valuable biblical letter and now nobody knows where it is. My question is, could he have given it to Lillian, and then they ended up fighting over it? And then he ends up dead? And Kathleen becomes the second victim— maybe of a setup?"

"If my father didn't speak with Lillian for five days, that's very significant," Mariah said quietly. "Father Aiden told me at the funeral that Dad had visited him on Wednesday afternoon and that Dad was sure the parchment was genuine but was also very troubled that one of the experts he showed it to was only interested in its monetary value. From what I gather, that person wanted to sell it through the underground market. Dad absolutely intended to return it to the Vatican Library."

"Do you know if your father went to confession that day with Father Aiden?" Alvirah asked.

"Father Aiden didn't say that, but I also know he wouldn't tell me if he did or he didn't, since that would be privileged."

"I'm not Catholic," Lloyd Scott said, "but if your father went to confession, wouldn't he be seeking forgiveness for something that he had done that he believed was wrong?"

"Yes," Alvirah said firmly. "And take it one step more. If Jonathan was going to go to confession, he must have made up his mind to give up Lillian. So let's suppose that's the way it happened. And let's suppose he told her it was over between them that Wednesday night, which is exactly when she told me that she last spoke to him."

"The police took boxes of papers out of his office today," Mariah said. "Some of them contained the documents he was translating, but I just don't think he would put something as valuable as the letter there. In fact, I don't think he would have kept it in the house since he knew that sometimes my mother rummages through his office. We certainly know that very well since she found the pictures of him and Lillian."

"It would seem to me," Lloyd said, "that it would have been logical of him to entrust the parchment to Lillian. We all know that they were very close. She could have kept it at her apartment or in some other secure location. My first thought is that Jonathan would have wanted the parchment that Wednesday evening, unless of course she was keeping it somewhere else and couldn't give it to him. In that case they would have had further contact in the next few days. So maybe she really *did* give it to him before he died and maybe he actually did have it in his study that night."

"I'll say it again. When Lillian called me she was trying to make up her mind about something," Alvirah replied positively. "Whatever she is holding back now has something to do with that parchment and maybe even with Jonathan's death."

"I would say we have to get the phone records of Jonathan's home and cell phones immediately," Lloyd said. "If he used either or both of those phones to call her, then we'll see if Lillian is telling the truth about having no communication with him in those last few days."

27

When she finally got to bed on Sunday evening, it occurred to Mariah that she had not phoned Rory to tell her that there would be no need for her to come in tomorrow. It was too late to call, but she rationalized that Rory had surely seen the evening news. If anything, Mariah was surprised that Rory had not contacted her to say how sorry she was.

At seven A.M. the next morning, already dressed, Mariah was having coffee in the kitchen when to her astonishment she heard the front door open and a moment later was greeted by Rory. "Mariah, I'm so sorry about all that has happened. Your poor, dear mother would never have hurt anyone if she had been in her right mind."

Why does her expression of sympathy sound so damn hollow? Mariah asked herself. "My poor dear mother didn't hurt anybody, Rory, in her right mind or not."

Rory looked flustered. Her graying hair was pulled back in its bun but as always a few strands were hanging loose. Her eyes, enlarged by wide-frame glasses, moistened. "Oh, Mariah, my dear, the last thing in the world I would want to do is offend you or your mother. I just thought that everyone believed the tragedy was caused by her dementia. I heard on the news she was in jail and she is going before the judge this morning. I was hoping he would let her come home on bail. I wanted to be here to take care of her."

"I doubt he did," Mariah said. "I caught him once using a cell phone that I knew was not his regular one. I just have the feeling that he would not have had his calls to Lillian showing up on any of the phone bills that went to the house. Frankly, he'd have been afraid I might see them."

"You know, I've seen a lot of this kind of thing," Alvirah said. "When people want to keep their communications private, they get one of those prepaid cell phones, then keep buying additional minutes for it as they go along."

"As I see it," Lloyd Scott said slowly, "it is entirely possible that Jonathan's last visit to Lillian Stewart was to break off their relationship. If that is the case and if she was in possession of the parchment, then she may have given it back to him, in which event the prosecutor's office will presumably find it in those boxes. I note that we only have her word for it that she and Jonathan didn't speak for those several days. Or, and this is entirely possible, Lillian may have refused out of anger to give it back to him and his further communications with her to try to get it returned were on that other phone."

Listening, Mariah felt as if a terrible weight was being lifted from her shoulders. "Until now, as much as I have fought it, I have believed in my own heart that my mother killed my father in a demented rage," she said quietly. "But now I just don't believe that's true. Now I think there is another explanation, and we have to find out what it is."

Lloyd Scott stood up from his chair. "Mariah, I need to digest all of this and decide what we share with the prosecutor at this point. I'll pick you up at seven thirty tomorrow morning. That will give us plenty of time to get to court before nine. Good night, everyone."

"That's very thoughtful," Mariah said. "If by any chance the judge lets Mom come home today, I will need your help. I didn't go into my office at all last week, and I've got to start taking care of some things there."

At precisely seven thirty Lloyd Scott rang the bell. "I hope you got some sleep last night, Mariah, but if you did, I suspect it wasn't much," he said.

"Actually, not much. I was exhausted, but I'm so worried about how we can prove that Mom is being framed."

"Mariah, in case Kathleen *is* released, would you like me to ride to the courthouse with you?" Rory asked.

Scott answered for Mariah. "Rory, that isn't necessary. I can almost guarantee that the judge will want to order a psychiatric evaluation before she's allowed to post bail. That will take at least two or three days."

"Rory, you go ahead home. Of course I'll pay you for these days, until we see when Mom is released. I'll let you know later on what's happening."

"But . . ." Rory started to protest leaving, but then she said, reluctantly, "Okay, Mariah, I hope to hear that you need me very soon."

When they arrived at the courthouse in Hackensack, Lloyd escorted Mariah to the fourth-floor courtroom of Judge Kenneth Brown. They waited quietly on a bench in the hallway until the doors were unlocked. It was now only eight fifteen and they knew that within the next half hour the media would be everywhere. "Mariah, they'll bring your mother to the holding cell adjacent to the courtroom a few minutes before the judge comes out," Lloyd told her. "I will go in and speak to her when she arrives. The sheriff's officer will let me know. When I do that, you just wait in the front row. And again, Mariah, it is most important that you say nothing to the press, no matter how much you want to."

By now Mariah's mouth was dry. She had been tempted to put on the black-and-white jacket she had worn to the funeral but instead chose a light-blue linen pantsuit. She wrapped her hands around the strap of the navy shoulder bag that now rested on her lap.

An incongruous thought came to her: This is the suit I was wearing two weeks ago when Dad met me in New York for dinner. He said that he always thought that blue was my best color.

"Don't worry, Lloyd. I won't say anything," she said finally.

"Okay. The doors are open. Let's go in."

As the next half hour passed, the courtroom began to fill with reporters and cameras. At ten of nine a sheriff's officer approached Lloyd and said, "Mr. Scott, your client is in the holding cell."

Scott nodded and got up. "Mariah, the next time I come out it will be just before your mother is brought in." He patted her shoulder. "She'll be all right."

Mariah nodded and kept her gaze resolutely forward, aware that she was being photographed. She watched as the prosecutor, a file jacket under his arm, took his place at the counsel table nearest the jury box. Now that she was here, the reality of what might be yet to come terrified her. Suppose by some crazy decision they actually put Mom on trial and the jury finds her guilty? she thought. I couldn't bear it. I couldn't bear it.

Lloyd emerged from the side door and went to his counsel table. At that moment the court clerk announced, "All rise!" and the judge entered from his chambers. The judge turned to the sheriff's officers and said, "Please bring in the defendant."

The defendant, Mariah thought. Kathleen Lyons, the criminal defendant whose only "crime" has been to lose her mind.

The same door Lloyd had used opened again. This time, two female sheriff's officers came out walking on either side of Kathleen and led her to where Lloyd was standing. Kathleen's hair was disheveled. She was wearing an orange jumpsuit with black lettering on the back: BCJ—for Bergen County Jail. She looked around and spotted Mariah. Her face crumbled into tears. Mariah was horrified to see that she was handcuffed at the wrists. Lloyd had not warned her about that.

The judge began to speak. "In the matter of *State versus Kathleen Lyons*, on warrant complaint 2011 dash 000 dash 0233, would you enter your appearances please?"

"Your Honor, appearing on behalf of the State, Chief Assistant Prosecutor Peter Jones."

"Your Honor, appearing on behalf of Kathleen Lyons, Lloyd Scott. I note that my client, Ms. Lyons, is present in court."

"Ms. Lyons," the judge said, "this is your arraignment and first appearance in court. The prosecutor will read the complaint into the record and then your attorney will enter a plea on your behalf. I will then consider the amount and conditions of bail."

Kathleen obviously realized that he was talking to her. She glanced at him but then turned to look at Mariah again. "I want to go home," she moaned. "I want to go home."

Heartsick, Mariah listened as the prosecutor read aloud the charges of murder and possession of a firearm for an unlawful purpose, and then Lloyd's firm "not guilty" response.

Judge Brown indicated that he would now hear from the attorneys regarding bail. "Prosecutor Jones, since Ms. Lyons was just arrested last night, bail has not yet been set. I'll hear your recommendations, then Mr. Scott can speak."

Mariah listened as the prosecutor argued that the State had a very strong case and that he recommended a five-hundred-thousand-dollar monetary bail. But before she could be released, he also wanted an inpatient psychiatric evaluation so that the judge could set "appropriate conditions to protect the community."

Protect the community from my mother? Mariah raged inwardly. She needs to *be* protected, *not* the other way around.

It was Lloyd Scott's turn. "Your Honor, my client is seventy years old and is in extremely fragile health. She suffers from advanced dementia. Five hundred thousand dollars' bail is extremely excessive, and unnecessary in this case. She is a thirty-year resident of Mahwah and poses absolutely no risk of flight. We guarantee the court that she will have round-the-clock care and supervision in her home. We beseech Your Honor to let her be released on bail today and schedule another hearing in a week regarding bail conditions after an outpatient psychiatric evaluation is completed. I note that I have already arranged with a bondsman to have the monetary bail posted in whatever amount Your Honor chooses to set today."

Mariah realized she was praying. Please, God, let the judge understand. Let him send her home with me.

The judge leaned forward. "The purpose of bail is to ensure the appearance of a defendant in court and the conditions of bail are set to protect the community. This lady is charged with murder. She is absolutely presumed innocent, but I conclude that under the circumstances, it is imperative that an inpatient psychiatric evaluation be performed and that I receive a detailed report so I can make an informed decision regarding the amount of bail as well as appropriate conditions of bail. She will be remanded to Bergen Park Medical Center for an inpatient evaluation, and I will have a further hearing in this court this Friday at nine o'clock. She may not be released on bail until this hearing is held. This is the order of the court."

Stunned, Mariah watched as the sheriff's officers escorted Kathleen back into the holding cell area, Lloyd following them. Mariah stood up as he turned and gestured for her to wait for him. The photographers who had been allowed to take pictures during the proceeding were being directed by the sheriff's officers to leave. Within a couple of minutes she was alone in the courtroom.

When Lloyd came out ten minutes later, she asked, "Can I see Mom?"

"No. I'm sorry, Mariah. She is in custody. They don't allow that."

"How is she? Tell me the truth."

"I won't lie to you. She's very frightened. She wants her scarf. Why would she want to tie it around her face?"

Mariah stared at him. "She's been doing that since Dad was killed. Lloyd, listen to me. Suppose she heard the shot and ran to the top of the stairs. Suppose she saw someone with some kind of covering on their face. Suppose that's what's going through her mind."

"Mariah, calm down. I really think she'll be released on Friday. Maybe we can somehow get through to her then."

"Lloyd, don't you see? If someone with their face covered came into the house, then either that person had a key, or the door was left unlocked. That lock is fixed now so that Mom cannot open it from the inside ever since she got out that time. We know the police said that there was no sign of forced entry. That's part of the reason that they're charging Mom.

"Betty, our housekeeper, told me she left at about seven thirty that night, after my parents had dinner and she cleaned the kitchen. She's been with us for over twenty years. I trust her implicitly. Rory has been with us for two years. She sat with Mom during dinner and then got her to bed. Mom hadn't slept well the night before and was agitated and tired. Rory said she fell asleep right away. Rory claimed she checked the lock on the front door, as she always does, then left. She said it was just a few minutes after Betty had gone."

"Maybe it's time to check on Rory," Lloyd replied. "I use a very good private investigator on some of my cases. I'll call him. If there's something in her background that we should know about, he'll find it."

28

Once again the collector received an unwanted phone call from Rory. "I was just at the house," she said. "Mariah and the lawyer were leaving to go to court. I have to tell you I'm getting nervous. They said something about Kathleen being framed. Before now, I thought they were just going to try to prove she was crazy. God knows *that's* true. Are you sure you didn't leave any evidence behind, like your fingerprints or something like that?"

"We already have a meeting scheduled for tonight. Couldn't you have waited to discuss this with me?"

"Listen, I don't need you talking to me like I'm dirt. You and I are both knee-deep into this. If for any reason they start checking into me, they'll find out about my prior record and I'll be a dead duck. I'll meet you tonight. Make sure you have my payment in full. It's getting too hot for me around here. I'm going to take off before it's too late. And don't worry about hearing from me anymore after tonight, because you won't."

"The fact that you have a prior record will not be proof that you had anything to do with any of this," he replied tersely. "But if you disappear, they'll know you were involved, and then they'll track you down. So just don't panic. If they talk to you, play the role of the loving caregiver who can't wait for dear Kathleen to come home."

"I can't do that. It won't work. I lied when I applied to the agency for the caregiver job. You know I made up a new name. I violated parole. I've got to get out of here."

"Suit yourself," he snapped. "I'll have the money for you tonight. As we agreed, you will take the subway downtown to the Chambers Street station. Be there precisely at eight o'clock. I'll pull up on the corner in a small black car, the same one you've seen before. We'll ride around the block. I'll give you the money; you can count it. Then I'll drop you right back off at the subway and you can go and live your life."

As Rory disconnected the call, she thought about how she had really planned never to get in trouble again after she had been released from prison the last time. If only Joe Peck had asked me to marry him, she thought. If he had, I'd never have taken that job in New Jersey. I never would have been in that house when this creep came to dinner and recognized me. And then blackmailed me into getting involved in this.

She permitted herself a grim smile. On the other hand, I've hated cleaning and feeding all those crazies since I got out of prison. At least I sometimes had a little fun, like the day I found those pictures of Jonathan and Lily and gave them to Kathleen. I guess I needed a little excitement in my life.

And now, with money in my pocket, I can find some real excitement, without a bedpan in sight.

29

From the last row of the courtroom, Detectives Simon Benet and Rita Rodriguez had observed the arraignment of Kathleen Lyons. When it was over, they went downstairs to their second-floor office and found Father Joseph Kelly, the biblical scholar they had hired, waiting for them. After they had spoken with Father Aiden and had learned of the possibility that a valuable ancient parchment had been in Jonathan's possession, they had contacted Father Kelly to let him know that his services might be needed and told him what they would be looking for.

During the search of the Lyons home yesterday, Mariah had pointed out the box of documents that her father had been working on. Simon had called Father Kelly last night and asked him to come to the prosecutor's office at nine thirty this morning.

"Father," Rita began, "we understand that this is the box of documents that Jonathan Lyons was translating when he died. We did a quick check early this morning of all the other items that we seized and this seems to be the only one containing this type of document."

Father Kelly, eighty-two years old but remarkably fit, said dryly, "I assure you that a letter that may have been written by Christ to Joseph of Arimathea must not be considered a 'type of document.' If I find it here, I will consider myself blessed to have even held it."

"I understand," Simon said. "I must explain that it is strict protocol to have a member of the prosecutor's staff present whenever an expert reviews evidence."

"That's fine with me. I'm ready to start."

"The office next door is ready for you. I'll carry it in."

Five minutes later, Simon and Rita, each with a fresh cup of coffee in hand, were once more alone in their shared office. "If Father Kelly finds the parchment, it tells me that the case begins and ends with Kathleen Lyons," Simon said. "The daughter told us when he wasn't home or wasn't working on those documents, he kept them locked in the file drawer in his desk. That's where they were when he was shot. But if that one parchment isn't there, whomever he may have given it to ought to have told Mariah by now. Even *she* admitted to us that he may very well have been afraid to have it anywhere near Kathleen after she found and cut up those pictures."

Rita was silent for a moment, then looked directly at him. "Simon, I'm going to be honest with you. Watching Kathleen Lyons in that courtroom today, it's hard to envision her managing to hide that gun from everyone, possibly load it herself, then sneak up behind him and shoot him—not to mention standing back ten to fifteen feet and putting the bullet squarely in the back of his head."

She knew that Simon was getting angry. "Look," she said, "before you jump all over me, let me finish. I know that she used to go shooting at the range with her husband so she certainly knew in the past how to fire that gun. But did you see her today? Physically she didn't seem coordinated at all. She was looking all over the place, completely bewildered. That was no act. I bet the shrinks find that her attention level is almost nonexistent. I say that if we don't have the parchment in that box then whoever has it wants to sell it and may have been involved in Jonathan's death."

"Rita, we arrested the right person last night." Simon's voice was raised. "Kathleen Lyons acted no different today than she has every time we saw her since she shot her husband. I do think she has some level of Alzheimer's, but that didn't prevent her from cutting up those pictures a while ago because she was angry at him, and it apparently didn't prevent her from shooting him in the head last week because she was still angry at him."

An hour later there was a knock on their door and Father Kelly entered. "There aren't many documents in the box and I was able to review them fairly quickly. There is nothing of any real value in there and certainly there is no letter written by Christ, I can assure you of that. Is there anything more you need me to do?"

30

On Monday afternoon, after her mother's appearance in court, Mariah returned to her parents' home and went up to her bedroom, changed into slacks and a cotton sweater, and twisted her hair up, fastening it with a comb. Then for a long minute, she stared into the bathroom mirror, seeing the reflection of her face with the deep blue eyes that were so like her father's. "Dad," she whispered, "I promise you, I *swear* to you, that I'm going to prove Mom is innocent."

Carrying her laptop, she went downstairs and headed to her father's study. Grateful for a certain sense of calm that was replacing the frantic emotions she had felt during the hearing, she settled in the dining room chair that had replaced the desk chair the police had seized on the night of the murder.

I did nothing last week with my clients, Mariah thought. I've got to get some work done before I have to start thinking about how Dad left things financially. I can do a lot of it from here. It was actually a relief to open her computer, check e-mails, and return calls to some of the clients whose investments she supervised. It feels like getting back to some degree of normality, she thought. Even though absolutely nothing in my life is normal, she added to herself wryly.

Betty Pierce, who was still busy putting the upstairs rooms back into order after the police search, brought her a sandwich and a cup of tea. "Mariah, I can stay tonight if you'd like company," she suggested tentatively.

Mariah looked up and saw the deep concern etched into the lines of their longtime housekeeper's face. This has been tough for her too, she thought. "Oh, Betty, thanks a million, but I'll be fine on my own. Tonight I'm having dinner next door with Lloyd and Lisa. But tomorrow night, I want to invite Dad's special group over for dinner. The usual four. Professor Callahan, Professor Michaelson, Professor West, and Mr. Pearson."

"I think that's a great idea, Mariah," Betty said heartily, now smiling. "Seeing them will give you a lift, and God knows you need one. What do you want me to cook?"

"Maybe salmon. They all like that."

By four o'clock Mariah felt that she had gotten up to speed with all of her clients. Dear God, it feels so good to get back into a routine, she thought. It's an escape. While she had been working, she had deliberately refused to allow herself to speculate on what was happening to her mother at the psychiatric hospital just a few miles away. As she began to make the calls for the dinner, she continued to push those thoughts away.

The first one she reached was Greg; as she heard his voice she thought about why she had so naturally called him first. She had truly appreciated being with him on Saturday night. His obvious admiration for her father and the amusing stories he told about him had made her realize she had been absolutely wrong in regarding Greg as bland and unemotional. She remembered her father had once said that although Greg was basically shy, he could also be really interesting and funny when he was with people he felt comfortable around.

When his secretary put her through to him, he sounded both surprised and pleased that she had called him. "Mariah, I've been thinking of you all day. I know what's been happening. I wanted to call you last night after I saw the news, but I didn't want to intrude. Mariah, I asked you Saturday night and now I'm asking you again. What can I do to help you?"

"You can start out by coming here to dinner tomorrow night," Mariah said as she pictured him in his spacious office, impeccably groomed, his brown hair always looking freshly barbered, his eyes that interesting shade of gray-green. "It would be so nice to have you and Richard and Charles and Albert here. You were all so close to Dad. We'll make it a sort of reunion in his honor."

"Of course, I'll be there," Greg answered promptly.

There was no mistaking the deep affection in his voice.

"Around six thirty," Mariah said hastily. "See you then." She broke the connection, realizing that she did not want to linger on the call. Dad, she thought, you told me more than once that Greg was sweet on me and that he had a lot to offer if I would just give him a chance . . .

Refusing to dwell on the thought, she dialed Albert West.

"I was camping over the weekend in your territory," he told her. "The Ramapo Mountains are really beautiful. I must have walked for miles." His booming voice reminded her that her father had told her that the odd combination of that voice and his small frame had earned Albert the nickname "Bellows." He readily accepted her invitation, then said, "Mariah, I have to ask. Did your father recently discuss with you the fact that he may have found a valuable ancient parchment?"

"No, I'm sorry, but he never did," Mariah said, her voice pained. "But over the years he told me about the Vatican letter, and now I understand he may have actually found it among those scrolls he was studying." Then she added sadly, "Albert, you know how it was. My relationship with Dad had been strained for the last year or so because of Lillian. If things had been the way they used to be, I know I'd have been the first one he told."

"That's absolutely true, Mariah. I'll be glad to be with you tomorrow. Maybe we can talk more about it."

Charles Michaelson's crisp "hello" brought a smile to Mariah's face. Charles always sounds at least mildly annoyed, she thought. She had never quite forgiven him for acting as if he was Lillian's date at so many of the dinners when he was really providing a cover for her father and Lillian in her parents' home.

He told her he'd very much enjoy coming to dinner, then echoed Albert's question about the parchment.

She repeated what she had told Albert. But then she said, "Charles, it would have been natural for Dad to have shown you what he thought was the Vatican letter. No one is more expert in this area than you are. Did you ever see it?"

"No," Michaelson answered sharply, almost before she finished asking the question. "He told me about it only a week before he died and promised to show it to me, but unfortunately he never got that far. Mariah, do you have it, or do you know where it is?"

"Charles, the answer to both of those questions is no." And why don't I believe you? she asked herself as she broke the connection. I would have bet that Dad would have gone to you first. She frowned, trying to remember why some years ago her father had mentioned something about being very disappointed in Charles. What could that have been about? she wondered.

Her final call was to Richard Callahan. "Mariah. Of course I've been thinking about you. I can't imagine what you and your mother must be going through. Have you been able to visit her?"

"No, Richard, not yet. She's going through the evaluation. I'm praying that she's back home on Friday."

"I hope so, Mariah, I hope so."

"Richard, are you okay? You sound so down or troubled or something."

"You're very perceptive. My dad asked me the same question last night. I've been doing a lot of thinking, and I've made a decision that I've put off for too long. I'll see you tomorrow night." Then he added quietly, "I'm very much looking forward to seeing you."

Richard has decided to go back and complete his training to be a Jesuit, Mariah thought, and wondered why she felt so much dismay. He brings so much to the table, and we won't see nearly as much of him once he rejoins the order.

At seven o'clock, she changed into a long blue skirt and white silk blouse, touched up her makeup, brushed her hair loose, walked across the lawn to the Scotts' home, and rang the bell. Lisa answered the door. As usual she looked glamorous in a designer multicolored shirt and slacks, with a silver belt that hugged her hips and silver slippers with five-inch heels.

Lloyd was on the phone. He waved to Mariah and she followed Lisa into the living room, where cheese and crackers were set out on the coffee table. Lisa poured glasses of wine for the two of them. "I think it's some kind of police call," she confided to Mariah. "They asked about our burglary. My God, wouldn't it be great if I got some of my jewelry back? I miss my emeralds so much. I'm still kicking myself that I didn't bring them with me on the trip."

When Lloyd joined them a few minutes later, he said, "Well, that was really interesting. The New York City police have been calling people who may have parked at the garage on West 52nd Street next to the Franklin Hotel. Our names are on the list from that charity ball we went to at the hotel a couple of months ago. An attendant at the garage was suspicious of one of the other employees and saw him attach what turned out to be a GPS tracker to a customer's car. The customer lived in Riverdale. The police checked his car, found the tracker, and arranged for him and his wife to drive to the Hamptons and stay there for a few days. They say this crook's modus operandi was to check the comings and goings of the car and, if it was some-where else or not used at all for a period of time he would case the house to see if was unoccupied. The local police kept the Riverdale house under surveillance. It only took three nights before this guy tried to break into it. They want me to see if there's a tracker on our car. They said if there is, then don't touch it, just in case they can lift some fingerprints off it."

Lloyd disappeared in the direction of the garage. When he returned, he said, "We've got a tracker on the Mercedes, too, which means that the guy who put it on has to be the one who got in here!"

"My emeralds!" Lisa cried breathlessly. "Maybe I'll get them back."

Lloyd did not have the heart to tell his wife that by now, the emeralds had undoubtedly been pried out of their settings by a fence and long since been sold to a willing buyer.

31

❧❦❧

On Monday evening, Kathleen was lying in bed in a single room in the psychiatric section of Bergen Park Medical Center. Several times she had tried to get up and now light restraints on her arms and legs were preventing her from making another attempt.

Besides her usual medicine, she had been given a light sedative to calm her, and so she was content to lie quietly as conflicting thoughts and memories mixed together in her mind.

She smiled. Jonathan was there. They were in Venice on their honeymoon walking hand in hand in Saint Mark's Square . . .

Jonathan was upstairs. Why didn't he come down and talk to her? So much noise . . . so much blood . . . Jonathan was bleeding.

Kathleen closed her eyes and stirred restlessly. She did not hear the door of the room open and close and was unaware of the nurse who was bending over her.

Kathleen was at the top of the stairs and the front door opened. Who was that? A shadow passed in the foyer. She couldn't see a face—

Where was her scarf?

"So much noise . . . So much blood," she whispered.

"Kathleen, you're dreaming," a soothing voice suggested.

"The gun," Kathleen mumbled. "Rory put it in the flower bed. I saw her. Did it have dirt on it?"

"Kathleen, I can't hear you. What did you say, dear?" the nurse asked.

"We're going to have lunch at Cipriani's," Kathleen said.

Then she smiled as she drifted off to sleep. She was back in Venice with Jonathan.

The nurse tiptoed from the room. She had been instructed to write down anything her patient said. Carefully, word for word, she wrote on the chart, "So much noise. So much blood. And then she was going to Cipriani's for lunch."

32

Rory spotted the car waiting at the corner as she reached the top step of the subway exit Monday evening. She had hurried up the stairs and was now short of breath. The sense that everything was closing in on her was overwhelming. She had to get the money and escape. Years ago she had disappeared and she could do it again. As soon as she got out of prison after serving seven years for stealing from that old lady, she skipped her parole.

I reinvented myself, she thought. She had taken on the identity of a cousin who had retired after years of being a caregiver and who had moved to Italy, then died suddenly. I worked hard, she thought angrily. Now even if they can't prove that I left the gun out and left the door unlocked, I'll go back to prison because of the parole violation. And I saw nutty Kathleen looking out the window when I put the gun in the flower bed. Did she see me? She has a way of blurting out stuff that you would think she didn't notice.

The passenger door of the car was being opened from the inside. The street was busy, and even though it was still hot people were moving swiftly. Everyone rushing toward air-conditioning, Rory thought as she felt sweat beginning to gather on her forehead and around her neck. She pushed back a strand of hair that was drooping over her chin. I'm a mess, she thought as she got in the car. Once I get away, I'll check into a spa and get myself back in shape. Who knows? If I look good and have money, there may be another Joe Peck around somewhere waiting just for me.

She reached for the handle of the door and pulled it closed.

"Eight o'clock," he said approvingly. "You're right on time. I just got here myself."

"Where's my money?"

"Look in the backseat. Do you see those suitcases?"

She craned her neck. "They look heavy."

"They are. You wanted a bonus. I gave you one. You deserve it."

His hand went to her neck. His thumb pressed with all his strength into a vein.

Rory's head slumped forward. She did not feel the needle he thrust into her arm nor hear the sound of the engine as the car sped downtown to the warehouse.

"It's too bad you won't be alive to enjoy the sarcophagus I've got all set for you, Rory," he said aloud. "In case you don't know what that is, it's a coffin. This one is fit for a queen. Not that there's anything regal about *you*, I'm sorry to say," he added with a smirk.

33

The detectives were coming to interview her at ten o'clock on Tuesday morning. Lillian did not sleep all Monday night. What was she going to tell them?

It had been stupid to tell Alvirah that she had not spoken to Jonathan since the Wednesday before he died. *Completely stupid!*

Could she tell them that Alvirah had misunderstood what she had said? Or could she say she had been so numb when they had had lunch together that what she really meant was that she had not *seen* Jonathan since Wednesday, because Kathleen was so agitated over the weekend that Jonathan didn't want to leave the house? But that they had spoken every day?

That would make sense, she decided.

She could tell them that they talked to each other only on prepaid phones and that after Kathleen killed him, she had discarded hers.

She thought about that last night they were together, when he left his prepaid phone with her. "I won't be needing this anymore. Please just throw it out and throw out yours," he had told her. But she had kept both of them. Terrified, she wondered if the police would get a warrant to search her apartment.

She was too nervous to do anything but swallow coffee, carrying the cup into the bathroom as she showered and washed her hair. It only took a few minutes to blow it dry, then she remembered the way Jonathan would playfully muss it when she was sitting on his lap in the big chair. "It looks too perfect," he would joke when she protested.

Jonathan, Jonathan, Jonathan. I still can't believe that you're gone, she thought as she carefully applied makeup, trying to cover the circles under her eyes. It will be good when classes start, she told herself. I need to be around other people. I need to be busy. I need to be tired when I come home.

I need to stop listening for the phone to ring.

The temperature had dropped overnight and was a seasonable seventy degrees. She decided to put on a running suit and sneakers to give the detectives the impression that she was on her way out as soon as they left.

Promptly at ten o'clock her doorbell rang. She recognized the two people who were standing there, the rumpled-looking guy with thinning hair and the olive-skinned woman who had been standing with Rory near the entrance to the room in the funeral parlor where Jonathan's casket had been placed.

Simon Benet and Rita Rodriguez introduced themselves. Lillian invited them in and offered coffee, which they refused, then all three went into the living room. Lillian felt vulnerable and alone as she sat on the couch while the detectives chose straight-backed chairs.

"Ms. Stewart, we spoke briefly last week on the phone but decided to wait to talk with you in person until now, since you were obviously extremely upset," Benet began. "I believe you told us you were home here in your apartment the night Professor Lyons died."

Lillian tensed. "Yes, that's right."

"Then did you lend your car to anyone else? According to the garage attendant downstairs, you took your Lexus out that evening at about seven thirty P.M. and returned shortly after ten P.M."

Lillian felt her throat close. Detective Benet had just said that when they phoned her last week she had been upset. That would be her excuse. Damn that garage guy!

Then she reminded herself that it was Kathleen who was under arrest for murdering Jonathan. But her E-ZPass . . . They could easily check to see what time she drove back over the George Washington Bridge to New York.

Be careful, be careful, she warned herself. Don't blurt out anything the way you did to Alvirah. "When I spoke with you I was so overwhelmed with shock and grief that I couldn't think straight. I was confused. You called me on Wednesday, didn't you?"

"Yes," Rodriguez confirmed.

"When I said I was home I was thinking of the night before your call. That was Tuesday evening when I was at home."

"Then you did go out on that Monday night," Benet said, pressing her.

"Yes, I did." Get ahead of them, she thought. "You see, Jonathan had become very suspicious that the Monday-through-Friday caregiver, Rory, was deliberately agitating his wife. He was convinced that she had snooped around his study and found that hollow book with the pictures of us both in it and then showed them to Kathleen."

"From what we understand, that happened over a year and a half ago. Why didn't Professor Lyons fire her then?"

"He didn't suspect her at the time, but only a few weeks ago he caught her in his study standing by while Kathleen rummaged through his desk. Rory claimed she couldn't stop her, but Jonathan knew she was lying. On his way into the room he had heard her telling Kathleen that maybe there were more pictures of us in there."

Simon Benet's face was impassive. "Again, why wouldn't he fire her immediately?"

"He wanted to talk to Mariah first. I gather they went through a couple of really indifferent caregivers who didn't keep Kathleen clean and mixed up her medications. He dreaded going through that again."

Then, feeling more confident, Lillian added, "Jonathan was working up his courage to tell Mariah it was time to put her mother in a nursing home and for him to get on with his life with me."

She widened her eyes and looked directly at Simon Benet and then at Rita Rodriguez. They remained impassive. No sympathy there, she thought.

"Where did you go that Monday night, Ms. Stewart?" Benet asked.

"I was restless. I wanted to have dinner out. I didn't want to be with anyone. I drove to a little restaurant in New Jersey."

"Where in New Jersey?"

"In Montvale." Lillian knew she had no way to avoid answering. "Jonathan and I used to go there together. The name is Aldo and Gianni."

"What time was that?"

"About eight o'clock. You can check. They know me there."

"I know Aldo and Gianni. It's not more than twenty minutes from Mahwah. And you just went there because you felt restless? Or was Professor Lyons planning to meet you there?"

"No—I mean yes." Watch out, Lillian thought, panicking. "We had prepaid phones to contact each other. He didn't want any calls to show up on his cell phone or landline to or from me. I imagine you've found his somewhere. He had planned to slip out for dinner with me after the caregiver got Kathleen to bed, but then it turned out she was leaving, so there would be no one home with Kathleen and of course she couldn't be left alone. So I had dinner myself and came home. I can show you my credit card receipt from the restaurant."

"What time did Professor Lyons call to say he couldn't come?"

"About five thirty, when he got home and learned that the care-giver would be leaving. I decided I'd go there anyway."

"Where is your prepaid phone, Ms. Stewart?" Rita asked, her voice warm.

"When I heard that Jonathan was dead, I threw it in the garbage. I couldn't bear to hear the sound of his voice again. You see, sometimes if he called and I couldn't answer right away, I'd save the messages from him on it. You must have found his prepaid phone?"

"Mrs. Stewart, what was your number, and what was his number?"

Shocked at the question, Lillian thought quickly. "I don't remember. Jon set it up so it went directly to him. We only used these phones for each other."

Neither detective visibly reacted to the answer. Simon Benet's next question came out of the blue. "Ms. Stewart, we have learned that Professor Lyons may have been in possession of a valuable ancient parchment. It was not among his belongings. Do you have any information about that?"

"A valuable parchment? He never said a word about that to me. Of course I know that Jonathan had been reviewing some documents that had been found in a church, but he never said anything about one of them being valuable."

"If he did have something valuable, are you surprised that he wouldn't have shown it to you, or at least told you about it?"

"You say Jonathan *may* have been in possession of a valuable parchment? You mean that you're not sure he was? Because I truly believe he would have shared that with me."

"I see," Benet answered crisply. "Let me ask you about something else. Professor Lyons was apparently a good marksman. He and his wife enjoyed going to a shooting range together, an activity that of course stopped when the signs of her dementia set in. Did *you* ever go to a shooting range with him?"

Lillian knew there was no use lying. "Jonathan started taking me out to a range in Westchester shortly after we met."

"How often did you go?"

They can check the records, Lillian thought. "About once a month." A mental image of the certificate she had received for marksmanship was burned in her mind, and before they could ask, she added, "I'm a pretty good shot." Then she burst out, "I don't like the way you two are looking at me. I loved Jonathan. I will miss him every day for the rest of my life. I'm not answering one more question, not one. You arrested his crazy wife for killing him and you were right. He was afraid of her, you know."

The detectives stood up. "Maybe you would answer this question, Ms. Stewart. You didn't like or trust the caregiver Rory, did you?"

"That I'll answer," Lillian said heatedly. "She was a snake. She found those pictures and started all the trouble. Jonathan's wife and daughter would never have suspected there was anything between us if it weren't for her."

"Thank you, Ms. Stewart."

They were gone. Trembling, Lillian tried to replay what she had told them. Had they believed her? Maybe not. I need a lawyer, she thought wildly. I shouldn't have talked to them without a lawyer.

The phone rang. Afraid to pick it up and afraid not to pick it up, she reached for it. It was Richard, but the tone of his voice was not the one she was accustomed to hearing.

"Lillian," he said forcefully, "I haven't been quite truthful with you and you certainly have been lying through your teeth to me. I saw the parchment. I know it is genuine. Jonathan told me he gave it to you for safekeeping. And that is what I am going to tell the police. I know you've had offers for it, but here's the price of my silence. I will give you two million dollars for it. I want it and I will have it. Is that clear?"

He did not wait for her response before breaking the connection.

34

On Tuesday morning at eleven A.M. Wally Gruber was brought before New York Judge Rosemary Gaughan for arraignment on charges of burglary and attempted theft. His round face was devoid of its usual friendly smile. His bulky body was garbed in an orange jail jumpsuit. His hands and legs were shackled.

The assistant district attorney began. "Your Honor, Mr. Gruber is charged with burglary and attempted theft at the residence specified in the complaint. He has a prior conviction for burglary, for which he served a prison sentence. We submit that the evidence here is extremely strong. Mr. Gruber was caught by the police as he broke into the home. We further note that the police are investigating another burglary in New Jersey for which he may be responsible. He is employed as a parking attendant at a city garage and there is evidence that he has been placing GPS trackers on cars so that he may be aware of when people are not home. The recent New Jersey burglary involved a theft of over three million dollars in jewelry while the family was away on vacation. We have been informed that a GPS tracker similar to the one surreptitiously placed on the vehicle of the owner of the New York home has been discovered on the vehicle of the owner of the New Jersey home. We anticipate criminal charges in New Jersey will be filed in the near future. I note further that the defendant is single and lives by himself in a studio apartment that he rents. Under all of these circumstances, we believe he is a high risk of flight and we request a two-hundred-thousand-dollar cash bail."

The defense attorney standing next to Wally, Joshua Schultz, then spoke. "First, Your Honor, Mr. Gruber is pleading not guilty. With respect to the district attorney's request for bail, I submit that it is clearly excessive. As of right now, no charges in New Jersey have been filed. Mr. Gruber is a longtime resident of New York City and has every intention of appearing at all court proceedings. He is a man of very limited means. Mr. Gruber has indicated to me that if you allow him to use a bondsman, he can make a fifteen-thousand-dollar bail."

Judge Gaughan looked down from the bench. "While the defendant is absolutely presumed to be innocent, the district attorney has proffered what appears to be strong evidence in this case. Given his exposure to a long custodial term if convicted, I conclude that there is a substantial risk of flight. I will not allow a bond. Bail is set at two hundred thousand dollars, cash only. Of course, if criminal charges are filed in New Jersey, additional bail will be set by a judge in that jurisdiction."

Three hours later, unable to post bail, Wally was on his way to Rikers Island. As he was hustled into the van, he breathed in the first hint of fall in the crisp breeze and compared it with the stale smell of the holding cell. I've got an ace in the hole, he reassured himself. They'll have to make a deal with me. When they hear what I know, they'll have to give me probation.

He smirked. I can sit down with their composite guy and give them every detail of the face of the person who blew away that professor, he thought. But if they don't want to play ball, I'll call the old lady's fancy lawyer and let him know I'm her ticket to go home.

35

The first thing Mariah did on Tuesday morning was call the hospital. The nurse at the desk of the psychiatric unit was reassuring. "Your mother was mildly sedated last night and slept quite well. She ate a little breakfast this morning and seems to be very calm."

"Is she asking for me or my father?"

"The notes on her chart indicate that last night she woke up several times and seemed to be carrying on a conversation with your father. She apparently thought that they were in Venice together. This morning she has been repeating the name 'Rory.'" The nurse seemed to hesitate, then asked, "Is she a relative or a caregiver?"

"A caregiver," Mariah answered, sensing that the nurse was holding something back. "Is there anything you're not telling me?" she asked bluntly.

"Oh, no. Of course not."

Maybe, maybe not, Mariah thought. Then, knowing that if she requested a visit with her mother before the next court hearing she would receive an automatic refusal, she asked, "Does my mother seem frightened? Sometimes she wants to hide in a closet when she's home."

"She is, of course, confused, but I would not say that she appears frightened."

Mariah had to be content with that.

She spent the rest of the morning on the computer in the study, thankful that so many of her accounts could be handled from home. Then she went upstairs to her father's bedroom and spent several hours removing his clothing from the closets and drawers and placing them, neatly folded, in boxes, to be given to a charitable distribution center.

Her eyes stinging with unshed tears, she remembered how her mother had not been able to bring herself to empty her grandmother's closet for nearly a year after her death. It doesn't make sense, Mariah thought. There are so many people who need clothes. Dad would want every stitch of his that could be passed on to be given away immediately.

She did keep the Irish cable-knit sweater coat that had been her Christmas present to him seven years ago. Once the cold weather arrived, it was his favorite at-home apparel. The first thing he did when he returned from the university was hang up his suit jacket, pull off his tie, and put on that sweater. He used to call it his second skin.

In his bathroom, she opened the door of the medicine cabinet and discarded the high-blood-pressure pills and the vitamins and fish oil he had taken religiously every morning. She was surprised to see a half-empty bottle of Tylenol for arthritis. He never told me he had arthritis, she thought.

It was another fresh and hurtful reminder of their estrangement.

She also decided to keep his aftershave lotion. When she unscrewed the cap and sniffed the subtle but familiar scent, it was momentarily as though he was in the room with her. "Dad," she pleaded softly, "help me to know what to do."

Then she wondered if an answer had come to her. Tonight for dinner, she should also invite Father Aiden and Alvirah and Willy Meehan. It was Father Aiden to whom her father had confided that he was sure the parchment was the one stolen from the Vatican

Library and that one of the experts he had shown it to was interested only in its monetary value. It was Alvirah to whom Lillian had admitted that she had not seen or spoken to her father in the five days prior to his death. In a happy coincidence, Alvirah and Willie had known Father Aiden long before they met Mariah.

Mariah went downstairs and made the calls to invite them. "Sorry for the last-minute notice, Alvirah," she said apologetically, "but you're a good judge of people. I cannot believe that Dad did not show that parchment to at least one or two of his dinner group. You've already met them at least half a dozen times. I want to bring it up tonight and see what their reactions are. I want to get your take on what happens. And certainly if Father Aiden is willing to repeat tonight what Dad told him, it would be hard for any of them to try to suggest Dad was mistaken about the authenticity of the parchment. God forgive me, and I hope I'm wrong, but I'm beginning to think that Charles Michaelson might be involved in some way. Don't forget that he and Lily used to come to dinner together and were pretty cozy. And I distinctly remember that one time Dad mentioned Charles had had some kind of legal or ethical situation that I gather had been a real problem."

"I'd love to be there," Alvirah said heartily. "And let me make it easy for you. I'll phone Father Aiden and if he can come, we'll pick him up. I'll call back in five minutes. By the way, what time do you want us?"

"Six thirty would be perfect."

Four minutes later, the phone rang. "Aiden can make it. See you tonight."

In the late afternoon Mariah went for a long walk, trying to clear her head, trying to prepare herself for what might come out of tonight.

The four most likely people to have been shown that parchment will be at my father's table, she thought. Charles and Albert have already asked me if I found it. The other night at dinner, Greg said that Dad talked about it but had not shown it to him. Richard has never even mentioned it to me.

Well, tonight, one way or the other, we are all going to talk about it.

Mariah picked up her pace, walking swiftly, trying to get the stiffness out of her limbs. The light breeze was becoming stronger. She had pinned her hair loosely into a bun but now she felt it slipping down around her shoulders. With a half smile she remembered how her father had told her that with her long black hair she reminded him of Bess, the landlord's daughter from the poem "The Highwayman."

When she got back to the house, Betty told her no one had called while she had been out. The first thing she did was to phone the hospital and receive virtually the same report as in the morning. Her mother was basically calm and not asking for her.

It was time to get dressed. The drop in temperature made a long-sleeved white silk blouse and black silk wide-bottomed pants feel like a good choice to wear at dinner. On impulse, she left her hair loose, again remembering her father's reference to Bess, the landlord's daughter.

Greg was the first to arrive. As she opened the door to let him in, he immediately embraced her. When he had dropped her off on Saturday night, his kiss on her lips had been brief and tentative. Now he held her tightly and stroked her hair. "Mariah, have you any idea how much I care about you?"

When Mariah pulled back, he immediately let her go. She gently put her hands on his face. "Greg, that means so much to me. It's just that, well—you know everything that's going on. Dad was murdered only eight days ago. My mother is locked up in a psychiatric hospital. I'm their only child. At least until this nightmare with the charges against my mother is resolved, I just can't think about my own life."

"And you shouldn't," he said crisply. "I completely understand. But you have got to realize that if there is anything you need, at any hour of the day or night, I will see you get it right away." Greg paused, almost as if he needed to catch his breath. "Mariah, I'll say it once and then I won't bring it up again while you're going through all of this. I love you and I always want to take care of you. But first I want to help you. If the psychiatrists who are evaluating your mother in the hospital don't do the right thing, I'll hire the best experts in the country. I know that the doctors I'd get would conclude that she has advanced Alzheimer's, is not capable of standing trial, and that with proper supervision she is no danger to anyone and should be at home."

As usual Albert and Charles had driven out together in Charles's car. As Greg finished speaking, the two were ringing the doorbell.

Mariah was profoundly grateful for the interruption. She had always known that Greg cared for her, but now she fully realized the intensity of his feelings. As much as she truly did appreciate his offer of help, his ardor added yet another layer of stress that both upset and smothered her. In the past few days, she had begun to understand subconsciously that for the past several years the terrible worry about her mother's deepening dementia and then the distress over her father's involvement with Lillian had wrung her emotionally dry.

I am twenty-eight years old, she thought. Since I was twenty-two, I have been heartsick over Mom, then for the past year and a half I have been basically estranged from the father I adored. I so wish I had a brother or a sister to share this with, but I do know one thing. I've got to get Mom home and comfortable and in the hands of a good caregiver. Then I need to have time to figure out my own life.

These thoughts were flooding her mind as she greeted Albert and Charles. She immediately sensed that there was tension between them. Charles was wearing his usual frown, only now it was more like a scowl. Albert, normally quite easygoing, seemed troubled. Quickly Mariah ushered them and Greg into the living room, where Betty had laid out a platter of hot and cold hors d'oeuvres. In the past, it had been their custom to have a cocktail in her father's study before dinner. Mariah sensed that they understood why they wouldn't be in that room tonight.

A few minutes later the bell rang again. This time it was Alvirah and Willy and Father Aiden. "I'm so glad you could all make it," Mariah said as she embraced each one of them. "Come on in. Everyone except Richard is here."

A little while later as they were all chatting, Mariah realized that the always punctual Richard was nearly half an hour late. "He's probably caught in traffic," she commented to the others. "As we all know, you can normally set your watch by Richard."

The thought crossed her mind that Richard had told her that he had just made a major decision. She wondered if he would tell her what it was tonight. She was also having a mixed reaction to the fact that Greg was taking over the role of host. It was he who offered to everyone the plate with the delicate sushi that Betty had prepared, and it was he who refilled glasses with the fine Merlot her father had enjoyed so much.

Then the chimes on the front door sounded again. Betty opened the door, and a moment later Richard stepped into the hallway and came directly to the living room. He was smiling. "Apologies, apologies," he said. "I had a meeting that ran over. It's so good to be with all of you." He was looking at Mariah as he said it.

"Richard, what can I get you?" Greg asked.

"Don't worry, Greg," he replied as he started walking toward the bar, "I'll get it myself."

A few moments later, Betty stood in the doorway and signaled to Mariah that dinner was ready.

Mariah had already decided that she would not bring up the subject of the parchment until they were having dessert. She wanted to create an atmosphere of warmth and closeness and had told a couple of them that this gathering would be a sort of tribute to her father. But she also wanted to loosen them up to the point where, no doubt with Alvirah's help, she would get some sense of who knew what about the parchment.

By the time that Betty was clearing the dinner plates from the table the anecdotes about her father had evoked both humor and nostalgia. Mariah did notice that Alvirah had switched on the microphone in her diamond pin when Albert talked about how much Jonathan enjoyed roughing it at excavation sites but despised the idea of camping for the sake of camping. "He asked me what in the name of God I could find pleasurable in sleeping in a pup tent with the possibility of bears visiting in the middle of the night. I told him that since I discovered the Ramapo Mountains, I could enjoy camping and keep an eye on him at the same time."

That was when Alvirah's hand brushed against the pin on her shoulder, but Albert did not say anything more about keeping an eye on Jonathan.

Usually after dessert they had coffee or espresso in the living room. This time Mariah had asked Betty to serve it at the table. She did not want the group separated when she brought up the subject of the parchment.

It was Greg who unwittingly gave her the opportunity to bring it up in a way that seemed spontaneous. "I was in awe of Jonathan's ability to read an ancient inscription and translate it, or see a piece of pottery and tell where it came from and how old it was," he said.

"That's exactly why the missing parchment my father told all of you about must be found," Mariah said. "Father Aiden, Dad talked to you about it. From what I understand, he mentioned it to Albert and Charles and Greg. Richard, did he ever show it to you or tell you about it?"

"He left word on my answering machine that he couldn't wait to tell me about his incredible find, but I never did see it."

"When did all of you receive those calls?" Alvirah asked, her tone casual.

"The week before last," Greg replied promptly.

"About two weeks ago," Charles said musingly.

"Two weeks ago yesterday," Albert said firmly.

"That would be the same day he left the message on my phone," Richard volunteered.

"However, he told none of you what it was and didn't show it to any one of you?" Mariah deliberately allowed the skepticism she felt to be heard in her tone.

"He left word on my machine at home that he thought he had found the Arimathea parchment," Albert said. "I was on a hiking trip in the Adirondacks and only got back the morning after his death. By then of course I had seen the headlines."

"The parchment was not in this house," Mariah said. "I think you all should hear what Dad told Father Aiden."

Before Father Aiden could speak, Charles Michaelson suggested, "Of course Jonathan may have jumped to the conclusion that it was the Arimathea letter, then after he made those calls realized he had made a mistake and never got around to calling any one of us back. We all know no expert ever wants to admit that he was wrong."

The priest had been quietly observing the others at the table. "Charles, you and Albert and Richard are biblical scholars. Greg, I know you have a deep interest in the study of ancient ruins and artifacts," he began. "Jonathan came to see me the Wednesday before he died. He was absolutely clear on the subject. He had found the Vatican letter, or the Arimathea parchment, as it is known." He glanced at Alvirah and Willy. "As I explained in the car on the way over, this letter is believed to have been written by Christ shortly before His death. In it He thanked Joseph of Arimathea for all the kindness he had extended to Him since He was a child. It was brought to Rome by Saint Peter and has always been a subject of debate.

"Some scholars believe that Joseph of Arimathea was at the temple in Jerusalem during Passover when the twelve-year-old Christ spent three days preaching there. Joseph was there when His parents came looking for Him and asked Him why He had not come home. Joseph heard him ask, 'Did you not know that I must be about my Father's business?' At that moment Joseph came to believe that Jesus was the long-awaited Messiah."

Father Aiden paused, then continued. "Later that year Joseph heard from his spies that King Herod's son Archelaus now knew Jesus had been born in Bethlehem and might be the King of the Jews whom the Wise Men had been seeking. Archelaus was afraid of His power and was planning to have Him murdered.

"Joseph hurried to Nazareth and persuaded Mary and Joseph to allow him to take Jesus over the border to Egypt, where He would be safe. Jesus studied at the temple of Leontopolis for a period of time, then afterward went back and forth from His home in Nazareth to Leontopolis for further study until His public mission began. The presence of Coptic Christians in this area of Egypt supports that theory of course."

Father Aiden's voice became emphatic. "That parchment belongs in the Vatican Library. It was stolen from there over five hundred years ago. Recent scientific tests have suggested that the Shroud of Turin is indeed the burial robe of Christ. Similar tests may prove that this parchment is authentic beyond any doubt. Think of it: a letter written by Christ to one of His disciples! Even now it is priceless beyond imagination. If Jonathan did not show it to any of you who were his closest friends, and also experts in this field, and whose opinions he could trust, then surely you must be able to think of some other expert or experts he might have consulted."

Before anyone could answer, the persistent ringing of the doorbell chimes startled everyone. Mariah jumped up and hurried to answer it. When she threw open the door, Detectives Benet and Rodriguez were standing on the porch. Her heart pounding, she invited them in. "Is my mother all right?" she demanded, her voice rising.

The others had followed her from the dining room. "Is Rory Steiger here, Ms. Lyons?" Benet asked tersely.

Relieved, Mariah knew their presence had nothing to do with her mother but then realized that Benet could have phoned and asked her that question. He did not have to come here.

"No, there's no need for Rory to be here when my mother's in the hospital," she said. "Why do you ask?"

"We called on Ms. Steiger today and she wasn't home. When we got there we were told by Rory's next-door neighbors that Rose Newton, a friend she was supposed to meet last night, had already rung their doorbell this morning. She was worried because they were going to have a special celebration dinner, but Rory hadn't shown up. She didn't answer her cell phone. At our request, the superintendent of the building checked the apartment while we were there. There was nothing out of order as far as they could tell. Ms. Newton had left her telephone number with the neighbor and the neighbor gave it to us. We contacted her. She still hasn't heard from Rory. She's very upset and believes that something is very wrong."

You didn't phone me because you wanted to see my reaction when you told me Rory was missing, Mariah thought. "I would agree," she said slowly. "If Rory was even fifteen minutes late coming here because she was caught in traffic, she'd phone to say she was on her way and she'd be terribly apologetic about the delay."

"That's what we understand," Benet commented, then looked around at the others who were standing in the foyer.

Mariah turned and introduced them. "I know you've met Father Aiden, Detective Benet." She gestured toward Richard, Albert,

Charles, and Greg, who were standing in a semicircle "My father's friends and colleagues," she said.

Richard's cell phone rang. With a murmured apology he stepped back and fumbled through his pockets for it. He did not realize that Alvirah, who was standing directly behind him, stepped back as well. Automatically she switched on the microphone in her sunburst pin, turning it to the highest amplifier setting.

By the time Richard finally answered the call, it had already gone to voice mail. Even without the microphone, Alvirah could hear Lillian's agitated and sullen voice as Richard played the message. "Richard, I've decided to accept your two-million-dollar offer. Get back to me."

The distinct click at the end of her message was echoed by the sound of Richard's phone as he snapped it closed.

36

As soon as Willy, Alvirah, and Father Aiden were in the car on the way home from dinner, Alvirah played back the message Lillian had left on Richard's cell phone. The shock and disbelief she had felt on hearing it was also the reaction of the two men. There was no question in the mind of any of them that when Lillian said she had decided to accept Richard's offer, she was referring to the Vatican letter.

"It sounds to me as if she's had other offers," Willy observed, "if Richard is willing to pay two million dollars for it."

"My guess is that any offers would have to be anywhere from one million on up," Alvirah said. "I wouldn't have thought Richard had that kind of money. Being a college professor isn't exactly like being on Wall Street."

"He was brought up on Park Avenue," Father Aiden said. "I know that his grandfather was a very successful businessman. My question is, what would Richard do with the parchment?"

"My guess is that he might want to see it returned to the Vatican Library," Alvirah said hopefully.

"That would be a noble thing, but the fact is Richard has denied ever having seen the parchment. Now we know he is not only aware that Lillian has it, but he has actually been trying to buy it," Father Aiden pointed out. "So that means Richard's motives are suspect.

I'm sure he knows collectors who would pay a fortune to get their hands on that parchment just for the thrill of owning it."

Alvirah sadly admitted to herself that what Father O'Brien had said made plenty of sense. "Those two detectives made appointments to meet with Richard and Charles and Albert and Greg tomorrow," she said. "That will keep them pretty busy. I wouldn't like to have them cross-examining me if I had anything to hide."

"They don't cross-examine anyone," Willy pointed out. "That only happens in a trial. But I guess they will try to pin them down." Then he added, "How about that missing caregiver? Alvirah, did we ever meet her?"

"Rory? I think once last year, but she was on her way upstairs with Kathleen. I didn't get much of an impression of her."

"She was at Kathleen's side in the funeral parlor and throughout the day of the funeral," Father Aiden said. "She was certainly very attentive to her."

"Maybe she forgot she had that dinner and took off," Willy suggested. "Mariah told the cops she was paying her for the week, but that it would be Friday at the earliest before Kathleen could be released to go home. Rory wouldn't be the first one to forget a dinner date. Maybe she just decided to go away for a couple of days. My bet is that she'll show up by Friday."

"I don't think it's all that simple," Alvirah said. "Even if she went away, why isn't she answering her cell phone?"

They were all silent for the next fifteen minutes until they reached the E-ZPass toll plaza at the George Washington Bridge leading into Manhattan. Then Willy asked, "Honey, do you think it might have been better if you had played your recording of that message for those detectives right on the spot?"

"I thought about it, but I decided it was too soon," she replied. "Richard could say the offer she was talking about was to buy Lillian's car, and they had joked about the amount. I have to pay another visit to Miss Lillian tomorrow morning. I'll take her by surprise and play the tape for her. You heard the way she sounds on it. She's nervous and frightened, and when someone is in that condition, she needs a good friend to help her see things clearly. I'll be that good friend."

Albert West and Charles Michaelson had quarreled on their way to the dinner. Albert's point-blank statement that he thought that Charles had seen the parchment and might even have it in his possession had evoked a scathing response from Charles.

"Just because you helped me out when I had that problem doesn't give you the right to accuse me of lying about the parchment," Charles had said, his anger blazing. "As I've said over and over again, Jonathan told me he was going to show me the parchment, but then he got killed. I have no idea where it is. My guess is he would have given it to Lillian for safekeeping so his nut-job wife wouldn't get her hands on it and tear it up. Do I need to remind you what she did to those pictures? And, Albert, while we're on the subject, what about *you*? How do I know that you don't know a lot more about what's happened? You've made some pretty good money over the years selling antiquities. You certainly would know how to connect to a buyer in the underground market."

"As you well know, Charles, I worked for interior designers buying antiques that had been offered for sale in the legitimate market," Albert had snapped. "I have never gotten involved with buying or selling or trading biblical documents."

"There's always a first time when big money is at stake," Charles retorted. "You've lived on a professor's salary. You're about to retire on a professor's pension. You won't be able to do much globe-trotting on that income."

"The same applies to you, Charles, but, unlike you, I've never made a nickel defrauding a collector."

That conversation had ended when they reached Mariah's home.

On the way back to Manhattan, the tension escalated. Each had now been asked to appear at the prosecutor's office tomorrow to give a statement to the detectives.

Both were aware that the detectives would inevitably check their cell phone records. Notwithstanding Kathleen's arrest, it was clear that the detectives were probing further into the circumstances surrounding Jonathan's death, the missing parchment, and now the missing caregiver.

Greg's apartment at the Time Warner Center overlooked Central Park South. When he arrived home after the dinner, he stood for a long time at the window watching the panorama of late-night strollers on the sidewalks rimming the park. By nature he was intensely analytical and he once again reviewed the events of the evening in his mind.

Was it too much to hope that Mariah was beginning to really care about him? He had sensed that, for just a moment, she had responded to his ardent embrace but then pulled back. The secret of winning her was to get her mother out of this mess, he thought. Even if the prosecutor had enough evidence to prove that Kathleen had killed Jonathan, if she was also found to be insane, then the judge just might let her come home as long as she had round-the-clock security. I can help Mariah get the right psychiatrists and I can also afford to provide the security for her mother, he thought.

How much money could Mariah possibly have at this point? he asked himself. Jonathan is dead. His pension can't be that much. He's been paying caregivers for a long time so he was probably getting pretty well drained. Mariah won't want to sell the house. She wants her mother to keep living in it. If her mother ends up back there, the security will cost a fortune. Even before any trial, if her mother is released on Friday, the judge is going to insist that the security start right now.

Those detectives seem to think that Rory's disappearance may have something to do with Jonathan's death. Do they think that Rory took off because she was somehow involved? Or do they think that somebody got rid of her because she knew too much about something?

Greg shrugged, walked into his den, and opened his laptop. It wasn't too soon to start looking up the leading court psychiatrists, he decided.

Richard drove back to his apartment near Fordham University, exultant that Lillian had decided to accept his offer. I'll keep my side of the bargain, he thought. I will never say that I got it from Lillian. She's told me that she has two other offers, but I believe her when she says she never actually admitted to anyone that she had it. Richard smiled as he pulled into his garage. She sure fell for the story I gave her, he thought.

She shouldn't be so gullible.

37

On Wednesday morning, Detectives Simon Benet and Rita Rodriguez were in their office reviewing the newest developments in the increasingly complex case of the murder of Professor Jonathan Lyons.

They had run a background check on the missing Rory Steiger. To their astonishment they learned that her real name was Victoria Parker and that she had served seven years in prison for stealing money from an elderly woman who had employed her as a caregiver.

"Well, our Rory is not only missing now but went missing from parole three years ago," Rita said, a hint of satisfaction in her voice. "She was a crook when she worked as a caregiver before, and maybe she's still a crook. She could easily have overheard Professor Lyons talking on the phone about the parchment. And she certainly knew how easy it would be to set up Kathleen as the killer."

"Kathleen Lyons is not off the hook," Simon said flatly. "I agree that Rory or Victoria, or whatever she wants to call herself, may very well have stolen the parchment. She certainly would be smart enough to know that we'd probably run a check on her as part of the whole investigation, and she was smart enough to take off."

"She was also smart enough to ditch her cell phone," Rita pointed out. "The telephone company reported that there's no signal coming from it, so we can't track it. That lady sure knows how to disappear. And if she did take the parchment, maybe she heard enough dinner conversation in that household to know about the underground market and how she could sell it." She hesitated, then said, "Simon, I know you weren't happy when I said it the other day. But particularly now, with this new information about Rory's record and her taking off, I am very concerned that Kathleen Lyons may be innocent."

For a moment Rita was afraid to look at Simon, half-expecting him to explode. But he didn't. Instead he said, "Let's look at it this way. If Rory took the parchment, she may already have found a buyer. Father Aiden said that Jonathan Lyons was upset because an expert he had consulted had only been interested in the monetary value of the parchment. I don't believe for one minute that those four guys who were in his house last night don't know anything more. I can't wait to talk to each one of them separately this afternoon."

"I think we should get an application in to the judge today to get their phone records for the last month," Rita said. "Lillian's convenient amnesia about the numbers of those prepaid phones means we can't check those records. But, Simon, we have to consider another possibility. If Rory got paid by someone to steal that parchment, then delivered it to that person, she would not only have outlived her usefulness, but she would be a threat. Maybe whoever it was got rid of her. There were a lot of personal items in her apartment that she could have easily taken with her if she left on her own. And don't forget that her car is still in the garage."

Rita began to speak more rapidly. "And her friend Rose said that Rory had invited her to a celebration dinner but hadn't said what it was about. Rory said she wanted to surprise her. Maybe Rory was going to celebrate that she'd been paid off for stealing the parchment. But I don't think she'd ever admit that to Rose. She was probably planning to tell Rose something like she'd gotten a job offer somewhere else for a lot more money. My gut says Rose was on the level when she told us that she has no idea why Rory didn't meet her."

"Who knows? Maybe Rory realized she was in danger, got nervous, and just took off." Simon drummed his fingers on his desk, always a sign that he was trying to make a decision. "I'm a long way from believing that Kathleen Lyons is innocent. Don't forget, that last night at dinner she was ranting about her husband and his girlfriend, then a few hours later he was dead. And don't forget that Kathleen knew how to use a gun. But I do think that we should meet with Prosecutor Jones and let him know about all this."

Rita Rodriguez nodded, careful not to show her satisfaction that Simon was clearly retreating from his original position that Kathleen beyond any doubt had murdered her husband.

38

On Wednesday afternoon, Assistant Prosecutor Peter Jones sat in his office with its floor-to-ceiling case files trying to absorb the information that had just been handed to him by Benet and Rodriguez. It was clear to him that Rita flat out believed that a mistaken arrest had been made. And it was clear that Simon was no longer confident that Kathleen Lyons was the killer.

Jones, forty-six, tall, and ruggedly handsome, a twenty-year veteran of the prosecutor's office, was hoping for the top job when the boss retired in five months. His reputation as an aggressive but fair trial attorney gave him every reason to believe that he was the strongest candidate. But now a tsunami of dread was engulfing him. He thought of his own seventy-two-year-old mother, who had been showing early signs of dementia. The thought of her being led away in handcuffs for an offense she did not commit made his throat dry. A mental image of the frightened and bewildered Kathleen Lyons trembling in front of the judge burned in his mind.

If we've made a big mistake the newspapers will have a field day, he thought as beads of sweat formed on his forehead. They'll run that picture of her looking pathetic over and over. It was on all the front pages yesterday. I might as well forget about the big job. I went over that evidence with a fine-tooth comb, he reminded himself grimly, and I still think she did it. For God's sake, she was in the closet holding the gun and covered with his blood!

But now with that caretaker woman turning out to be an ex-con and disappearing, it's a whole new ball game, he admitted to himself.

The buzzer on his office phone sounded. He was about to tell his secretary that he didn't want to talk to anybody when she told him that a Mr. Joshua Schultz, an attorney from Manhattan, was on hold and was asking to speak to him about the Kathleen Lyons case. "He claims that he has some important information for you, Peter," she said, her voice skeptical. "Do you want to talk to him?"

What more can be coming? Peter asked himself. "Put him through, Nancy," he said.

"Assistant Prosecutor Peter Jones speaking," he said briskly.

"First, Mr. Jones, thank you very much for accepting my call," a smooth voice with a distinct New York accent said. "I'm Joshua Schultz and I practice criminal defense in Manhattan."

"Yes, I have heard of you," Peter said. And from what I've heard you're no great shakes in court, he thought.

"Mr. Jones, I am contacting you with information that I believe is of the utmost importance in the Jonathan Lyons murder case. I represent a defendant named Wally Gruber, who is charged with a residential attempted burglary in Riverdale and also a residential burglary in Mahwah. My client is in custody at Rikers Island, and there is a detainer from New Jersey for the Mahwah case."

"I'm aware of the Mahwah case," Peter Jones said tersely.

"I have spoken to my client and he recognizes that he has little defense to the case in your jurisdiction. We have been informed that his fingerprints have been recovered from the scene. We have also been made aware that there is an ongoing investigation by the New York City police regarding other house burglaries in which the owners had parked their cars at the Manhattan garage where Mr. Gruber was employed prior to his recent arrest."

"Go on," Peter said, unable to even guess where the conversation was going.

"Mr. Jones, I am proffering to you that my client has informed me that when he was on the second floor of the Mahwah home during that burglary, he heard a gunshot coming from the house next door. He hurried to the window and saw someone running out of that house. I am not going to divulge now whether it was a man or woman, but I *can* say that the person's head and face was covered by a scarf, which the person then pulled down, and that my client was able to see the face clearly. Mr. Gruber explained to me that there is a lamppost halfway down the front walkway that illuminated the area."

There was a long pause as Peter Jones digested the fact that Schultz was obviously referring to the murder of Jonathan Lyons. "What are you trying to tell me?" he demanded.

"What I am saying to you is that Mr. Gruber has seen the picture of Kathleen Lyons in the newspaper, and he is emphatic that she is *not* the person who ran from the house. He is confident that he could sit with your composite officer and assist in producing a very accurate sketch of the person he saw. Of course, in exchange for his cooperation, he would expect considerable assistance from you in receiving reduced sentences in both New York and New Jersey."

Peter felt as if the world was caving in on him. "It sounds pretty convenient that Mr. Gruber just happened to be there on that night and at that moment," he said sarcastically. "The owners of the house next door to the Lyons residence were away for several weeks and that burglary could have been committed at any time during that period."

"But, Mr. Jones, it *wasn't* committed, as you put it, at any time during that period." Schultz's voice was now equally sarcastic. "It was being committed at the same time that Jonathan Lyons was being murdered. And we can prove that to you. Mr. Gruber drove his own car to New Jersey that night, but he was using stolen license plates and a stolen E-ZPass tag. At my request, his cousin went to a storage unit that Mr. Gruber rents and retrieved the plates and the tag. I have them. The tag is from an Infiniti sedan owned by an Owen Morley, a long-time customer of the garage where Mr. Gruber worked. Mr. Morley is in Europe this month. The tag will show a debit for that night. I am sure that if you check the account tied to the E-ZPass tag he used, it will corroborate my client's admission that he drove across the George Washington Bridge from New Jersey to New York approximately forty-five minutes after Jonathan Lyons was shot."

Peter Jones struggled to choose his words carefully and to sound calm. "Mr. Schultz, you must understand that your client's credibility is at best highly suspect. Based upon what you have told me, however, I believe that I have an ethical obligation to interview him. We will see where it goes. Mr. Gruber might have been there at the same time, but how do I know that he isn't simply going to invent a face and claim it's the one he saw leaving the Lyons home?"

"Mr. Jones, this is a fascinating case that I was following even before Mr. Gruber retained me. It seems to me that if Mrs. Lyons was not involved, then that shot might have been fired by someone else who was close to the victim. From what I have read, this case has no markings of a random intruder. I believe that it is very possible that if a high-quality composite is made, the face may end up being recognized by the family or friends of the victim."

"As I just told you," Peter snapped, "I recognize my ethical duty to follow up on this, but I am certainly not promising you anything in advance. I want to speak to Mr. Gruber, and I want to see those license plates. We will check out the E-ZPass charge to Mr. Morley's account. If, after that, we decide to have him sit down with our composite officer, we will see where the sketch takes us. You have my word that any meaningful cooperation will be brought to the attention of his sentencing judges. I absolutely refuse to get any more specific at this point."

Schultz's voice became angry and cold. "I don't think Mr. Gruber will be very responsive to such a vague offer. Perhaps I should simply give this information to Mr. Scott, who represents Kathleen Lyons. It is most ironic that he is the victim in this burglary, and I assume he would have to advise Mrs. Lyons to obtain new counsel. But I have read that the families are close friends, and I am sure any information that would assist in exonerating this innocent woman would be most welcome. And I have no doubt that Mr. Scott would ensure that my client's cooperation is brought to the attention of the sentencing judges."

Peter sensed that Schultz was about to hang up. "Mr. Schultz," he said emphatically, "you and I are both experienced criminal lawyers. I have never laid eyes on Mr. Gruber, but I do know he is a criminal and looking to benefit himself. It would be totally irresponsible of me to make more specific promises at this point and you know it. If any information he gives us turns out to be of importance, I assure you that his cooperation will be brought to the attention of his sentencing judges."

"Not good enough, sir," Schultz retorted. "Let me suggest something. I will wait two days before contacting Mr. Scott. I suggest that you reflect further on my offer. I will call you again on Friday afternoon.

"Have a good day."

39

On Wednesday morning one of Lillian's prepaid phones rang at six o'clock. Knowing who would be on the other end of the line, she reached across the pillow to pick it up from the night table. Although she was already awake, she still resented the early-morning intrusion. Her "Hello" was abrupt and sullen.

"Lillian, did you phone Richard last night?" the caller asked, his tone frigid and even threatening.

Lillian debated about whether to lie, then decided it was not worth it. "He knows I have the parchment," she blurted out. "Jonathan told him he gave it to me. If I don't sell it to him, he'll go to the police. Do you realize what that could mean? When the cops were here, I had to admit that the night Jonathan died I was having dinner only twenty minutes from his house in New Jersey. We both know that Kathleen killed him, but if Richard tells them I have the parchment, they could turn it all around and say I went to the house, that Jonathan let me in, then I killed him and took the parchment."

"You're getting hysterical and jumping to absurd conclusions," the caller snapped. "Lillian, how much is Richard going to pay you?"

"Two million dollars."

"And I am offering you four million dollars. Why are you doing this?"

"Don't you see why I'm doing this?" she screamed. "Because if

I don't sell it to Richard, he'll go straight to the detectives. He's already seen the parchment. He trusts Jonathan's judgment that it's authentic. Jonathan told him that he gave it to me. And of course Richard would deny he ever tried to buy it from me. He'll tell them he's been trying to persuade me to give it back."

"Richard has already denied to both Mariah and those detectives just last night that he ever *saw* the parchment. If he changes his story they'll start suspecting him. You should call his bluff and tell him to get lost."

Lillian pushed herself up to a sitting position. "I have a splitting headache. I can't deal with this much longer. I already lied to the cops when I told them that Jonathan was going to try to sneak out and meet me for dinner the night he was shot. I already told Alvirah I didn't speak to Jonathan during those last five days, and I'm sure she's passed that on to Mariah and the cops."

"Lillian, listen to me. I have an alternate plan that can make this a win-win situation for you. I'll give you four million dollars for the parchment. Stall Richard until Friday. I can have a first-class expert make a perfect copy of it on two-thousand-year-old parchment, and you can give that one to Richard. He'll pay you two million, so you end up with six million dollars. That should help dry your tears over Jonathan. And when Richard finds out that it's a fake, he'll just think that Jonathan was wrong about it. What do you expect he's going to do? Go to the police? He'd be knee-deep in trouble himself. Don't forget, we're talking about a parchment that was stolen from the Vatican Library. Dear Richard will just have to swallow the whole thing."

Six million dollars, Lillian thought. If I decided to give up teaching, I could travel. Who knows? I might even meet a nice guy who doesn't have a crazy wife.

"Where is the parchment, Lillian? I want it today."

"It's in my safe-deposit box at the bank a couple of blocks from here."

"I warned you that the police may very well be getting a search warrant for your apartment and any safe-deposit box in your name. You've got to get that parchment out of your box now. Be at the bank when it opens at nine o'clock. Don't even think about bringing it back to your apartment. I'll call you in an hour and tell you where to meet me after you're finished at the bank."

"What about the four million dollars? When do I get it and how do I get it?"

"I'll wire it to an overseas account and I'll have the paperwork for you when I give you the copy Friday morning. Look, Lillian, we have to trust each other. Either one of us could blow the whistle on the other. You want the money. I want the parchment. You give Richard the phony parchment Friday afternoon and collect your money from him. Then everybody's happy."

40

Kathleen was sitting up in bed, a tray with tea and juice and toast in front of her. The smell of the toast made her think of sitting at the breakfast table with Jonathan. He was with her now, but he wasn't looking at her. He was sitting on a chair next to the bed, and his head and arms were leaning against her legs.

Any minute now he will start to bleed, she thought.

She pushed aside the tray, unaware that the nurse grabbed it in time to prevent the tea and juice from spilling.

A voice asked, "What do you want, Kathleen? Why are you doing that?"

Kathleen was clawing at the pillow, trying to yank the pillowcase off.

She did not realize that the nurse made a gesture to stop her, then stepped back.

Her fingers shaking, Kathleen pulled the pillowcase free and tied it around her face.

"Kathleen, you're frightened. Something is frightening you."

"I can't see his face," Kathleen wailed. "Maybe if he can't see mine, he won't shoot me, too."

41

At a quarter of nine on Wednesday morning, Lloyd Scott dropped in on Mariah. He had phoned at eight thirty hoping that she was up. "Lloyd, I'm on my second cup of coffee," she had told him. "Come on over, I was going to call you anyhow. There are some things you should know."

When he arrived he found her in the breakfast room, with neatly laid-out files spread across the table. "I told Betty to take the day off," she explained. "She stayed late last evening because I had people in for dinner. She's been practically living here since Dad died, but now it's time to get back to whatever you'd call normal."

"I'm sure it is," Lloyd agreed. "Mariah, you'll remember I told you I was going to look up Rory Steiger. Well, the report is in and it turns out her real name is Victoria Parker and she has a prison record. She spent seven years in jail in Boston, for stealing money and jewelry from an elderly woman who hired her as a caregiver."

"Those two detectives were here last night. They told me about the prison record and that Rory is missing," Mariah said. "They wanted to know if I had heard from her, which I hadn't."

Lloyd Scott had learned to keep his face impassive in court even when a witness he was counting on said something unexpected on cross-examination. Even so, his pale blue eyes widened and he unconsciously smoothed back the few strands of hair that nature had permitted him to keep. "She's missing? Wait a minute. I'll be right back."

With the familiarity of an old friend, he went into the kitchen, poured himself a cup of coffee, returned to the breakfast room, and sat down. Mariah briefly explained that Rory had not shown up for a dinner date with a friend and was not answering her cell phone, but that when her super checked on her apartment nothing looked disturbed.

"Lloyd," she said, "the question seems to be, did Rory disappear on her own or did something happen to her?" Then she added, "It's funny. I never felt warm about Rory the way I do about Delia, the weekend caregiver, but Rory did seem to take good care of Mom. And Mom listened to her. Delia had to beg Mom to shower or to take her medicine. With Rory there were no arguments."

"Rory stole from her employer in Boston," Lloyd said. "Is there any possibility she's been stealing in this house and is now afraid of getting caught?"

"I think Dad would have noticed if money was missing from his wallet. Betty has a credit card for food shopping. Mom's jewelry is in the safe-deposit box. Dad caught Mom trying to throw it out and took it away from her." Mariah's voice became strained. "What occurred to me is that Rory must have heard talk about the parchment when Dad was on the phone in his study. Last night at dinner, Richard, Greg, Albert, and Charles all admitted that Dad had called and told them about it. Mom loved to sit in the study with Dad, and Rory was always hovering around her. Suppose after Dad died, Rory helped herself to the parchment and found a buyer for it? That would be a good reason to disappear."

"Do you think that's what happened?" Lloyd asked incredulously.

"We know that she's a thief." For a moment Mariah turned her head so that she was looking out the back window. "The impatiens grew so beautifully," she said. "And in a few weeks they'll be gone.

I can still see Dad planting them in June. I came out and wanted to help him, but he turned me down. I had just delivered another zinger about Lillian. He turned away from me, shrugged, and went outside. God, Lloyd, if we could only take back the hurtful things we say." She sighed.

"Mariah, listen to me. I was close to your father. You were the voice of his conscience. He knew he shouldn't have been involved with Lillian and that it was hurting Kathleen and you. Don't forget, I've lived here for more than twenty years and witnessed how in love he and Kathleen were. I think he knew that if the positions were reversed, there wouldn't have been anyone else in her life."

"I still wish I had been more understanding. And the fact is that if those damn pictures hadn't surfaced, Mom and I would have been blissfully unaware that there was something between Dad and Lillian and a lot happier for it. I always thought that it was Lillian and Charles who were involved. Lillian is and was a good actress, which is what I was planning to bring up with you." Mariah looked straight into Lloyd's eyes. "I have done nothing but think about this and, despite what you just told me, I would bet everything I have that Dad gave the parchment to Lillian to hold for him. Whether he did or did not break up with her after he visited Father Aiden that Wednesday two weeks ago, Lillian admitted to Alvirah that she and Dad were not in touch for the next five days, and then he was killed."

Lloyd nodded. "Alvirah was emphatic about that and if there's one thing I'm sure of, Alvirah doesn't misunderstand what she's being told."

"Lloyd, suppose they had a quarrel? Lillian might have refused to give the parchment back to him. Suppose she didn't keep it in her apartment. Maybe she put it in a safe-deposit box for safekeeping?"

"Then you think that Lillian may have the parchment?"

"I'd stake my life on it. Lloyd, think about it. If Dad told her it was over, she'd be hurt and angry. I saw those pictures. They were in love. Now Dad had taken five years of her life and was walking away from her. She might have felt that he owed her plenty."

Lloyd waited, then decided to voice the possibility that had occurred to him. "Mariah, suppose Lillian came here on that Monday night, ostensibly to give back the parchment. There was no caregiver here. Is it possible that your father let her in, that a quarrel began and that she was the one who pulled that trigger?"

"Except for the fact that my mother is completely innocent, I think anything is possible," Mariah said. "And this morning I'm driving into New York and I'm going to have it out with Lillian. My father found a sacred and priceless artifact that belongs to the Church and to the generations of people who will be able to view it in the Vatican Library. One way or the other I'm going to make sure they get it back."

Tears welled in her eyes. "If I can get that letter from Christ to Joseph of Arimathea back and send it to where it belongs, I know that Dad will be aware of it and it will help make up for all of the nasty remarks I've been giving him this past year and a half."

42

On Wednesday morning at eight thirty Alvirah and Willy were sitting in their car parked across the street from the entrance to Lillian's apartment opposite Lincoln Center. "There's only one exit from the building," Alvirah said, more to herself than to Willy, who was reading the *Daily News*. "I just hope the cops don't chase us away. I'll wait until nine, then I'll march in and give my name to the doorman. When Lillian gets on the intercom, I'll tell her that I have information that may save her from a stint in the pokey."

That statement was enough to get Willy's attention. He had been reading the sports pages and was consumed by the articles covering the closeness of the race for the division championship between the Yankees and the Boston Red Sox. "You didn't tell me you had that kind of dirt on her," he said.

"I don't," Alvirah admitted matter-of-factly. "But I'm going to make her think that I do." She sighed. "I love the summer, but truth to tell I'm glad it's a little cooler the last few days. You can just take so much of the ninety-five-degree weather. This outfit is light, but even with the air-conditioning it feels like a blanket."

She was wearing a cotton pantsuit that, after the delicious and never-ending food on the cruise, was feeling a bit tight. She was also painfully aware that telltale white roots were springing up like weeds in her artfully colored red hair and that Dale of London, her colorist, was on vacation in Tortola. "I can't believe I let it go this long, and now Dale won't be back for another week," she complained. "I'm starting to look like the old lady in the shoe."

"You always look gorgeous, honey," Willy assured her. "At least you and I have hair to worry about. Kathleen's lawyer is a nice guy but he should get rid of those three strands he combs across his dome and cave in and just go bald. He'd look like Bruce Willis—"

Willy interrupted himself. "You're too late, Alvirah. Lillian's on her way out."

"Oh, no," Alvirah moaned as she watched the slim figure of Lillian Stewart, dressed in a lightweight running suit and sneakers, walk from the door to the sidewalk and turn right. Her shoulder bag was dangling on her left side and she was carrying something resembling a tote bag tucked under her right arm.

"Follow her, Willy," Alvirah ordered.

"Alvirah, there's a lot of traffic on Broadway. I don't think I can trail her for long. I'll keep half the buses and taxis in New York backed up behind us."

"Look, Willy, she's heading north. It looks as if she's going at least another block on Broadway. Drive ahead and pull up at the corner. Everybody else around here double-parks. Why not you?"

Knowing it was useless to protest, Willy did as he was told. When Lillian reached the next block, she did not cross at the intersection but turned right.

"Oh, good," Alvirah said, "it's a one-way, going that way. Turn left, Willy."

"Roger, over and out," Willy deadpanned as he made a precariously sharp maneuver across two lanes of oncoming traffic.

At the next corner, Alvirah let out a triumphant gasp. "Look at that, Willy. She's going into the bank. I'd bet anything she's going to pay a visit to her safe-deposit box. Dollars to donuts, when she comes out, there'll be something in that bag she's carrying. Don't forget she accepted Richard's offer for two million dollars. Shame on both of them."

Once again Willy double-parked, this time a few doors down from the entrance to the bank. Moments later, an unsmiling face rapped on the driver's window. "Move along, sir, right now," a traffic policeman ordered. "You can't stay here."

Willy knew he had no choice. "What do you want me to do, honey?" he asked. "There's no place to park around here."

Alvirah was already opening the passenger door. "Drive around the block. I'll get out here. I'll hide behind that fruit stand and follow her when she comes out. My guess is she'll be heading back to the apartment or going somewhere to meet Richard. If I have to leave here before you get back, I'll call you on the cell."

She was gone and the traffic cop was again at the window, ordering Willy to move. "Okay, Officer, okay," he said. "I'm pulling out."

43

At nine A.M. Richard was in the wealth-management office at Roberts and Wilding at Chambers Street, arranging to withdraw two million dollars from his trust fund and have it wired into the account of Lillian Stewart.

"Richard, as we have discussed, in your lifetime you are allowed to give away several million dollars without tax penalties. Do you want this gift to be part of that lifetime allowance?" Norman Woods, his financial adviser, asked.

"Yes, that would be fine," Richard said, recognizing that he was very nervous and hoping he wasn't showing it.

Woods, white-haired, dressed as always in a dark blue suit, white shirt, and patterned blue tie, was approaching his sixty-fifth birthday and was close to retirement. It was on the tip of his tongue to do something totally out of character and say, "Richard, may I ask if Ms. Stewart is a romantic interest? I know that would delight your mother and father."

Instead he kept his face impassive as he confirmed that when Richard got back to him with the information about Ms. Stewart's bank account, the money would be wired directly to her.

Richard thanked him and left the office.

As soon as he was in the lobby of the building, he dialed Lillian's cell phone.

44

From her perch behind the fruit stand, Alvirah waited for Lillian to come out of the bank. At ten after nine Willy drove around the corner, waved to her, and once again began to circle the block. At twenty after nine, when the door of the bank opened, Lillian stepped out onto the sidewalk. As Alvirah had expected, the folded tote bag she had been carrying under her arm was now firmly grasped in her left hand and obviously contained something.

Willy should be back any second now, Alvirah thought, then realized with dismay that Lillian was walking up the one-way street against the traffic. She's probably going home, Alvirah decided. The best thing I can do is follow her and call Willy on the cell.

But at the corner of Broadway, Lillian darted across the avenue, and Alvirah realized that she might be heading for the subway entrance.

Lillian was moving quickly. Alvirah picked up her own pace, puffing from the effort of keeping up but staying a short distance behind. With one eye she was trying to catch Willy when he came around the block again, but when he sailed past he was not looking in her direction. He'll just have to keep driving around. I can't start fishing in my pocketbook for my cell phone now, she thought.

It was with a tremendous burst of energy that she managed to keep as close to Lillian as she dared without Lily's seeing her as they both descended the subway steps. There was no train there, but the platform was crowded and the sound of an approaching train could be heard. Alvirah watched as at the same moment, she and Lillian reached into their pockets for their MetroCards. Then, standing a few people back from Lillian in the line, Alvirah followed her through the turnstile and saw that a train was pulling in. Lillian hurried onto the platform to board the train. Grateful that it was already crowded, Alvirah slipped onto the same subway car, careful to conceal herself behind several portly riders.

From the other end of the car Alvirah observed as Lillian stood, her eyes downcast, holding onto a pole with one hand and tightly clutching the tote bag with the other. But then as the train approached the Chambers Street station some twenty minutes later, Lillian began to move toward an exit door. When the train stopped, Alvirah waited for a moment to be sure that Lillian was getting off, then left the train herself in the middle of a large group.

The large exodus onto the platform meant that she was half a flight of stairs behind Lillian, who was hurrying up the subway steps to the street. Alvirah fumed with frustration as directly ahead of her a heavyset woman with a cane ascended the stairs, one step at a time. Try as she might, with the two-way traffic on the stairs, Alvirah could not make her way past or around her.

When she finally made it to street level, Alvirah frantically spun her head in all directions.

There was no sign of Lillian.

45

At twenty minutes after ten, he drove up to the heavy metal delivery doors at the back of the warehouse, Lillian beside him in the front passenger seat. It had taken less than ten minutes from where he picked her up at the subway exit to get to this isolated industrial neighborhood two blocks from the East River.

His corporate shell companies, created on paper for the sole purpose of hiding his identity, owned the boarded-up buildings on either side of this one. It was here that he had created his own splendid and secret world of antiquity. In a way he mourned the fact that he had never been able to share the magnificence of his priceless collection with another human being. Today it would happen. Lillian would be dazzled and awed. He could picture her eyes widening when she took in all the treasures of the second floor. And he knew that the greatest treasure of all was in the bag that she was grasping so tightly.

Jonathan had shown it to him, had let him remove it from the protective glassine envelope he had placed around it, had allowed him to touch it and to feel it, and to validate its authenticity.

It *was* authentic. There was no doubt about it. It was the one and only letter written by the Christ, and it had been written to the man who had befriended Him from His boyhood. Christ knew that soon He would be lying in Joseph's tomb. He knew that even after His death, Joseph would once again be caring for Him.

The entire world would be mesmerized to see this, he thought. And it is mine.

"Where on earth are we going?" Lillian asked querulously.

"As I told you when I picked you up, I have an office in my warehouse where we can have complete privacy. Would you have wanted me to explain the details of the overseas account that I set up for you on a crowded sidewalk on Chambers Street?"

He could tell that she was only impatient, not yet nervous.

He pushed the button on the visor of the car and the massive delivery door lumbered noisily upward. Then he drove inside and pushed the button again to close the door behind them. It became pitch-dark as the door slid back down and he heard Lillian's quick gasp, unmistakably the first sign of her realization that something might be terribly wrong.

He hurriedly reassured her. He wanted to observe and savor her reaction upon seeing his treasures, but she wouldn't even look at them if she knew what was going to happen to her. From his pocket, he took the remote that activated the garage overhead light and clicked it on. "This is pretty barren, as you can see," he said, smiling. "But my office is upstairs, and I assure you that it is much more inviting."

He could see that she was not completely at ease. "Are there other people upstairs?" she asked. "I don't see any other cars here. This place seems deserted."

He allowed a touch of annoyance to creep into his tone. "Lillian, do you think I wanted an audience for this transaction?"

"No, of course not. Let's go right to your office and get this done. Classes start next week, and I have a lot of errands to do."

"With all this money, you're still going to deal with students?" he asked as they got out of the car. He motioned her to the back wall. He slipped his hand under her arm as they walked across the cavernous windowless room. "This is the main level," he explained. Then, leaning down, he pushed the hidden button at the bottom of the wall and the large lift began to descend.

"My God, what kind of setup is this?" Lillian asked, startled.

"Inventive, isn't it? Come upstairs with me," he said as he nudged her onto the lift. The two of them rode it to the next level, then stepped into the room. He waited until she was right beside him. "Ready?" he asked as he turned on the light. "Welcome to my king-dom," he announced.

His eyes never left her face as she stepped into the enormous room and looked incredulously from one of the glorious antiquities he had gathered there to the next.

"However did you collect all of this?" she asked, stunned. "And why do you keep it here?" She spun around to face him. "And why did you bring me to a place like this?" she demanded. "This isn't an office!" She stared at him, her face and lips suddenly turning pale. From the triumphant smile on his parted lips she knew that he had entrapped her. Panicking, she dropped the tote bag and made a quick move to shove past him.

Instantly, she felt his viselike grip pinning her body to him. "I'm going to be merciful, Lillian," he said softly as he reached into his pocket for the syringe.

"You'll just feel a prick and then nothing. I promise you. Nothing at all."

46

As soon as Alvirah realized she had lost Lillian, she phoned Willy.

"Where have you been, honey?" he asked. "I was getting worried about you. I've circled the block a million times. The traffic cop thinks I'm a stalker. What's going on?"

"Willy, I'm sorry. I chased behind her into the subway. I got on the same train and ducked down behind some big guys. She got off at Chambers Street, but I lost her in the crowd going up the stairs."

"That's too bad. What do you want to do now?"

"I'm going to come back uptown and sit in her lobby. If it takes all day, I'm going to have a showdown with that lady. Why don't you go on home?"

"No way," he replied firmly. "I don't like this whole business, and with Rory missing, who knows who's doing what? I'll park the car at Lincoln Center and come in and sit with you."

Alvirah knew that when Willy used that tone of voice, there was no changing his mind. Taking one last look around in the hope that Lillian might emerge from one of the many office buildings in the area, she sighed in resignation and retraced her steps back down into the subway.

Twenty-five minutes later she was at the door of Lillian's apartment building across from Lincoln Center again. The doorman told her that Ms. Stewart was not home and then added, "There's a lady and a gentleman already waiting for her in the lobby, ma'am."

That would be Willy, Alvirah thought. I wonder who the woman is? On quick reflection, she decided that it would be Mariah.

She was right. Mariah and Willy were seated on leather chairs on opposite sides of a round glass table in a corner of the lobby. They were deep in conversation, but both looked up when they heard her footsteps clicking on the marble floor.

Mariah stood up and embraced Alvirah. "Willy's been filling me in," she explained. "I gather that we've all come to the same conclusion, that Lillian does have the parchment and that it's time to confront her."

"Has or *had* the parchment," Alvirah said grimly. "As I'm sure Willy told you, she left the bank carrying a tote bag with some kind of package in it. My guess is that the parchment was in her safe-deposit box and she was delivering it to somebody this morning."

Alvirah caught Willy's questioning glance and knew she would have to tell Mariah that she had overheard and taped Lillian's phone message to Richard last night. "Mariah, I think this is going to be a nasty surprise," she said as she sat down next to her. She reached for the playback button on her sunburst pin and activated the tape.

"I can't believe what I'm hearing," Mariah said, biting her quivering lip as shock and disappointment flooded her. "That means Lillian was probably on her way to meet Richard this morning. He absolutely *swore* to me that he had not seen the parchment. Now I find out he struck a deal for it. God, I feel so betrayed, not just for myself, but worse still for my father. He really loved and respected Richard."

"Well, we'll just sit here and wait her out," Alvirah said. "I'd like to see how she tries to weasel her way out of this one."

Resolutely, Mariah blinked back the tears that were welling in her eyes. "Alvirah, on my way here at about ten o'clock, Greg called me. He wanted to see how I was and if I had heard anything more about Rory. I told him I was actually in my car and heading into the city to have it out with Lillian because I believe Dad gave her the parchment to hold for him. I told Greg that if Lillian wasn't here, I intended to spend the whole day waiting in the lobby if necessary. He said he'd walk over here at about twelve thirty, unless I called him back to change it."

At twelve twenty Greg walked into the building. Alvirah noticed with approval his protective embrace of Mariah as he leaned over her chair and kissed the top of her head. "Have you seen her yet?" he asked.

"No," Willy said, "and I have a suggestion. Greg, why don't you take the girls to lunch and bring me back a sandwich? Alvirah and Mariah, I promise I'll call you right away if she shows up. We can't get around the fact that the doorman will tell her that I'm here. But even if she bolts for the elevator, you can phone her when you get back here and play that tape. You can tell her we're going straight to the cops with it. Trust me, she'll talk to us."

"I think that's a good idea," Greg said. "But after lunch I have to head out to New Jersey. My appointment with those detectives is at three o'clock."

47

On Rikers Island, Wally Gruber sat in an attorney conference room listening sourly as Joshua Schultz related the conversation that he had had with Assistant Prosecutor Peter Jones.

"You're telling me I should hand him the sketch of the guy who wasted that professor and all I get out of it is some half-baked promise that he'll put in a good word for me before the judge buries me?" Wally shook his head. "I don't think so."

"Wally, you're not in much of a position to call the shots. Suppose you come up with a picture of someone who looks like Tom Cruise and say, 'That's the guy I saw'? Are they going to say thanks a lot and give you some kind of free ride?"

"The guy I saw did *not* look like Tom Cruise," Wally snapped, "and I bet you a million to one that when I sit down with that artist, we'll come up with someone the family recognizes. Why do you think that guy had his face covered? Maybe he thought that if he ran into that old lady, she'd know who he was, even though she's nuts."

Joshua Schultz was beginning to wish he'd never taken the case of *State of New York vs. Wally Gruber*. "Look, Wally, you have a choice," he began. "Either we take our chances with the prosecutor, or I call the old lady's lawyer. If you think he can somehow pay you off or fight to get you probation, forget it. That won't happen."

"There's a reward of a hundred grand out there from the insurance company for any leads about the jewelry I took," Wally pointed out.

"And you have the nerve to think they're going to give it to the person who took it in the first place?" Schultz asked incredulously.

"Don't get smart with me," Wally snapped. "What I'm talking about is they probably think that the gems have been pried out of the settings by now. I know they're still just like when I got them."

"How do you know that?"

"Because the fence I deal with has a lot of customers in South America. He told me he was going to take the stash to Rio next month. He told me it's worth a lot more intact than it would be broken up. The Scott woman is a jewelry designer, right? Suppose I give up the fence and they get the jewelry back. The insurance company would be off the hook. That Scott woman would be thrilled. And on top of all this, I give the face of the killer to the husband, who's defending the old lady. They'll all be ready to forgive and forget. They'll make me man of the year."

"Sounds good on paper, Wally, but you seem to ignore a couple of very important points. First, the lawyer for Kathleen Lyons is also the husband of the woman who owned the jewelry. He'd have to disqualify himself from the murder case because he'll have a world-class conflict, the likes of which I've never seen before. Second, your information about the fence and jewelry would have to go to the prosecutor, because they're the ones who would have to investigate it further. So what you're suggesting is that we give some information to Lloyd Scott and other information to the prosecutor. That's not going to work."

"All right. I'll give the prosecutor another chance. We'll start with him, and when he sees I can give him the lowdown on the jewelry, maybe his attitude will change. Then we decide if we stay with him on the murder case or go to Lloyd Scott. One way or the other in the next few days, I'll be sitting down with a cop."

"Then you want me to call the prosecutor and tell him you're also willing to provide information about recovering the jewelry?"

Wally pushed back his chair, clearly impatient to end the conversation. "You got it, Josh. Maybe this will convince him that I can solve the murder for him too."

48

❧⚜❧

Detectives Simon Benet and Rita Rodriguez spent a busy Wednesday morning at the prosecutor's office. After they'd left Mariah Lyons's home on Tuesday evening, they'd decided to apply for the last month's phone records of four of the men who had been at dinner with Mariah: Richard Callahan, Greg Pearson, Albert West, and Charles Michaelson.

"They were the closest associates of Professor Lyons," Rita observed, "and I don't buy that not one of them got a look at the parchment. Somebody's lying, or maybe even they're *all* lying."

On Wednesday morning they applied in chambers to Judge Brown to obtain the phone records and their request was granted. "We know Professor Lyons called and told every one of them about the parchment," Benet pointed out. "Now we'll be able to see if they called him back and how often they may have spoken to him."

Their first interview was going to be with Albert West at eleven A.M. He was twenty minutes late arriving. Apologetically, he explained that the traffic on the George Washington Bridge had been unexpectedly heavy, and he hadn't allotted enough time for the drive from Manhattan.

Benet glanced at Rodriguez, aware that she too was picking up the fact that West was nervous. Is it because he's late for the meeting, or is it because he has something to hide? Benet wondered. He made a mental note to check what the traffic conditions on the bridge had been for the last hour. West was casually dressed in jeans and a short-sleeved shirt. Benet watched as he clenched and unclenched his hands, noticing that even though the man was not more than five feet six in height and slight of build, the sinewy muscles in his hands and arms hinted at steely strength.

"Professor West, when we spoke on the phone last week, you told me that you never saw the parchment that Professor Lyons had found, is that correct?"

"Absolutely. I heard about the parchment from Jonathan a week and a half before he died. He was wildly excited. I warned him that so-called discoveries often turn out to be clever forgeries. That was our last conversation."

"Professor West," Rita said, her voice hesitant, as if the question she was going to ask had just occurred to her. "You were with your colleagues last night at dinner with Ms. Lyons. Do you think that any one of them might have seen the parchment and, because of the murder of Jonathan Lyons, is afraid to admit that fact?"

The two detectives watched Albert West's expression become impassive as he seemed to be weighing how to answer the question.

"Professor West," Rita said softly, "if that parchment is as valuable as Jonathan Lyons believed, whoever has it now and is choosing not to come forward is committing a serious crime. It's not too late for whoever has it to give it up and avoid getting in any deeper."

West looked around the crowded office as though trying to find a place to hide, then cleared his throat nervously. "It is very hard to point a finger at a colleague and friend," he began, "but I think in this case it may have become necessary. As Father Aiden told us last night at dinner, the parchment is the property of the Vatican Library, and if further scientific tests absolutely prove it to be authentic, it should be on display there for generations to come. Literally until the end of time."

"You think you know who has the parchment?" Benet queried. "Because if you do, it is your responsibility to tell us and help us get it back."

West shook his head and slumped in his seat. "Charles Michaelson," he said. "I believe he may have it now, or at least *did* have it."

Simon Benet and Rita Rodriguez were too experienced to show emotion, but both were thinking that this could be the first break in locating the parchment.

"Why do you think Professor Michaelson has it?" Benet asked.

"Let me backtrack," Albert West said slowly. "Fifteen years ago, a wealthy collector of antiques who regularly hired Charles as a consultant asked him for his professional opinion as to the authenticity of an ancient parchment. Charles was paid five hundred thousand dollars by the seller to tell the collector that it was genuine. In fact, it was a clever forgery."

"Was Michaelson or the seller ever prosecuted?" Benet asked.

"No. I personally interceded with Desmond Rogers, the buyer. Frankly, other experts had warned him that the parchment was a fraud, but Rogers considered himself very knowledgeable and had absolute faith in Charles. He did not file charges against Charles or the seller because he did not want the public humiliation of having been duped. As you can imagine, Desmond Rogers now considers Charles nothing more than a common thief and beneath contempt."

Where is this leading? Rita Rodriguez wondered, but Albert West was already answering her unspoken question.

"This morning, just before I left my apartment, I received a call from Desmond Rogers. As you would expect, he knows quite a few other wealthy collectors. One of them has been in touch with him. He heard that Charles is shopping the Joseph of Arimathea parchment and has received several enormously high bids for it from unscrupulous collectors."

"He's shopping the parchment!" Benet could not keep the surprise from his voice.

"So I am told." Albert West looked both drained and relieved. "That is all I know. I have no proof beyond what I just told you. I am simply relaying to you what Desmond said to me. But frankly, it makes a great deal of sense. I stress that there is nothing more that I can tell you. May I leave now? I have a one o'clock meeting with my department chairman."

"Yes, that's all, except for one thing," Benet told him. "Do you remember the exact date on which you last spoke to Jonathan Lyons?"

"I think it was the Tuesday before he died, but I'm not sure."

He's being evasive, Rita thought, and she took a chance on asking a question that might get her in trouble with Simon Benet. "Don't worry, Professor West," she said reassuringly, "we'll be checking your phone records, so if you're mistaken, we'll know."

Out of the corner of her eye, she caught Benet's furious stare, but then Albert West sank back into the chair. "Full disclosure," he said, his voice now high-pitched. "As I told you, I had been in the Adirondacks the weekend before Jonathan died. I *was* planning to stay up there until Tuesday, but it was very hot and humid, and so on Monday I decided to return home. I was very curious about Jonathan's supposed find and so I impulsively drove down through New Jersey, debating about calling him and asking if I might stop in."

"What time was that?" Rita asked.

"It was later than I expected it to be. I drove past Mahwah a few minutes before nine."

"Did you visit Professor Lyons the night he died?" Benet asked.

"No. I realized Jonathan did not like surprises. Upon reflection I thought that he might very well not welcome a visit on such short notice, and so I continued home."

"Did you phone him to ask if you could stop in?" Rita demanded.

"No. The only reason I bring this up is that I made a phone call while I was in the vicinity of the Lyons home, in case anyone is checking the location of my cell phone at that time."

"Professor West, who did you call?"

"I called Charles Michaelson. He did not answer and when his answering machine came on I did not leave a message."

49

After lunch, Mariah and Alvirah went back to wait at Lillian's apartment building. Alvirah brought a sandwich and coffee for Willy. They sat for the rest of the afternoon in the lobby. At five o'clock it was Willy who voiced their growing sense of apprehension. "If Lillian was meeting Richard to sell that parchment to him, it's sure taking a lot of time," he commented as he got up to stretch his legs.

Mariah nodded. At lunch she had tried to keep up with the conversation, but she felt crushing disappointment after hearing Lillian's message to Richard. It had robbed her of the faint optimism she had been allowing herself to feel that, given a showdown with Lillian, she might be able to persuade her to quietly return the parchment.

Now she wondered if the revelation that Lillian had the parchment and that Richard was willing to buy it might not be enough to have criminal charges brought against both of them.

Dad, this is the woman you loved, she thought, realizing that the bitterness she had been trying so hard to overcome was returning in full measure. She knew that during lunch Greg had recognized how quiet she had been and had tried to reassure her that the parchment would be recovered and returned to the Vatican Library.

"I never would have thought of Richard as capable of doing something so underhanded," Greg had observed. "I'm absolutely stunned." Then he'd added, "Nothing Lillian did would ever surprise me. Even while she was involved with Jonathan, I always wondered if she didn't have something going with Charles too. Maybe it was just because they were both big moviegoers. But still, when Lillian wasn't with Jonathan, it seemed to me that she spent an awful lot of time with Charles."

Mariah knew the last thing Greg wanted to do was upset her, but the thought that Lillian might have been involved with Charles as well was galling. It was all she could think of as they waited hour by hour in the lobby. Finally, at five thirty, she said, "I think what we need to do is to let Detective Benet hear your recording of that phone call, Alvirah. I guess if he hears it, it would be enough to have him confront both Lillian and Richard. I think I'll go home now. For all we know, Lillian and Richard are out together celebrating somewhere."

"I'll be right back," Alvirah said. "The new doorman just came on duty. I'll have a talk with him." When she returned a few minutes later, she was obviously pleased with herself. "I gave him twenty bucks. I told him that we have a surprise for Lillian, that her cousin is in town unexpectedly. That's you, Mariah. I gave him my number. He's going to tip me off when she gets back."

Mariah reached into her purse and pulled out Benet's card. "Alvirah," she said, "I don't think we should wait any longer. It's time to call Detective Benet. You can play the tape for him as soon as you get home and let the chips fall where they may."

50

❦❧

On Wednesday afternoon, Kathleen Lyons was sitting in a chair by the window in her hospital room, a cup of tea by her side. She had been dozing, and when she woke up, she looked out listlessly at the trees and the way the sun was flickering through the leafy branches. Then she leaned forward. She could see that there was someone half-hidden behind one of the trees.

It was a woman.

It was Lillian.

Kathleen stood up, leaned her hands on the windowsill, and narrowed her eyes so that she could see Lillian more clearly.

"Is Jonathan with her?" she mumbled. Then as she watched, she could see that Lily and Jonathan were taking pictures of each other.

"I hate you!" Kathleen screamed. "I hate both of you!"

"Kathleen, what's wrong, dear, what's wrong?" A nurse was hurrying into the room.

Kathleen grabbed the spoon from the saucer of the teacup and spun around in her chair. Her face savage with fury, she pointed the spoon at the nurse.

"Bang . . . bang . . . Die, damn you, die! I hate you, I hate you, I hate you . . . ," she shrieked, then collapsed back into the seat. Her eyes closed, she began to moan, "So much noise . . . so much blood," as the nurse quickly injected a sedative into her thin and trembling arm.

51

Greg Pearson's interview with Detectives Benet and Rodriguez had none of the drama of Albert West's blurted-out accusation against Charles Michaelson.

He explained that he considered himself to be a good friend of Jonathan Lyons and that he had met him six years ago when, on an impulse, he signed up for Jonathan's annual archaeological dig.

"For Jon and Albert and Charles and Richard, it was a passion," he said. "I was in awe of their knowledge of antiquities. By the end of that first trip, I was hooked and I knew I would sign up for the next one."

He verified that about once a month they were invited to the Lyons' home for dinner. "It was an evening we all thoroughly enjoyed," he said, "even though it was painful to watch a beautiful and charming woman like Kathleen deteriorate before our eyes."

In response to questions about Lillian, he said, "The first time she signed up for one of Jonathan's annual expeditions was five years ago. We could all see that Jonathan was instantly enchanted with her, and she with him. Within three nights they were sharing a bedroom and making no bones about it. Frankly, given their relationship, I felt quite uncomfortable watching her interact with Charles when they were at Jonathan's dinners. But of course when Kathleen found those pictures, Lillian was banished from ever setting foot in that house again."

Greg readily admitted to Benet and Rodriguez that Jonathan had told him about his supposed find. "Jon didn't actually offer to show it to me. He said he was having it evaluated. I told him that at some point I'd love to see it and he promised that after he had gotten the opinions of the experts, he'd let me have a look at it."

"Where were you on the Monday night that Professor Lyons was murdered, Mr. Pearson?" Rita asked.

Greg looked straight at her. "As I told you last week, Detective Rodriguez, I was in the Time Warner Center in Manhattan, where my apartment is located, all of Monday evening. I had dinner at Per Se on the fourth floor at about six and afterward went directly up to my apartment."

"Did you have dinner with anyone?"

"After a busy day at my office, I was content to eat quietly by myself, and to forestall your next question, I was alone in my apartment all night."

Benet's final question to Greg was about Charles Michaelson. "Do you think it's possible that Professor Lyons might have entrusted the parchment to him?"

As he and Rodriguez watched, Greg's face became a study in conflicting emotions. Then he said, "I believe that Jonathan would have entrusted the parchment to Lillian and I believe she would have confided that to Charles. I'm not prepared to speculate any further than that."

52

An hour later Charles Michaelson was sitting in the chair earlier occupied by Albert West and Greg Pearson. His portly body shook with anger as he got into a fiery exchange with the detectives: "No, I never saw the parchment. How many times do I have to tell you that? If someone says I was shopping it, he's a liar."

When told by Benet that they were planning to interview the source of the rumor, Michaelson snapped, "Go ahead. Whoever he is, tell him for me that there are laws about slander and he should look them up."

When asked where he was on the night Jonathan Lyons died, he retorted, "Once again, let me tell you, and I will speak slowly so that you'll get it straight. I was at home on Sutton Place. I got there at five thirty and didn't go out again until the next morning."

"Was anyone with you?" Benet asked.

"No. Happily, since my divorce, I live alone."

"Did you receive any phone calls that evening, Mr. Michaelson?"

"No, I did not. Wait a minute. The phone rang around nine o'clock that evening. I could see that the caller was Albert West and I was not in the mood to speak to him so I didn't answer."

Abruptly, Michaelson stood up. "If you have any more questions for me, you can submit them in writing to my lawyer." He reached in his pocket and flipped a card onto Benet's desk. "Now you know how to reach him. Good afternoon to both of you."

53

Richard Callahan's interview was scheduled for four P.M. When he had not arrived by four forty-five, Simon attempted to reach him on his cell phone. It went directly to voice mail. Frustrated, Simon left a brusque message for Richard regarding his missed appointment. "Mr. Callahan, I don't know why there would be any confusion about the fact that you were supposed to be here at four o'clock. It is imperative that you contact me as soon as you receive this message so we can reschedule, preferably for tomorrow.

"Once again I am leaving my cell phone number . . ."

54

After Mariah, Alvirah, and Willy had given up on waiting for Lillian and left the lobby of her apartment building, they crossed the street together and went down into the Lincoln Center garage, where they'd parked their cars only a few rows apart. Alvirah promised to call Mariah immediately if Lillian's doorman phoned to say that she had come home.

All the details of her day were running through Mariah's mind as she drove back to New Jersey. She wanted to be close by her mother in case she was allowed to visit her. When she got to her parents' home she left the car in the driveway, and, with a feeling of infinite weariness, she made her way to the front door and took out her key. As she stepped into the house, the thought ran through her mind that until the last few days, she had almost never been there alone. Better get used to it, she told herself as she dropped her shoulder bag on the table in the foyer and walked back to the kitchen. She had given Betty the day off, so she put on the kettle, made herself a cup of tea, then carried it outside to the patio.

Mariah settled into a chair at the umbrella table and watched the early evening shadows slant across the bluish-gray cobblestones. The colorful umbrella was closed now, and it brought back the memory of the night, about ten years ago, when her parents were out and a sudden summer storm had come up. The wind had toppled the umbrella over. It had taken the table with it, causing the glass tabletop to shatter in a hail of windblown shards.

Like my life now, Mariah thought. Another sudden storm just over a week ago and now I'm left to pick up the pieces. When Alvirah plays that recording for the detectives, she wondered, will it be enough proof for them to charge Lillian and Richard with conspiracy to buy and sell stolen property? Or will Lillian and Richard be smart enough to come up with another explanation for why she was accepting some offer from him?

And I don't think the safe-deposit records at her bank will give any hint to what she took out today, Mariah decided as she slowly sipped the tea.

What's going to happen to Mom at the court hearing on Friday? was the next question that rushed into her mind. From what the nurses are telling me, she seems to be pretty quiet. Oh, God, if only she could be allowed to come home, she thought.

Then, realizing that it was cooling down rapidly, she carried her empty cup into the house. She was barely back in the kitchen when Alvirah phoned.

"Mariah, I tried you on your cell phone and you didn't answer. Are you all right?" Alvirah asked anxiously.

"Sorry. My cell phone is in my bag in the foyer and I didn't hear it ring. Alvirah, have you heard anything?"

"Yes and no. I called Detective Benet and he was very interested. He wants to make a copy of Lillian's message to Richard. In fact, he's on his way in to our apartment now. Boy, that guy wastes no time! But here's what he told me: Richard had an appointment with him in the prosecutor's office this afternoon and he didn't show up or call."

"What does that tell you?" Mariah asked numbly.

"I don't know what it tells me," Alvirah said, "except to say that all of this is so out of character for the Richard I know. I can't believe it's happening."

"Out of character for the person I know too." Mariah bit her lip, afraid that her voice was breaking.

"Any word about Kathleen?"

"No. I'm going to call the hospital now, not that they really tell me anything," Mariah answered, swallowing over the lump in her throat. "But as I told you, this morning they said Mother had slept reasonably well."

"Okay. That's about it for now, but I'll call if I reach Lillian or hear from her doorman."

"I don't care what time it is. Please call me. I'll be sure to have my cell phone in my pocket if I go out again."

A few minutes later the doorbell rang. It was Lisa Scott.

"Mariah, we just got home. We saw your car in the driveway. Lloyd's going out to pick up some Chinese food. Come on over and have something to eat with us," she offered.

"Okay, but I'd better not read the fortune cookies," Mariah said with a weak smile. "I'd love to be with you. This has not been the best day of my life, as I'll explain to you and Lloyd. I'll be over in a few minutes. First I want to call the hospital and check on my mother."

"Sure thing. Maybe just this once we'll have a glass of wine," Lisa said jokingly. "Or two," she added.

"Sounds good to me. See you in a bit."

It was getting dark. Mariah switched on the outside lights, then went into the study and turned on the lamps on the tables at each end of the couch. She hesitated, then knew she did not want to make the call from her father's study. She went back into the kitchen and dialed the hospital. When she reached the nurse at the desk on the psychiatric floor and inquired about her mother, she could sense from the pause that the nurse's response was guarded.

"Your mother had a difficult afternoon and had to be given some extra sedation. She is resting quietly now."

"What happened?" Mariah demanded.

"Ms. Lyons, as you know, there is an ongoing court-ordered evaluation of your mother and I am not at liberty to say very much. She was quite agitated, but I can assure you she is calm now."

Mariah did not try to keep the frustration out of her voice. "As you can surely understand, I am sick with worry about my mother. Is there nothing else you can tell me?"

"Ms. Lyons, the judge has ordered that the report be faxed to his chambers by two o'clock Thursday afternoon. That's tomorrow. My understanding from past experience is that the attorneys will get a copy of it. Your mother's behavior and the doctor's conclusions will be detailed in the report."

Mariah knew she could not push any further. Thank you, I guess, she thought as she politely said good-bye to the nurse and hung up the phone.

A half hour later, over wonton soup, she filled Lloyd and Lisa in about everything that had happened since Lloyd had stopped by to see her that morning. "I feel as though this morning was a week ago," she said. "And now we have every reason to believe Lillian went to the bank to get the parchment and that she was on her way to deliver it to Richard. If that's the case, and if it's proven that they have basically stolen it, can't they both be charged with a crime?"

"You bet they can, and if it can be proven, they will be," Lloyd replied emphatically. "It would seem that Jonathan gave the parchment to Lillian for safekeeping and Richard either knew that or figured it out. The one thing I can't understand at this point is where Rory fits into the whole picture. It may be as simple as the fact that she knew that the detectives would be checking out everybody, and with that parole warrant from years ago hanging over her head, she simply took off."

"On the other hand, maybe she's involved in some way," Mariah speculated. "If anybody was in a position to set up my mother, it was Rory."

Lisa had not yet said anything. "Mariah, it would make sense if your father and Lillian were breaking up that Lillian might want to get rid of your father, so that she could hang on to the parchment. Did you ever notice any quiet conversation between Lillian and Rory?"

"I can't say that I did, but on the other hand Rory had only been my mother's caregiver for six months when those photos of Venice were found. Lillian was never in the house again. But we don't know if Lillian and Rory were calling each other."

"Rory vanished forty-eight hours ago. No one has seen her since," Lloyd said slowly. "Now you say Lillian left her apartment a little before nine this morning, and as of about forty minutes ago when you spoke to Alvirah, she still hadn't returned."

"That's right," Mariah said. "I can't help but think that maybe she and Richard are out somewhere celebrating."

"You told me that Richard missed his appointment with the prosecutor's office. That doesn't sound right to me. If anything, you'd think he'd get there early, to appear cooperative and cover his tracks."

"Lloyd, when I talked about speaking to the nurse, I told you that she said that the judge would have the psychiatric report by two tomorrow afternoon and the attorneys would get a copy. But I didn't think to ask you, at what time do *you* get it?"

"I'm sure the judge will give it to the prosecutor and me before the end of the day, so that we can look at it overnight."

"Can you show it to me when you get home?"

"Of course, Mariah. Now, for heaven's sake, have some of that sesame chicken. You hardly even touched the soup."

With an apologetic smile, Mariah started to reach for the plate when her cell phone rang. She grabbed it out of her pocket, murmuring, "I hope it's Alvirah." But then she saw the caller ID and said, "If you can believe it, it's Richard. I'm not going to answer. Let's see if he leaves a message and what lie he comes up with."

The three sat silent until her phone chimed, indicating that there was a new voice mail. Mariah played it on speakerphone: "Mariah, I am so very sorry. I have made a terrible mistake. *Please* call me."

"Mariah, maybe you should call him back," Lloyd began, then stopped.

Mariah's face was buried in her hands and her shoulders were shaking with sobs.

"I can't talk to him," she whispered. "I can't."

55

❧❦❧

On Wednesday evening at eight o'clock, Father Aiden opened the door of the friary of Saint Francis of Assisi Church to find Richard Callahan standing in the doorway. "It's good of you to see me on such short notice," Richard said as the priest motioned for him to come in.

Father Aiden looked at the troubled face of his visitor, noting that in place of his usual black slacks and white shirt, Richard was wearing a blue sport shirt with a designer logo and tan slacks. There was a light shadow on his face indicating that he had not shaved recently. When he took Aiden's extended hand, Aiden could feel that his palm was moist.

It was obvious to him that something was terribly wrong. "My door is always open to you, Richard," he said mildly. "The other friars are lingering over coffee. Why don't we go into the sitting room? We'll have privacy there."

Richard nodded without speaking. It was clear to Father Aiden that Richard was trying to compose himself. "Richard, I know you're a coffee drinker," he said. "I'm sure there's still some left in the pot in the dining room. Let me get you a cup. In fact, I'll bring a second cup in for myself. I know how we both like it, black and no sugar."

"That sounds good."

At the door of the modest sitting room, Aiden gestured for Richard to go in and said, "I'll be right back." When he returned, he put the cups on the coffee table, then closed the door. Richard was sitting on the couch, his shoulders slumped forward, his elbows propped up on his knees, and his hands clasped. Wordlessly, he reached for the coffee. Father Aiden noticed that his hand was trembling. He sat down in the wing chair facing the couch. "How can I help you, Richard?" he asked.

"Father, I've made a terrible mistake." As Father Aiden listened, Richard told him that he always believed that Jonathan had given Lillian the parchment. Then he admitted that he had lied to her. "Father Aiden, I told her that Jonathan had shown it to me, and that he said that he was going to give it to her for safekeeping.

"I knew that there was no way anyone could prove that she had it, and I was desperate to get it back," Richard explained. "She believed me. She even told me that after Jon dropped her so abruptly that Wednesday evening, she was heartsick. She said that Jon asked her to give the parchment back to him, but she had already put it in her safe-deposit box. She told me she begged him to wait a week before she returned it and pleaded with him to take that time to think more about whether he really wanted to end their relationship."

Father Aiden nodded without commenting. He thought back to that same day, when, in the late afternoon, Jonathan had told him he could no longer endure the pain of his estrangement from Mariah and the heartbreak Kathleen continued to suffer because of his relationship with Lillian. He had said he was going directly to Lillian's apartment to tell her of his decision.

Aiden O'Brien remembered sadly that Jonathan then had spoken about his plan to take Kathleen to Venice and said that he would ask Mariah to go with them. Aiden was stunned when Jon said at the time that he had an odd sense that he might not live very much longer, and he needed and wanted to repair the damage his affair with Lillian had inflicted on his family.

"I never saw the parchment and Jonathan never told me he had given it to her," Richard repeated, then paused, as if too embarrassed to go on. "But Lillian believed me."

"When did you tell her this?" Father Aiden asked.

"Let me explain. After the funeral, I waited in the cemetery when the others drove to the club for lunch. I had a hunch that Lillian would show up there and I was right. She visited Jonathan's grave and when she went back to her car, I followed her. That was when I asked her if she had ever seen the parchment. I knew she was lying when she said no. I knew that she almost certainly had it, and I was afraid she would sell it now that Jonathan was dead. But of course I had absolutely no proof."

Richard reached for the coffee cup that until now he had ignored. He took a long sip before he said, "Father Aiden, as we both know, that parchment is the property of the Vatican Library. That was when I decided to take a different approach with Lillian. I called her and got tough. I told her I knew Jonathan had given it to her, and I was going to the cops to tell them that. She believed me and finally admitted that she had it. I told her that I would give her two million dollars for it."

"Two million dollars! Where would you get that kind of money?"

"A trust fund my grandfather set up for me. I am *sure* Lillian must have had at least one other offer, but I promised her I would never disclose that I had actually paid her for it. I told her she could tell people that she realized that it would be wrong to keep it and that she wanted to do the right thing. She was afraid because she had already told the detectives that she didn't have it. I said to her that I really believed that the prosecutor's office wouldn't pursue it any further if she returned it quickly. I swore to her that I would give the parchment back to the Vatican Library and said no matter how much Jonathan had hurt her, she owed it to him to see that it went back there."

"How were you going to make the payment?" Father Aiden inquired. "If you did it on the level, wouldn't you or she or both of you have to pay some kind of tax on all this money?"

Richard shook his head. "As the tax laws stand today, I am allowed to give away up to five million dollars in my lifetime. I would report the two million dollars to the IRS as a gift to her. That way she could have the use of the money without having the worry that if she sold the parchment under the table and it somehow came out, she might end up in prison for tax evasion."

Richard hesitated, then took a long sip of his coffee. "Last night, as we were leaving Mariah's house, Lillian phoned me and said she would accept my offer. This morning I went downtown to my trustee's office to sign the paperwork to move the money into her account. But I've been calling her all day, and she still hasn't answered."

"Why wouldn't she answer after she agreed to accept your offer?"

"My guess is that she is greedy, she reconsidered, and she probably decided to sell it to some underground collector for a lot more money. I spent the whole day hanging around outside my trustee's office because if I had reached her, I was going to have her meet me there. At five o'clock, I gave up and went uptown to my parents' apartment. They were on their way out, but I stayed there for a while, calling Lillian every half hour. Then I decided to come and talk to you."

"Richard, what I don't understand is, why are you blaming yourself? You were willing to spend a very considerable amount of your own money to get that parchment back and then return it to the Vatican."

"I'm blaming myself, Father, because I should have gone about it another way. I should have hired a private detective to follow Lillian around the clock and see where she was going and whom she was meeting. She did admit she had put the parchment in her safe-deposit box. I'm afraid that once she sells it, it will be gone for good. Then if I go to the detectives, it will be her word against mine. I'm already on record with them that I never saw the parchment."

Richard stopped and looked startled. "My God, I forgot. I was supposed to go talk to the detectives again today. It absolutely went out of my mind. I'll call them in the morning. But here's what I need. Father Aiden, you met Lillian at Jonathan's home a number of times before those pictures were found. I know she respects you. Will you try to talk to her? I'm sure she's avoiding my calls."

"I don't know if it will do any good but of course I will. Do you have her number?"

"It's right here on my cell," Richard said.

Father Aiden quickly jotted it down on a slip of paper, then picked up his phone and dialed it and listened as Lillian's voice mail greeting came on: "You have reached Lillian Stewart. I'm not available to take your call. Please leave a message and I'll get back to you as soon as possible."

A computerized voice immediately announced that the mailbox was full.

Richard had been able to hear the recording. "Probably her voice mail is full because of all the messages I left for her today," he said as he stood up to leave. "Will you try her again in the morning, Father?"

"Of course," Father Aiden said as he put the receiver down and walked Richard to the door, promising to get in touch with him as soon as he reached Lillian. Then he slowly walked back to the sitting room and settled again into the wing chair, his arthritic knees emitting sharp pains as he lowered his body. He picked up the cup of now less-than-warm coffee. Frowning in concentration, and disappointed, he sadly acknowledged that all of his long experience in dealing with human beings was warning him that his valued friend Richard Callahan had been less than truthful.

"But why?" he asked himself aloud.

56

On Thursday morning, Detectives Benet and Rodriguez began to consider the possibility that Lillian Stewart had been a victim of foul play.

When they'd met with Alvirah at her Central Park South apartment the previous evening, they had listened to the tape of Lillian's message to Richard Callahan again, which Alvirah had already played for them over the phone. Then they reviewed with Alvirah everything she had told them during that call.

She had repeated the exact timeline of following Lillian to the bank, then downtown on the subway, and finally losing her at Chambers Street. "It made me so mad," Alvirah told them, "but this poor old soul was crawling up the steps, one at a time, leaning on her cane. And with so many people rushing down the other way, I could no more have passed her than I could have jumped over her. And when I got to the sidewalk, Lillian had disappeared into thin air."

"Do you think she might have gotten into a car that was waiting for her, Mrs. Meehan?" Benet asked.

"Call me Alvirah. As I told you, when Lillian walked out of the bank with something in her tote bag, she was holding a cell phone to her ear. Who knows if she was making a call or receiving one? I can't say. Maybe she was agreeing to meet someone. It's a possibility."

"And I kept driving around the block," Willy offered from his

comfortable lounge chair. "By the time Alvirah got back to me I felt
as if I was on a carousel."

From the Meehans' apartment on Central Park South, Benet
and Rodriguez drove directly to Lillian's apartment building and
learned from the doorman that Ms. Stewart had not returned home
yet that day.

"The doorman said that since Professor Lyons died, he doesn't
remember anyone, man *or* woman, coming to visit her," Rita
pointed out.

Simon did not respond. Rita knew her partner well enough to
have a pretty good idea of what the disgruntled look on his face
meant. After they had interviewed Lillian Stewart on Tuesday morning, they should have requested a search warrant on her apartment
immediately. Whether or not she admitted to having a safe-deposit
box, with a search warrant they would have been able to trace it.
Simon was beating himself up because if Lillian had taken the
parchment from the safe-deposit box yesterday, it might well have
slipped through their fingers for good now.

"I should have gotten a search warrant Tuesday," Simon Benet
said, confirming Rita's guess at what he had been thinking. "And
now Stewart's been gone for twenty-four hours. At least we know
that Alvirah Meehan tracked her to Chambers Street yesterday
morning."

The phone on Simon's desk began to ring. "What now?" he mut-
tered as he picked up the receiver.

It was Alvirah Meehan. "I couldn't sleep, so I walked over to Lillian's apartment this morning at eight o'clock. It's only six blocks or
so from Central Park South. I'm not much for early morning walks.
Willy likes them but today I just couldn't stay in bed."

Simon waited patiently, somehow sure that Alvirah was not calling to discuss her exercise routine.

"Just as I got there, the doorman pointed out to me Lillian's cleaning woman, who was on her way in. I told her I was worried about Lillian, and she let me go upstairs to the apartment with her. She has a key, of course."

"You were in Lillian Stewart's apartment!" Benet exclaimed.

"Yes. It's all in perfect order. I have to say Lillian's very neat. But can you believe that her cell phone, I mean the one with the phone number she gave me, is sitting on the coffee table in the living room?"

Benet knew it was a rhetorical question.

"I turned it on, of course, to check the cell phone's number, and I recognized it. Then I looked to see if she had listed anything in the phone's daily calendar for today."

Benet pushed a button on his phone. "Mrs. Meehan, I mean Alvirah, my partner Detective Rodriguez is here. I'm putting you on speakerphone."

"That's a good idea. She's a very smart young woman. Anyhow, Lillian's calendar shows that she had scheduled an eight o'clock breakfast meeting this morning with some of the professors in her department at Columbia. I've already phoned there. She didn't show up and she didn't call them. She also has an appointment with her hairdresser at eleven o'clock this morning at Bergdorf Goodman. Let's see if she keeps that one."

"Wait a minute, Alvirah," Rita interrupted. "You told us yesterday morning that when Ms. Stewart came out of the bank, she was talking on her cell phone."

"She *was* talking on a cell phone and I *did* tell you that. But she sure wasn't talking on the cell phone that's sitting on the cocktail table in her apartment, so she must have more than one."

The detectives waited as Alvirah hesitated, then said firmly, "You want to know my opinion? Lillian Stewart is going to turn out to be a vanishing act, just like Rory Steiger. And you know what else I think? Sad to say, when she promised to sell that parchment to Richard Callahan, she may have been putting herself in mortal danger."

"I think you may be right," Benet said quietly.

"All right. That's all I have for now. I'll be at Bergdorf's in the beauty salon at eleven o'clock. Whether she shows up or not, I'll call you." With a decisive click as she disconnected, Alvirah was gone.

The detectives looked at each other, but before they could react to what they had just heard, the phone on Simon's desk rang again.

He picked it up and identified himself.

"Detective Benet, this is Richard Callahan."

"Where are you, Mr. Callahan?" Simon asked brusquely.

"I've just parked outside the courthouse. I apologize for not keeping my appointment with you yesterday. If you hadn't been there now, I would have asked to speak to someone else in the prosecutor's office."

"That won't be necessary," Benet said curtly. "I'm here and so is Detective Rodriguez. Our office is on the second floor. We'll be waiting for you."

57

Kathleen's mind was filled with images that came and went fuzzily. People were moving all around and talking to her.

Rory was angry. "Kathleen, why are you standing at the window? Why aren't you in bed?"

"The gun will get dirty . . ."

"Kathleen, you're dreaming. Go to bed now."

Jonathan's arms around her. "Kathleen, it's all right. I'm here."

The noise.

The man looking up at her.

The door closing.

The girl with the long black hair.

Where is she?

Kathleen began to cry. "I want to . . . ," she moaned. What was the word? The girl was in that place. "Home," she whispered. "I want to go home."

Then the man with his face covered came back. He was floating across the room to her and the girl with the black hair.

Mariah.

He was pointing the gun at them both now.

Kathleen sat up in bed and grabbed the water glass from the table. She pointed it at the man and tried to pull the trigger but couldn't find it.

She threw it across the room at him.

"Stop!" she screamed. "Stop!"

58

Chief Assistant Prosecutor Peter Jones was in his office, not far from where Richard Callahan was being questioned by Simon Benet and Rita Rodriguez. After discussing with them the call from Wally Gruber's defense attorney Joshua Schultz, he had gone to his boss, Prosecutor Sylvan Berger, and filled him in on what was developing. Berger decided that he should call Schultz back. "Tell him to give us the stolen plates and the E-ZPass tag information, and if it checks out, we'll go to the next step with him," Berger had said.

Schultz had agreed and the report had been quickly received. The plates had been stolen six months ago. The stolen E-ZPass that Gruber claimed to have used when he drove back from Mahwah after he burglarized the home of Lloyd Scott had been on a car that had been driven from New Jersey the night Jonathan Lyons died. The time that the car traveled city-bound over the George Washington Bridge coincided with the approximate time it would have taken Gruber to reach the GW Bridge from Mahwah if he had been in the Scott home and heard the shot that killed Lyons.

Now, at the direction of the prosecutor, Jones was calling Joshua Schultz back. When Schultz answered, Jones said, "Give us the name of the fence who has the Scott jewelry. If your client is telling the truth, and we get the jewelry back, this office will make a recommendation to the judge that Mr. Gruber's cooperation be taken into consideration at his sentencing."

"How much consideration?" Schultz demanded.

"We will make a significant recommendation to the judge in New Jersey who will be hearing the Scott burglary and to the judge in New York who hears the case of the burglary charges against Mr. Gruber there. But he absolutely has to do some prison time."

"What does he get for giving you the face of the person who ran out of the house after that professor got shot?"

"Let's make this a two-step process. If Gruber's story checks out on the jewelry, we'll talk more about what further consideration we can give him for the sketch. As you well know, Mr. Schultz, your client is remarkably clever at inventing ways to track wealthy people, break into their homes, and, in the Scott case, ransack their safes without setting off the alarms. So he may be clever enough to invent this story about the face he claims he saw, too."

"Wally didn't invent it," Schultz snapped. "But I'll talk to him. If you get the jewelry back, you'll go to bat for him in New York and New Jersey?"

"Yes. And if he ends up doing a composite that leads to something, there's no question that he'll get more consideration."

"Okay, that sounds all right for now." Schultz laughed, a short gruff bark. "You know, Wally's kind of vain. He'll be flattered to hear you think he's so clever."

Now we wait and see, Peter Jones thought as he hung up the phone. He leaned back in the chair in his small office, thinking that for months, every time he had walked into the prosecutor's roomy office, he had had the feeling that one day soon it would be his.

Now that feeling was fading.

And there was something else the prosecutor had told him to do. It was time to inform Lloyd Scott that the man who broke into his house claimed he saw someone fleeing from the Lyons home seconds after Jonathan Lyons was shot. And that someone wasn't Kathleen Lyons.

59

Mariah's office was on Wall Street. After another sleepless night and unable to stay in her parents' house any longer, despite wanting to be near her mother, she had driven into New York at six A.M. Thursday morning and gone into work. Long before anyone else came into the suite where she rented her own space, she was at her desk going through her e-mail and the regular mail that the receptionist/secretary had left for her.

It was pretty much as she had expected. The e-mails she had been receiving and sending to her clients basically covered anything of importance. But it was good to be here with the television on, watching the markets all over the world as they began to open or close. It was also a place that was a refuge from everything that had happened during the last week and a half, particularly the bombshell that Richard had been planning to buy the parchment from Lillian.

She could vividly see the look on Richard's face when they were all sitting at the dinner table only the night before last and he had again denied ever having seen the parchment. She had watched his expression as he nodded in agreement with Father Aiden's stern reminder that the parchment, which probably would be proven to be sacred, was the property of the Vatican.

The once and maybe future Jesuit, she thought scornfully. Well, the Bible says that the soldiers cast dice for Christ's robe. Now, two thousand years later, some of my father's so-called dear friends may have been casting dice for the letter Christ may have written to Joseph of Arimathea. A letter thanking Joseph for his kindness.

Mariah thought about Lillian's message to Richard: "I've decided to accept your two-million-dollar offer. Get back to me."

His offer, Mariah thought. How many offers did she have, and where did they come from? If nobody at the table except Richard was lying, who are the other experts Dad may have consulted? The detectives were checking Dad's phone records. I wonder if they came up with anyone?

If Lillian doesn't show up, has something happened to her?

It was unthinkable that Richard would harm Lillian, just as unthinkable as it was that her mother had shot her father.

There, at least, I can take some comfort, Mariah promised herself. Richard may be the antithesis of everything I thought him to be, but he isn't a murderer. Dear God, let Lillian show up. Let us be able to find the parchment.

There were a few letters she should answer. She turned off the television, drafted her responses, and e-mailed them to her secretary to print out and mail. It was almost eight A.M., and she knew the early birds would be arriving soon. She didn't want to run into anybody. At the wake she had told her friends that she understood how much they grieved with her, but for the immediate future, she needed to concentrate on taking care of her mother and assisting her defense attorney.

Since then, she had received many e-mails that began in a similar way. "Love you, Mariah. Thinking of you. No need to respond." Nice, but no help.

She left the office and took the elevator down to the main floor. She decided that her next stop would be her apartment in Greenwich Village.

She retrieved her car from the parking lot and drove the short distance to Downing Street. Her apartment was on the third floor of a town house that had been a private residence eighty years ago. She had been here only once, to get clothing, since the fateful night she had rushed out to New Jersey when her second call to her father at ten thirty P.M. had not been answered.

Her apartment was small. It consisted of a living room, a bedroom, and a kitchen, which barely accommodated a stove, a sink, a microwave oven, and a few cabinets. Dad helped move me in here, she thought. That was six years ago. Mom had already been diagnosed as having signs of early Alzheimer's. She was getting repetitive and forgetful. I offered to move home and commute. Dad practically threw me out. He said I was young and had my own life to live.

Aware that the apartment felt stuffy, Mariah opened the window and welcomed the sound of the street noise. Music to my ears, she thought. I love the house, but what happens now? Even when this nightmare is over and Mom is allowed to come home permanently, she certainly couldn't come live here. I'll have to move back to Mahwah. But how long can I pay full-time caregivers?

She sat down on the club chair that her father used to sit in before he retired. Once every week or ten days, he would walk over from NYU and have a drink with her here at around six o'clock. Then they would go out to their favorite Italian restaurant on West 4th Street. By nine o'clock, he would be on his way home.

Or on his way to Lillian's, an uncomfortable voice in her mind whispered.

Mariah tried to push aside her speculation on that possibility. Eighteen months ago, when she'd found out about Lillian, the intimate dinners they had both enjoyed had stopped. I told Dad I didn't want to interfere with his precious time with Lillian . . .

To distract herself from the guilt she felt at that memory, she looked around the living room. The walls throughout the apartment were a soft yellow shade that gave an illusion of space. Dad went through the swatches of paint with me, she remembered. He had a much better ability to judge the finished product than I ever did.

The painting over the couch had been his gift to her on move-in day. It was one he had bought in Egypt on an expedition and depicted the sun setting over the ruins of a pyramid there.

Everywhere I look, either here or at the house, something reminds me of him, she thought. She walked into the bedroom and picked up the picture of her parents taken about ten years ago, before the onslaught of the Alzheimer's. Her father's arms were locked around her mother's waist and they were both smiling. I hope that in some way his arms are still around her and protecting her, Mariah thought. She needs his protection now, more than ever.

What will happen to Mom in court tomorrow?

She was about to call Alvirah to see if she had heard anything more when the land line on the night table beside her bed rang. It was Greg. "Mariah, where are you? I called the house and Betty said you had left before she came in and you're not answering your cell phone. I've been worried about you."

Mariah had turned off her phone because she was afraid that Richard might contact her again. She did not want to repeat her performance of the night before, when she had broken down at the sound of his voice at Lloyd's dinner table. Now she said apologetically, "Greg, my cell phone was off. As you can imagine, I'm not thinking straight."

"Neither am I. But I *am* worried about you. Your father's girlfriend and your mother's caregiver have both disappeared in the last few days. I can't let anything happen to you."

He hesitated, then said, "Mariah, I'm a pretty good judge of people. I know you are devastated at the thought that Richard would buy the parchment from Lillian. I don't know whether he did or he did not, but if anything has happened to Lillian, I doubt very much that Richard is responsible."

"Why do you say that, Greg?" Mariah asked quietly.

"Because it's what I believe." Greg paused, then said slowly, "Mariah, I love you and I want your happiness above everything. At all of your father's dinners, I sensed that there was a growing attraction between you and Richard. If it turns out that he would buy a stolen and sacred object, I frankly hope that whatever your feeling is for him, it will change."

Mariah chose her words carefully. "If you saw a growing attraction between us, I have never been aware that it existed. And certainly, judging from that phone message, if Richard is what I think he is, I want no part of him ever."

"That's good news," Greg said. "And I'm going to give you plenty of time to think of me as a guy worth spending your life with."

"Greg," Mariah began to protest.

"Forget I said that. But, Mariah, I am dead serious now. I've done some of my own investigation. Charles Michaelson is a fraud. He's been trying to find a buyer for the parchment. I can even give you the name of the man who heard about it from his contacts. He's Desmond Rogers, a well-known collector. Mariah, I beg you, don't let Michaelson get *near* you. I wouldn't be surprised if he turns out to be responsible for Lillian's disappearance and the disappearance of your mother's caregiver, too. And, Mariah—maybe even for your father's death."

60

Lloyd Scott was in his office on Main Street in Hackensack, a block away from the courthouse, when he received a call from Assistant Prosecutor Peter Jones.

"You're telling me that the crook who broke into my house may have seen someone running from Jonathan's house right after he was shot!" Lloyd exclaimed. Anger creeping into his tone, he demanded, "When in God's name did you find this out?"

Peter Jones had been fully anticipating the hostile response. "Lloyd, I got the call from Gruber's attorney, Joshua Schultz, a little less than twenty-four hours ago. As you well know, many defendants with serious charges pending try to tell us that they have valuable information on some other case. As you also well know, they're not trying to help the prosecutor out of the goodness of their hearts. They're looking to get their sentences reduced."

"Peter, I couldn't care less about what this guy's motives are, and I'm speaking as the owner of the house he broke into," Lloyd answered, his voice rising. "Why didn't you call me right away?"

"Lloyd, calm down and let me tell you what happened yesterday. After I got the call from Schultz, I spoke to the prosecutor immediately. We followed up right away on Gruber's claim that he was using a stolen E-ZPass tag when he drove back to New York after breaking into your house. His attorney gave us the information about the stolen tag and the record checked out. E-ZPass only activates on the George Washington Bridge going from New Jersey to New York, not the other way around. So we don't know when Gruber drove out to New Jersey, but we know when he drove back."

"Go on," Lloyd said brusquely.

"We know he was on the bridge going back at ten fifteen. Mariah Lyons spoke to her father at eight thirty, and she panicked at ten thirty when she called him again and only got his voice mail. We know he was dead at that point. So, with this time frame, it is very possible that Gruber was in your bedroom emptying your safe when he claims he heard the shot."

"All right. So what's next?"

"Gruber gave us the name of the fence he says he used to get rid of the stolen jewelry. His name is Billy Declar and he runs some kind of dumpy secondhand furniture store in lower Manhattan. He lives in the back room. He's got a long criminal record and was Gruber's cell mate the one time he served a prison term in New York. We're working with the Manhattan DA's office to get a search warrant for his place."

"When are you going to execute the search warrant?"

"They promised us they'd get it from the judge by three o'clock, and our guys will go right over there with them. For what it's worth, according to Gruber, Declar has your wife's jewelry intact. He was planning to take it to Rio in the next couple of weeks and sell it there."

"Getting the jewelry back would be fine, but, obviously much more important, can Gruber give any kind of description of whoever he claims he saw leaving the house?"

"So far, he's holding back on that because he's still trying to make a deal, but I must tell you that he has already stated through his lawyer that it was not Kathleen Lyons. So, if the information about the fence turns out to be true, then Gruber will have established sufficient credibility for this office to arrange for him to sit down with our composite officer immediately and come up with a face."

"I see."

Jones knew that in the next minute, Lloyd Scott would be delivering an impassioned protest about the arrest of Kathleen Lyons. Hastily Jones added, "Lloyd, you must understand something. Wally Gruber is one of the most cunning crooks I have ever come across. The Manhattan DA is looking into other unsolved residential burglaries that he may have committed using the same kind of GPS tracker he put on your car. This guy knows if he can convince us that he was in your house at the approximate time of Professor Lyons's death, it might work for him big-time."

"I understand what you are telling me," Lloyd Scott snapped. "Nevertheless, there was an ungodly rush to arrest and handcuff and incarcerate a frail, sick, and bewildered grieving woman, and you know it."

Trying to keep his voice from rising, Scott paused, then added, "At this moment, I don't care whether the jewelry is returned or not. I demand that you go immediately to the next step. I want Gruber to sit down with that composite officer and I want it to happen by tomorrow at the latest. If you don't, I will immediately make such arrangements myself. And, frankly, I don't care what you have to promise him. At the very least, you owe Kathleen Lyons that much."

Before Peter Jones could respond, Lloyd Scott added, "I want to know right away what develops from that search warrant. I'll be waiting for your call."

As he heard the click that ended their conversation, Peter Jones saw his dream of becoming the next county prosecutor evaporating in front of his eyes.

61

At eleven o'clock, Alvirah was sitting on a chair near the receptionist's desk in the beauty salon at Bergdorf Goodman waiting for, but not expecting, Lillian Stewart to keep her appointment there.

When she'd arrived fifteen minutes earlier, she'd explained to the receptionist why she was there. "I'm an old friend. I help Ms. Stewart out by covering at her apartment when she has a repairman coming in. She's not answering her cell phone, and she told me a couple of days ago that she had a refrigerator guy coming in today at one o'clock and she might need me to let him in."

The receptionist, a trim sixtyish woman with ash-blond hair, nodded. "I understand. I waited my whole day off for the television guy and he never showed up. And you know what drives me crazy? They give you a window of time for when they'll be there and it doesn't mean a thing."

"You're so right," Alvirah agreed. "Anyhow, since I couldn't reach her, and you know how impossible it is to even get an appointment with anyone who fixes anything, never mind reschedule it, I decided to come over here and find out when she'll be finished. If she has a long appointment, I'll meet the repair guy. The way I figure it, with school starting next week, she's probably getting the whole works done today."

The receptionist smiled and nodded. "Yes, she is. Manicure, pedicure, haircut, coloring, highlights, and blow dry. She'll be here at least three hours."

"That's my Lillian," Alvirah said, smiling broadly. "She always looks so perfectly put together. How long has she been coming here?"

"Oh, my goodness." The receptionist frowned in concentration. "She was already a regular client when I came to work here and that's almost twenty years ago."

At a quarter past eleven, Alvirah went back to the desk. "I'm getting a little worried," she confided. "Is Lillian usually on time?"

"You can set your clock by her. She's never forgotten any appointment before, but maybe something important came up. If I don't hear from her in the next twenty minutes, I think I'll have to cancel the rest of her appointments."

"Maybe you should," Alvirah said. "Maybe something important really did come up."

"I just hope it wasn't any big problem, like a death in her family." The receptionist sighed. "Ms. Stewart is such a nice person."

"I hope there wasn't a death in her family," Alvirah agreed quietly. Including Lillian's own, she thought grimly.

62

After the call from Greg, Mariah sat on the edge of the bed in her apartment and tried to sort out her emotions. It was a relief to realize that she agreed with him. No matter how bad it was that Richard had tried to buy the parchment, she simply could not believe that he was a killer.

Was Greg right when he claimed that he sensed an attraction between her and Richard? In the past six years, ever since Richard had been on the first archaeological dig with her father, he'd come to the house at least once a month.

Was he the real reason why I always came home for those dinners? she asked herself. I don't want to go there, she decided. She looked at the picture of her mother and father on the dresser. I felt so betrayed when I saw those pictures of Dad and Lillian. I feel the same sense of betrayal with Richard now.

She remembered an evening three years ago when she'd gone to the wake of a close friend's husband. He had been killed in a car crash by a drunk driver speeding the wrong way on the Long Island Expressway. Her friend Joan was sitting quietly near the casket. When Mariah spoke to her, all she could say was, "I hurt so much. I hurt so much."

That was the way I felt when I learned about Dad and Lillian,

Mariah thought. That's the way I feel now about Richard. I am beyond tears. I hurt so much.

Is Greg right that Charles Michaelson might have been one of
the bidders for the parchment? That made sense too. He did something illegal years ago. I don't know what it was, except that Dad was
upset when he mentioned it. And Charles was the one who covered
for Lillian whenever they were at our house . . .

She could hear him now. "Lillian and I went to see the new
Woody Allen film. Try to catch it." Or, "There's a great new exhibit
at the Met. Lillian and I . . ."

I could believe anything about Charles, Mariah thought. I've
seen him explode when Albert disagreed with him about something.
I guess he knew enough not to pull that sort of behavior with Dad or
Greg. Or Richard.

She got up slowly, feeling as if everything was an effort, then remembered that she still hadn't turned on her cell phone. She took
it out of her purse and saw that there were seven new messages since
last night. Alvirah had tried to reach her three times this morning,
the latest only twenty minutes ago. Two of the other four were from
Greg. Richard had called again last night and early this morning.

Without taking the time to listen to any of the messages, she dialed Alvirah, who filled her in about going into Lillian's apartment
with the cleaning woman and then going to Bergdorf's. "I called
Columbia, and the head of Lillian's department is going to file a
missing person report with the New York City police," Alvirah said.
"They're terribly worried. The New Jersey detectives already know
she's still not home. Mariah, I'm at home with a cup of tea in front
of me, trying to figure this whole thing out, but I don't think there's
much more we can do right now."

"I don't think so either," Mariah agreed. "But let me tell you
what Greg has found out. Charles has been shopping the parchment around to underground collectors. Greg has been doing his

own check on Charles. He heard it from a friend of his who is a well-known collector."

"Now, that gives me something to go on," Alvirah said with satis-faction. "What are you up to today, Mariah?"

"I stopped at my office and now I'm in my apartment. I'm about to head back to New Jersey."

"Do you want to have a quick bite of lunch?"

"Thanks, but I don't think so. I'd better get home. This afternoon Lloyd will be able to get the psychiatric report on Mom."

"Then I'll call you later. Hang in there, Mariah. We love you."

Later, as she was getting into her car, Mariah called Alvirah back. "I just heard from Lloyd Scott. There may be a witness who saw someone running out of the house right after Dad was shot. He was in the middle of robbing the Scotts' house when he says he heard the shot and looked out the window. He claims he clearly saw the face and can describe the person to the prosecutor's sketch artist. Oh, Alvirah, pray, pray."

An hour after that conversation, Alvirah still had not moved from her chair at her dining room table. As she looked out unseeingly at Central Park, Willy finally broke into her reverie. "Honey, what's going on in that mind of yours?"

"I'm not sure," Alvirah said. "But I think it's time for me to make a friendly visit to Professor Albert West."

63

When Richard Callahan arrived at the receptionist desk of the prosecutor's office, Detectives Simon Benet and Rita Rodriguez were waiting for him. After a curt greeting, they escorted him to an interrogation room at the end of the hall. Without referring to specific details, Simon coldly explained to him that, based upon certain developments that had occurred since they had initially asked him to give a statement, they now believed it would be appropriate to read him his Miranda rights.

"You have the right to remain silent. Anything you say can and will be used against you. You have the right to consult with an attorney . . . If you do choose to speak, you can decide to stop the questioning at any time."

"I don't need a lawyer and I do want to talk to you," Richard Callahan said firmly. "That's why I'm here. I am going to tell you the exact truth and we'll take it from there."

The detectives looked him over carefully. He was wearing a long-sleeved light-blue shirt, a sleeveless sweater, tan gabardine pants, and leather loafers. His features, strong and attractive, and dominated by intense blue eyes and a firm chin, had a calm but determined expression. His full head of salt-and-pepper hair had recently been trimmed.

Benet and Rodriguez had done a full background check on

him. Thirty-four years old. The only child of two prominent cardiologists. Raised on Park Avenue. Attended Saint David's School, Regis Academy, and Georgetown University. Two doctorates from Catholic University, one in Bible history, the other in theology. Entered the Jesuits at age twenty-six and left the order after a year. Currently teaching Bible history and philosophy at Fordham University. This guy was raised on Park Avenue, went to private schools, and wouldn't know anything about applying for a school loan, Benet thought.

Annoyed at himself, but unable to shut off that sentiment, Benet continued his introspection about the man he now strongly considered to be a person of interest in the apparent disappearance of Lillian Stewart. He's dressed like a guy coming out of a country club. He sure didn't get those clothes at a discount store.

Simon Benet thought of his wife, Tina. She loved to read those captions in fashion magazines. " 'Understated elegance.' 'Saturday-night casual.' They're talking about us, honey," she would joke.

Callahan reeks of privilege, Benet thought. When he was around people like Richard, he recognized that he would become momentarily envious and painfully aware of his own hardscrabble background. College at night. Police officer at twenty-three. Years of working those midnight shifts and holidays. Detective at thirty-eight after getting shot during a robbery. Three great kids but school loans that would take him years to pay off.

Never mind all that. I'm a damn lucky guy, he reminded himself. Ready to shut his mind off from any more distractions, he began his questioning of Richard.

"Where were you yesterday at nine thirty A.M., Mr. Callahan?" Benet asked. Two hours later, he, Rita, and Richard were still going back over every detail of his account of his activities.

"As I have told you," Richard repeated, "or to reiterate again," he added with a touch of sarcasm, "I was downtown in the office of my trustee at nine o'clock and spent the entire day hanging around outside the building and calling Lillian constantly."

"Is there anyone who can verify what you're telling us?"

"Not really. Around five o'clock I finally left and stopped in at my parents' apartment."

"And you claim that you are not aware that Lillian Stewart got off the subway at the Chambers Street station shortly after nine thirty yesterday morning, just about the time you were supposedly hanging around outside your trustee's office nearby?"

"No, I have no idea when or where Lillian may have gotten out of the subway. You can check her cell phone. I called her every half hour all day and I also left messages on the landline in her apartment."

"What do you think may have happened to her?" Rita asked, her voice concerned and thoughtful, in direct and intentional contrast to Simon's hostile tone.

"Lillian told me that she had other offers for the sacred parchment. I believed her. I tried to convince her that whoever wanted to pay her illegally might get caught someday and she could end up in prison for selling stolen property. I told her that if she sold it to me, I would never tell anyone that I had gotten it from her."

"And what would you have done with the parchment, Mr. Callahan?" Benet asked, his own voice sarcastic and disbelieving.

"I would have given it back to the Vatican, where it belongs."

"You say you have something around two million, three hundred thousand dollars in your trust fund? Why didn't you offer all of it to Lillian Stewart? Maybe that extra three hundred thousand dollars might have made a difference."

"I would hope that you can understand that I wanted to have something left of my trust fund for my own life. And it would not have made a difference," Richard said emphatically. "I was appealing to Lillian on two levels to sell it to me. First, the fact that it would be in both her best interest and mine for her to receive the money as a gift, since I am allowed under tax law to give away that amount of money without penalties. I told her that I would be returning the parchment to the Vatican. I said that I didn't think that there would be any further stolen property investigation that she would have to worry about. I would simply say that the person who had had it was afraid to admit it to anyone but me.

"My other plea to her was that I knew that she and Jonathan loved each other very much. He trusted her with that parchment. I told her that she owed it to him to see that it was returned to the Vatican Library. I said that if we did it this way, she would have money for the future and I would take care of the rest of it."

Richard stood up. "As of now, I have been answering the same questions for over two hours. Am I free to leave?"

"Yes, you are, Mr. Callahan," Benet said. "But we will be in touch with you shortly. You're not planning to take any trips or otherwise leave the immediate area, are you?"

"For the most part I will be at home. You have my address. I am going absolutely nowhere, unless here in New Jersey you consider the Bronx to be outside of the immediate area."

Richard paused, by now clearly upset. "I am very concerned that a woman I consider to be a friend is missing. I am completely floored that you obviously think that I had something to do with her disappearance. I assure you that I will be available to you at any hour of the day or night until the first day of class next week and then I will be in my lecture hall at Fordham University on the Rose Hill campus. If necessary, you can reach me there."

He turned and walked out of the interrogation room, forcibly closing the door behind him.

Benet and Rodriguez looked at each other. "What do you think?" Benet asked.

"He's either completely truthful or completely lying," Rita said. "I don't think there's any in-between."

"My gut says that he's an accomplished liar," Benet declared. "He claims he was hanging around all day outside an office until five o'clock, when he left to go to Mommy and Daddy's Park Avenue apartment. Come on, Rita, get real."

"Should we get him back tomorrow and see if he'll take a lie-detector test?" Rita asked. "The way we talked to him, I wouldn't be surprised if he lawyered up."

"Let's check with Peter about any polygraph. I'm not sure what he's going to want to do."

64

Billy Declar had been dismayed to hear that his old friend and prison cell mate, Wally Gruber, had been caught dead in the act of breaking into a house in Riverdale.

"Stupid, stupid, stupid," he kept muttering to himself as he shuffled around his secondhand furniture store in lower Manhattan. "He's as dumb as they come because he thinks he's so smart." At seventy-two years old, having endured three separate stints in the slammer, Billy was not looking forward to going back there.

I gave him big bucks for the stuff from New Jersey, Billy thought. Four days later the greedy lowlife goes after another haul. I know Wally. He'll rat me out to get a better deal for himself. I'd better move up my trip to Rio. I'm out of here now.

As usual there had been no customers for the tired and well-worn couches and chairs and headboards and dressers that were placed in forlorn groupings in the so-called showroom. Whenever one of the guys who had stolen jewelry came in and sold it to Billy, he'd offer them a choice of furniture. He would call it their "bonus."

"Select any piece that you may desire to grace your home," he would say grandly.

Their suggestions as to what he could do with his furniture made Billy roar with laughter.

But he was not laughing now. The jewelry he planned to sell in

Rio was hidden under the floor in the back room of the store. It was two o'clock. I'll put the "Closed" sign on the door, get the jewelry, and go straight to the airport, he thought. I've got my passport and plenty of cash. I'm ready to go. So what if I stay in Rio for a while? It's winter there but that's okay with me.

Billy hobbled as quickly as he could, wincing in pain from his chronically swollen left ankle. It was the result of his leap out of a second-story window, when he was sixteen years old, to avoid the police who had come to arrest him for stealing a car.

He grabbed his fully packed suitcase, which he always kept ready for any such emergency departure, from the closet. He knelt down, rolled up the rug, and lifted up the floorboards that covered the safe he kept hidden there. He punched in the code, opened the door of the safe, and pulled out the large canvas bag containing the jewelry from the Scott home. Then he quickly closed the safe and put the floorboards and rug back in place.

Scrambling to his feet, he grabbed the suitcase, flung the canvas bag over his shoulder, and turned off the light in the back room.

Billy was halfway across the showroom when the buzzer at the front entrance went off several times in quick succession. His stomach churned. Through the bars on the window of the door, he could see a cluster of men outside. One of them was holding up a shield.

"Police," someone shouted. "We have a search warrant. Open up the door immediately."

Billy dropped the bags on the floor with a sigh. The image in his mind of Wally's round face, and his phony ear-to-ear smile, was as clear as if Wally was standing in front of him. Who knows? Billy asked himself, resigned to being a guest of the state of New York once more. Maybe we'll end up bunking together again.

65

At three fifteen P.M. Peter Jones received a call from the law clerk of Judge Kenneth Brown. "Sir," the young woman said in a very respectful tone, "we wanted to let you know that the report on the Kathleen Lyons case has come in and you can pick it up now if you wish."

What I really wish is that the Kathleen Lyons case would go away, he thought wryly. "Thank you very much," he replied. "I'll come right up."

As he waited for the elevator to take him to the fourth floor, he thought fleetingly of when he had started his legal career as a clerk to a judge in the criminal division. Judge Brown is sitting in the same courtroom where my judge used to sit, he thought. Mom knew how much I wanted that job. When I got it, the way she carried on, you'd think that they had made me chief justice.

At the end of his one-year clerkship, he had been ecstatic to be hired as an assistant prosecutor. That was nineteen years ago. Since then he had worked in several units, including Major Crimes, before being appointed chief of the trial section five years ago.

Thane of Glamis, thane of Cawdor, and hereafter king of Scotland, he thought, reflecting on one of his favorite lines from Shakespeare. That's the track I thought I was on. Until now.

Shrugging, he got into the elevator, went up two flights, got off, and went into the judge's office. He knew that Judge Brown was on the bench conducting a jury trial. He greeted the secretary, turned the corner, and went over to the law clerk's desk.

She was a small, very attractive young woman who could have passed for a college freshman. "Hello, Mr. Jones," she said as she handed him the ten-page report.

"Has the judge had a chance to look at it yet?" Peter asked.

"I'm not sure, sir."

Good answer, Peter thought. Never say anything that might return to bite you. Three minutes later, back in his office, he closed the door. "Hold the calls," he told his secretary. "I need to concentrate."

"You've got it, Peter." Gladys Hawkins had worked in the prosecutor's office for thirty years. In the presence of outsiders, she addressed both Prosecutor Sylvan Berger and Peter Jones as "sir." Otherwise, when they were among themselves, the prosecutor was "Sy" and Assistant Prosecutor Jones was just "Peter."

With trepidation, Peter Jones carefully absorbed the psychiatric report. As he did, the burden of carrying the weight of the world on his shoulders began to lessen.

The doctor had written that Kathleen Lyons was clearly in a worsening stage of Alzheimer's and had, on two occasions while in the hospital, exhibited symptoms of violent tendencies. Both awake and in her sleep, she had demonstrated severe antagonism toward her late husband and his companion Lillian Stewart. It was the recommendation of the treating doctors that, at the present time, and as a result of underlying mental illness, she was a danger to both herself and others and required full-time and intense supervision. It was their opinion that she should remain in the inpatient setting for further observation, medication, and therapy.

With a deep sigh of relief, Peter leaned back in his chair. There's no way the judge is going to cut her loose, he thought. He can't with this kind of report. Sure, we'll go through the charade with Wally Gruber and the composite artist. This is just what I've suspected. Gruber knows how to play the system. I wonder what face he'll decide to invent. I don't care if it's Tom Cruise or Mickey Mouse. It's a total dead end.

Peter stood up and stretched. Kathleen Lyons killed her husband, he thought emphatically. I'm sure of it. If she ends up incompetent to stand trial, so be it. If she ends up not guilty by reason of insanity, so be it. Either way, she'll never get out of a mental hospital.

He turned on the intercom. "I can take calls now, Gladys."

"That was a pretty short deep-think session, Peter. Wait a second. There's a call coming in. It's Simon Benet's extension. Do you want to take it?"

"Put him through."

"Peter, I just got a call from the New York guys," Benet said tensely. "They just arrested Gruber's fence. They got him at his shop. In another minute he would have been on his way to the airport. They recovered the missing Scott jewelry. All of it."

66

At one o'clock on Thursday afternoon, Mariah arrived back at her parents' home and walked into the kitchen. There was a note from Betty on the table. "Mariah, I stopped in and left some cold cuts for you in case you came home for lunch. Tidied up quickly but feeling under the weather and leaving now — 8:20 A.M."

The message light on the kitchen phone was flashing. Mariah pushed the button to retrieve the messages and punched in the code. Her parents had kept it easy to remember by choosing the year of her birth. "The happiest event in our lives," her father had told her.

Besides his attempts to reach her on her cell, Richard had also called on this phone at nine fifteen that morning. "Mariah, please, we have to talk." She quickly deleted the rest of the message, not wanting to hear the sound of his voice.

As Greg had told her, he had tried to reach her twice on this line. "Mariah, you're not answering your cell phone. I'm worried about you. Please call me."

Alvirah's three calls, made before Mariah had spoken to her from the apartment, were first about trying to trace Lillian and then wondering why Mariah wasn't calling her back.

Mariah made a turkey and cheese sandwich from the assortment of cold cuts that Betty had brought in. She took out a bottle of cold water and carried it and the sandwich into her father's study. This was Dad's favorite sandwich, she remembered, and then realized that no matter what she did or where she went she always felt his presence.

She ate the sandwich and realized that her eyes were heavy. Well, I did get up early and I haven't exactly been sleeping much lately, she thought. She leaned back in the chair and closed her eyes. I can't concentrate on anything until Lloyd calls about that report. I wouldn't mind dozing off for a while.

At three thirty she was awakened from a surprisingly deep sleep by the ring of the phone on her father's desk. It was Lloyd. "Mariah," he began, "it almost sounds like a cliché, but the truth is that I have good news and bad news. Let me tell you the good news first, because I think it will soften the rest of what I have to tell you."

Afraid of what she was about to hear, she clutched the phone as Lloyd explained the developments surrounding Wally Gruber.

"You mean to tell me that this guy says he saw somebody running out of here right after Dad was shot? My God, Lloyd! What does this mean for Mom?"

"Mariah, I just got off the phone for the second time today with Peter Jones. He told me that the New York police have arrested Wally Gruber's fence and all of Lisa's jewelry has been recovered. Of course, Lisa and I are relieved about that, but much more important, it does give at least some credibility to this Gruber fellow."

"Did he get a good look at that person? Was it a man or a woman?"

"So far, he's not even getting that specific. He's been trying to make a deal to get time taken off the sentences he'll get for the burglaries. Jones has agreed to have him brought from the New York jail to the prosecutor's office tomorrow morning so that he can sit with their composite officer. Hopefully, they'll get a good sketch and with any luck at all it will help Kathleen."

"You mean that it would prove Mother didn't kill Dad?" Mariah had a vivid flash of the image of her mother arriving at the courthouse in a prison uniform.

"Mariah," Lloyd cautioned her, "we don't know where this is going, so don't get your hopes up too high. But of course, if the sketch turns out to be someone whom you recognize or the detectives recognize, it would go a long way to proving that she had nothing to do with your father's death. Don't forget, his closest friends swore that they never saw the parchment. If they're telling the truth, Jonathan may have consulted a different expert or experts in the field and we don't even know who they are. And there's always the possibility that Gruber was telling the truth about the jewelry but the rest of his story is a sham."

"Lloyd, there's something you don't know yet. Greg told me that he's had a tip that Charles Michaelson has been shopping the parchment. He said he heard it from a collector in the field. That's all I know."

There was momentary silence on the other end of the phone, then Lloyd said quietly, "If that is proven to be true, then at the very least Michaelson is guilty of possession of stolen property."

Mariah's relief at the possibility that someone whose face they might recognize would be revealed on the sketch gave way to the frightening thought that Lloyd had also told her that he had bad news.

"Lloyd, you said you had bad news for me. What is it?" she demanded.

"Mariah, the psychiatric report recommends that your mother be kept in the hospital for further observation and therapy."

"No!"

"Mariah, it indicates that several times your mother has exhibited very aggressive behavior. 'Further observation' could mean her staying there as little as a week or two more. I've had other defendants with psychiatric problems who've been in that hospital. They were well treated and safe there. The report says that she not only needs round-the-clock care but additional security measures as well. You would have to make all of those arrangements before the judge would agree to release her. I've already consented to putting off tomorrow's hearing."

"Lloyd, most of the time when she seems to be aggressive, it's because she's so frightened. I want to see her." Mariah knew her voice was rising. "How do I know for sure that she's being treated well?"

"You can start by seeing it for yourself. I told Peter Jones that I wanted you to have the right to visit her. He had no problem with that. He promised that he'll get an order from the judge by the end of the court day. They'll fax the order to the hospital. There are visiting hours this evening from six to eight."

"When we do we get to see that sketch that Gruber will do tomorrow morning?"

"Jones promised me that I could come to his office after it's done and look at it. He said he'll give me a copy. I'll bring it directly to you."

With that, Mariah had to be content. She called Alvirah, told her about the conversation with Lloyd, and then, unable to even think about trying to do any work on her computer, went upstairs to her father's bedroom. She looked sadly at the handsome four-poster bed. They bought this house and this furniture when Mom was expecting me, she thought. They told me that when I was born, they were so afraid that I might stop breathing they kept me in a crib right next to their bed for the first six months.

Until four years ago, her parents had shared this room. It had then become necessary, because of her mother's nocturnal wanderings, to create a separately secured two-bedroom suite for her and her caregivers.

When Mom comes home, I know that Delia will fill in for me during the week until I can get a new Monday-to-Friday person, she thought. God knows where Rory's disappeared to. But one thing is for certain. I'm giving up the apartment in New York and moving back here. So I might as well get settled into this room now. I've got to do something to keep myself busy. It'll help keep me sane.

She was relieved that she had already gone through her father's clothing. With feverish haste, she moved back and forth between the bedrooms, bundling in her arms the hanging garments from her closet and transferring them to the large walk-in closet in her father's room. Then she pulled out the drawers from her own dresser and, not even noticing how heavy they really were, carried them down the hall and emptied their contents into her father's mahogany dresser.

At five minutes of five, she was finished. Her father had never moved her mother's vanity table from this room. In the early stages of her dementia, Kathleen had been frightened by the mirror over the table. Sometimes when she saw her own reflection, she had been afraid that there was an intruder in the house.

Now Mariah's cosmetics and comb and brush were neatly arranged on its glass top. I'll get a new spread and dust ruffle and curtains for in here, she decided. And I think I will eventually redo my old room, with those red walls and the red-and-white flowered coverlet. She recalled the Bible verse that began, "When I was a child, I spake as a child," and ended with, "when I was a man, I put away childish things."

Realizing what time it was, she began to worry. Why hadn't Lloyd called again? Surely the judge wouldn't refuse to allow her to visit her mother. That can't happen, she thought. It simply can't.

Ten minutes later, the phone did ring and it was Lloyd. "They just faxed me the judge's order. Permission granted. As I said earlier, the visiting hours are from six to eight."

"I'll be there at six," Mariah said. "Thanks, Lloyd." She heard her cell phone ringing in the study. She hurried downstairs and looked at the caller ID. It was Richard. With a mixture of anger and sadness, she decided not to take the call.

67

It's a blessing that Albert West lives only a few blocks away from us and we don't have to bother with the car," Alvirah remarked as she and Willy left their apartment building, walked to the corner, and turned onto Seventh Avenue. They were meeting Albert at five o'clock for a cup of coffee at a diner on Seventh Avenue near 57th Street.

Hoping against hope that she would catch Albert at home and that he would agree to meet them right away, she had been pleasantly surprised on both levels. "Willy, unless he's a good actor, he sounded like he actually wanted to come," she remarked.

Puffing a bit as he endeavored to keep up with Alvirah's quick strides, Willy asked himself why these emergency meetings always seemed to come up in the middle of a Yankees game. Although Alvirah had insisted it would be perfectly okay for her to meet him in a public place by herself, Willy was taking no chances. "I'm coming with you. End of discussion."

"Do you think that little guy is going to kidnap me in the middle of a coffee shop?" Alvirah had joked.

"Don't be so sure he wouldn't be capable of it. If he's mixed up in this whole thing and he thinks that you're onto him, he could offer to walk you home, but you might not make it."

As they crossed the street, they could see Albert entering the diner. He was already seated at a booth when they got inside and he waved his hand to get their attention.

As soon as they settled in, a waitress came over and took their orders. All three decided on caffe latte. Alvirah could see the disappointment on the face of the young woman, who had obviously hoped for a food order that would run up the tab and bring a bigger tip.

She was surprised that after the waitress was out of earshot, Albert, in a tone that was both nervous and abrupt, said, "Alvirah, I know your reputation as a darn good detective. You certainly didn't call me to socialize over coffee. Have you come up with anything?"

"I've heard a rumor. I'm not going to say where I heard it. From what I understand, you and Charles had been driving to Jonathan's dinners together for the last year and a half since Lillian was banned from his house."

"Yes, that's true. Before that, Charles would go alone with Lillian and I would drive my own car."

"Albert, the rumor I heard is that Charles has been shopping the parchment. Do you think that there is any chance that could be happening?"

She and Willy could both see in Albert's expression his reluctance to answer.

Finally he said, "I not only think it's happening, but I actually spoke about it to the detectives in New Jersey yesterday. I have always considered Charles to be a good friend, so it was very painful for me to talk about him in this vein."

Alvirah sat back as the waitress placed the tall glasses of latte in front of them on the table. "Albert, what did you tell the detectives?"

"Exactly what I'm going to tell you now. Desmond Rogers, a wealthy collector beyond reproach, whom Charles defrauded a number of years ago, was the source of my information. He didn't volunteer how he knew and I didn't ask."

Albert took a sip of his latte and, knowing that he was about to be cross-examined by Alvirah, repeated to her and Willy what he had told the detectives about the previous fraud involving Charles and Desmond.

"Albert, this is very important. Will you try to get Desmond on the phone right now and ask him where he got that information?"

Albert frowned. "Quite frankly, Desmond Rogers pays confidential sources in the antiquities world to keep him informed of what's coming on the market. I am sure that he would never buy anything without impeccable provenance—which is why he would never have bid for the parchment."

Alvirah replied, "Albert, I'm not suggesting that Rogers has done anything wrong. But you've told us that he lost a lot of money because of Charles. Maybe he was only too happy to pass on this kind of information. But if he or one of his sources truly does have solid proof about this, you have to know it's probably tied in with Jonathan's death. It's important that he fully understand that Jonathan's murder and the disappearance of two women who were close to him all may be connected to that parchment."

Albert shook his head. "And you don't think that all this hasn't occurred to me?" he asked wearily as he pulled out his cell phone. "I absolutely trust Desmond's integrity. He would never touch that parchment or any other stolen property, but I assure you he'll never betray his sources. If he did, the word would get around and he'd never be able to use them again. Now, if you'll excuse me, I'll step outside and make the call. I'll be right back."

He was gone a full ten minutes. When he returned, his face was flushed and angry. "I never thought that Desmond Rogers would pull this on me. I've been sick ever since I told the cops what he told me about Charles. Now I find out that Desmond *didn't* hear this from a reliable source. When I asked him about it, at first he hedged around and then finally admitted that he had received an anonymous call. He couldn't even tell if it was a man or woman. The voice was husky and low. The caller said that Charles was accepting bids on the parchment and that if Desmond was interested he should give him a call."

"I thought that might be the case," Alvirah said with satisfaction in her voice. "What did Desmond say to that person?"

"I can't repeat to a lady what he claims he said. And then he hung up."

Studying Albert intently, Alvirah watched as the veins in his forehead began to bulge.

"I'm going to call those detectives first thing in the morning," he said angrily, slapping his hand on the table. "They should know this. And I have to decide whether to admit to Charles what I said about him."

They finished their lattes and left the diner. On the way home, Alvirah was unusually quiet. Willy knew that the wheels in her head were turning. "What did you get out of all that, honey?"

"Willy, this doesn't mean that Charles is innocent. And this doesn't mean that Albert was telling the truth. With all of his so-called reluctance, my gut tells me he had no problem telling the prosecutor's office about that quote-unquote rumor. Don't forget, he's on their radar screen too."

"So do you think our meeting with him was a waste of time?" Willy asked.

"Not at all, Willy," Alvirah said as he took her arm to cross the street. "Not at all."

68

Wally Gruber and Joshua Schultz sat across from each other, separated by an old wooden table, in the attorney-client conference room. "You look nervous, Josh," Wally said. "I'm the one in Rikers Island, not you."

"You're the one who should be nervous," Schultz snapped. "There isn't one guy locked up in this rat hole who doesn't hate a snitch. Billy Declar is already passing the word that you gave him up. You did it for a reason, but you'd better watch your back."

"Let me worry about that," Wally said dismissively. "You know, Josh, I'm kind of looking forward to driving out to New Jersey tomorrow. It's supposed to be a nice day and I could use a breath of fresh air."

"You're not driving out, Wally. You're being hauled out there in handcuffs and chains. It's not an outing. No matter what you come up with, you're still going to do some hard time. Okay, you were on the level about the jewelry. But if you're lying about the face you claim you saw and nothing ends up coming out of the sketch, who knows? They might ask you at that point to take a lie-detector test to check out your story. If you refuse, or you take it and fail, they'll think you've played around with them on a homicide case. If that happens you'll be lucky if getting back that jewelry takes six months off your sentence."

"You know, Josh," Wally said with a sigh as he signaled to the guard standing outside the door that he was ready to go back to his cell, "you're a born pessimist. I saw a face that night. I can see that face as clear as I'm seeing yours. And by the way, the person was better looking than you. Anyhow, if nobody they show the sketch to recognizes it, then the shooter was probably hired to get rid of Lyons, right?"

The guard had entered and Wally stood up. "Josh, I got one more thing to tell you. I got no problem at all if they want me to take a lie-detector test. My blood pressure won't rise and my heart won't skip a beat. That graph with all those lines running through it will be as smooth as a baby's bottom."

Joshua Schultz looked at his client with grudging admiration. Completely undecided in his own mind as to whether Gruber was pulling a fast one, he said, "I'll see you in the prosecutor's office to-morrow morning, Wally."

"I can't wait, Josh. I miss you already. But don't go in there with a long face and act like you don't believe what I'm saying. If you do, the next time I get in trouble, I'll find a new lawyer."

He means it, Schultz thought as he watched the retreating figure of his client being escorted back to his cell. He shrugged. I guess I should look on the bright side, he decided.

Unlike a lot of my other clients, Wally always pays my bill.

69

❧✿❧

At six P.M. Thursday, Mariah stepped off the elevator on the psychiatric floor of Bergen Park Medical Center. A guard was sitting at a desk at the end of the corridor. She walked over to him, aware that her heels were making a clicking sound on the polished floor.

He looked up, his expression neither pleasant nor hostile. She gave her name, as she had to the receptionist in the lobby, and showed him the pass that she had been given. Then, with rising concern, she watched as he made a phone call. Don't let them tell me at the last minute that for some reason I can't see Mom, she thought nervously. Don't let that happen.

The guard put down the phone. "A nurse will be right out to escort you to your mother's room," he said, his voice hinting at a degree of compassion.

Do I look as upset as I feel? Mariah asked herself. After Lloyd's call earlier confirming that she could visit, she had realized that there was enough time to shower and change her clothes. After lugging the dresser drawers and the contents of her closet from one room to the other, she had felt hot and rumpled.

Now she was dressed in a red linen jacket and white slacks. She had twisted her long hair up and fastened it with a clip. Remembering how her mother had never left the house in the old days without putting on makeup, she'd gone to the dressing table and reached for the mascara and eye shadow. Maybe it will please Mom if she realizes I spruced up for her, she had thought. It's the sort of thing that she just might notice. She had debated for a minute, then opened the small wall safe in the walk-in closet and took out the strand of pearls her father had given her for her birthday two years ago.

"Your mother believes that old superstition that pearls are tears," he had said, smiling. "My mother always loved them."

Thank you, Dad, Mariah thought as she clasped them around her neck.

She was glad she had taken the time to change, because Greg had called while she was driving to the hospital. He'd insisted that he would meet her back at the house around eight thirty. "I'm taking you to dinner," he said protectively. "I know the way you've been eating, or, more accurately, *not* eating. I'm not going to let you get to the point where you don't even cast a shadow."

"I hope I'll be getting my appetite back by tomorrow night," she had told him as she pulled into the hospital parking lot. "I have a feeling that by then Charles Michaelson will be under arrest."

Then, before he could speak, she'd added, "Greg, I can't talk now. I'm at the hospital. I'll see you later."

As she waited at the security desk, she remembered that Lloyd Scott had warned her not to talk about the potential witness to anyone. Well, I didn't say much, she thought as the door behind the guard's desk opened. A petite Asian woman in a white jacket and slacks, with an identification tag on a cord around her neck, smiled and said, "Ms. Lyons, I'm Nurse Emily Lee. I'll take you to your mother."

Swallowing over a lump in her throat and a sudden stinging in her eyes, Mariah followed her past a row of closed doors. At the last one, the nurse tapped on it lightly, then opened it.

As she followed her into the room, Mariah was not sure what she expected to see, but it was certainly not the small figure in a hospital gown and robe sitting at the window in semidarkness.

"She doesn't want the light any brighter," the nurse whispered. Then in a cheery tone, she said, "Kathleen, Mariah is here to see you."

There was no response.

"Is she heavily medicated?" Mariah asked angrily.

"She has been given some very light sedation, which helps to calm her when she's been angry or frightened."

As Mariah walked toward her, Kathleen Lyons slowly turned her head. The nurse turned up the lights, making Mariah clearly visible, but there was no sign of recognition in her expression.

Mariah knelt down and took her mother's hands in hers. "Mom, Kathleen, it's me."

She watched as her mother's face became puzzled.

"You're so pretty," Kathleen said. "I used to be pretty too." Then she closed her eyes and leaned back. She did not open them, nor did she speak again.

Mariah sat on the floor, her arms around her mother's legs, slow tears streaming from her eyes, until ten minutes of eight, when a voice on the intercom requested that visitors leave by eight o'clock.

Then she got up, kissed her mother gently on her cheek, and embraced her. She smoothed back the gray hair that had once been a stunning shade of golden blond. "I'll be back tomorrow," she whispered. "And maybe by then we'll be able to clear your name. There isn't much else I can do for you except that."

At the nurses' station, she stopped to speak to Emily Lee. "The report to the judge said that my mother was angry and aggressive," she said accusingly. "I certainly don't see any evidence of that kind of behavior."

"It will happen again," Lee said quietly. "Anything may set her off. But there have been several times when she thought she was at home with you and your father. She was so animated and happy then. Until this disease set in, I imagine her life was pretty wonderful. Trust me, that's a lot to be grateful for."

"I guess so. Thank you." With an attempt at a smile, Mariah turned and left the secured patient area, passed by the guard, and waited at the bank of elevators. A few minutes later, she was in her car on the way home. She was sure Greg would already be there waiting for her.

She also knew that no matter what happened when Wally Gruber sat down to do that sketch, she had to make some painful decisions about the future.

70

From his interrogation at the prosecutor's office on Thursday morning, Richard had gone directly home to his apartment in the Bronx and tried to concentrate on finalizing the lesson plans that he had been preparing for his fall semester classes.

It was a wasted afternoon. He had accomplished nothing. Finally, at four thirty, he'd telephoned Alvirah. The reception he received from her was uncharacteristically cool. "Hello, Richard. What can I do for you?"

"Look, Alvirah," he said heatedly, "I've been dragged over the coals at the prosecutor's office today because I gather you were able to overhear the message Lillian left on my cell phone the other night. I'll tell you what I told those detectives. You can believe me or not believe me, but at least let me know how Mariah and Kathleen are doing. Mariah won't talk to me and I'm worried sick about her."

His voice passionate, he repeated every word of what he had told the prosecutors.

Alvirah's tone softened a little. "Richard, you sound on the level, but I have to tell you that in my mind you're not coming clean about your motive for trying to make a deal with Lillian for the parchment. On the other hand I'm beginning to form my own suspicions about someone else, but I'm not ready to discuss them yet because I may be wrong. From what Mariah tells me, there's a good chance that tomorrow this will all be over. I'm not saying anything else now."

"I certainly hope you're right," Richard said fervently. "Have you seen Mariah? Have you spoken to her? How is she?"

"I spoke to her a couple of times today. She's just gotten the judge's permission to visit her mother tonight." Alvirah hesitated. "Richard . . ." Her voice trailed off.

"What is it, Alvirah?"

"Never mind. My question can wait for another day. Good-bye."

What was that all about? Richard asked himself as he pushed the chair back from his desk and stood up. I'll go out for a walk on the campus, he decided. Maybe I can clear my head.

But even a long walk on the shaded paths between the beautiful Gothic buildings on Rose Hill did not have its usual effect of helping him to think calmly. At three minutes of six, he was back in his apartment, a paper bag from the nearby deli under his arm. He turned on the television as he unwrapped the sandwich that was going to be his dinner.

The opening words of the CBS six o'clock evening news startled him: "Potential bombshell in the Jonathan Lyons murder case. An eyewitness may have seen the face of the killer. Now these messages."

Sitting bolt upright, Richard waited with frantic impatience for the commercials to be over.

The two anchors, Chris Wragge and Dana Tyler, came back on screen. "A spokesperson for the Bergen County prosecutor's office has confirmed that jewelry stolen during the burglary of the home of the next-door neighbor of murdered professor Jonathan Lyons has been recovered," Wragge began. "They will neither confirm nor deny that Wally Gruber, a convicted felon who was arrested for the burglary, claims that while he was inside the neighbor's home next door, he witnessed someone fleeing from the Lyons residence immediately after Professor Lyons was shot. He reportedly also says that he can clearly describe that person. Sources tell us that Gruber, who is now on Rikers Island after being arrested for an attempted burglary in New York, is being transported to New Jersey tomorrow morning. He will be taken to the prosecutor's office in Hackensack to describe to their composite technician the face he claims he saw that Monday night, nearly two weeks ago."

"Imagine if he's telling the truth and comes up with a sketch of a face that someone does recognize," Dana Tyler said. "That could lead to the charges against Kathleen Lyons being dropped."

As she spoke, they replayed the tape of Kathleen's arraignment in the courtroom from the other day, with Kathleen standing before the judge in bright orange jail garb.

So that's what Alvirah meant when she said that by this time tomorrow, all this may be over, Richard thought. Kathleen could be free. He began to switch from channel to channel. They were all carrying the same story.

At six thirty he grabbed his car keys and went rushing out of the apartment.

71

At six o'clock Alvirah and Willy were listening to the same CBS broadcast. Willy watched as Alvirah's normally cheerful countenance took on a worried frown. After speaking to Mariah earlier, Alvirah had told him that the crook who stole that jewelry might have seen someone leaving Jonathan's house after he was shot.

"Honey, I thought you told me this was a big secret," Willy said. "How come it's all over the news?"

"It's hard to keep this kind of stuff quiet," Alvirah said with a sigh. "There's always somebody who tips off the press." She pushed a stray lock of hair back behind her right ear. "Thank God Dale of London will be back next week," she said. "Otherwise my roots will be so white I'll have to wear a hood."

"It's hard to believe that Labor Day is this weekend already," Willy commented as he gazed out over Central Park, its blanket of lush green leaves still thick on the trees. "Before you can blink an eye, winter will be here and they'll all be gone."

Alvirah could see that he was looking down at the park. Ignoring his observation about the changing seasons, as he had ignored hers about the white roots of her hair, she asked, "Willy, if you were the one running out of the house that night, what would you be thinking now?"

Willy turned from the window to give his full attention to his wife's question. "If I had something like that to worry about, I'd try to figure which way to play it. I could say that the crook saw my picture with Jonathan and picked me out to blame."

He sat down in his comfortable chair, deciding not to mention that he was getting hungry and they'd gone light on lunch. "After Jonathan was murdered, there was a big picture of him in some of the newspapers with the group that was with him on his last trip to Egypt," he pointed out. "The article said they were his closest friends. If the cops were after me, I would say that it was easy for this guy to have seen me in that picture, then try to frame me so he could help himself."

"That's a possibility," Alvirah agreed. "But suppose that sketch really is of the right person and it turns out that it is one of Jonathan's friends? They've all given the prosecutor a story of where they were that night. Once somebody recognizes the sketch, the prosecutor will haul that guy in for more questioning two minutes later. What I'm thinking is, if the guy who killed Jonathan is watching the news right now, he'll be scared to death about the sketch they're going to do. Will he be scared enough to go on the run? Or will he try to bluff it? What would you do?"

Willy stood up. "If I were him, I'd think it over while I was having dinner. Let's go, honey."

"Well, I want you to have a good dinner and a good night's sleep," Alvirah said. "Because I can tell you right now, you're going to have a busy day tomorrow."

72

Greg was waiting when Mariah pulled into her driveway. He jumped out of his car and stood ready to open her door when she braked and released the lock. He put his arms around her and kissed her lightly on the cheek. "You look beautiful," he said.

She laughed. "How can you tell? It's dark out."

"Your outside lights are pretty bright. Anyhow, even if it was pitch-dark and I couldn't see you, I'd know you couldn't look anything but beautiful."

Greg is so shy, Mariah thought. He's so sincere, but a compliment from his lips somehow sounds awkward and rehearsed.

Not spontaneous, and teasing, and fun—the way it would be if Richard said it, a sly voice whispered in her mind.

"Do you want to go inside for a few minutes?" Greg asked.

Mariah thought about how she had sat in the hospital parking lot sobbing after she left her mother and opened her compact to pat away the traces of smeared mascara under her eyes. "No, I'm fine," she said.

She got into his car and sank back against the soft leather passenger seat. "I have to tell you this feels a lot more luxurious than the interior of my car," she said.

"Then it's yours," he told her as he started the engine. "We'll switch when we get back from dinner."

"Oh, Greg," she protested.

"I mean it." His tone was intense. Then, as if he realized he was making her uncomfortable, he said, "Sorry. I'll keep my promise not to crowd you. Tell me about Kathleen."

He had reserved a table at Savini's, a restaurant ten minutes away in the neighboring town of Allendale. On the way there she told him about her mother. "Greg, she didn't even recognize me today," she said. "It was heartbreaking. She's getting worse. I just don't know what will happen after she's released to come back home."

"You can't be sure she will be released, Mariah. I saw the news about that so-called witness. That guy has a record, a whole bunch of other charges, and he's looking for a deal. I think he's probably bluffing when he says that he saw someone running out of the house the night your father was shot."

"That was on the news?" Mariah exclaimed. "I was told to say nothing about it. After I started to tell you about him, when you called me as I was arriving at the hospital, I stopped because I realized I was supposed to keep quiet."

"I only wish you had wanted to trust me and confide in me," he said sadly.

They were at the entrance to Savini's and the valet was opening the door, saving her from the need to answer. Greg had made a reservation for the cozy fireplace room of the restaurant. One more place where I've had so many pleasant evenings with Dad and Mom, Mariah thought.

A bottle of wine was already chilling at the table. Anxious to dispel the strain between her and Greg that was quickly becoming apparent, when the maître d' had poured the wine, she held up her glass. "To this nightmare ending soon," she said.

He clinked his glass with hers. "If only I could make that happen for you," he said tenderly.

Over salmon and a salad, she tried to steer the conversation to other topics.

"It felt good to get to my office today—I swear I love being in the investment business. And getting to my apartment felt so good."

"I'll give you money to invest," Greg answered. "How much do you want?"

I can't do this, Mariah thought. I've got to be fair with him. He's not going to be able to keep our friendship on an even keel. And I know I'll never be able to give him what he wants.

They drove back to Mahwah in silence. He got out of the car and walked her to the door. "A nightcap?" he suggested.

"Not tonight, Greg. I'm awfully tired."

"I understand." He did not attempt to kiss her. "I understand a lot, Mariah."

The key in her hand, she unlocked the door. "Good night, Greg," she said. It was a relief to be inside and alone. From the living room window she watched him drive away.

A few minutes later, the doorbell rang. It has to be Lloyd or Lisa, she thought as she looked through the peephole. She was startled to see Richard standing there. For a moment she hesitated, but then she decided to open the door.

He stepped in and put his hands on her shoulders. "Mariah, you've got to understand something about that phone message you overheard. When I tried to buy that parchment from Lillian, I did it for you and your father. I was going to give it back to the Vatican. You have got to believe me!"

She looked up at him and, as she saw the tears glistening in his eyes, her intense feelings of anger and doubt evaporated. "I *do* believe you," she said quietly. "Richard, I do."

For a moment they stared at each other, then with joy and relief she felt his arms wrap around her.

"My love," he whispered. "My dear love."

73

Richard did not leave her until midnight.

At three A.M. Mariah was woken from a dead sleep by the ringing of the phone on her night table. Oh God, something's happened to Mom, she thought. She spilled her water glass as she grabbed the phone. "Hello!"

"Mariah, you have to help me." The voice on the other end sounded frantic. "I have the parchment. I couldn't sell it and betray Jonathan like that. I want you to have it. I promised it to Charles, but I changed my mind. He was in a rage when I told him. I'm afraid of what he'll do to me."

It was Lillian Stewart.

Lillian is alive! And she has the parchment! "Where are you?" Mariah demanded.

"I've been hiding at the Raines Motel on Route 4 East just before the bridge." Lillian broke into a sob. "Mariah, I beg you. Come and meet me now. Please. I want you to have the parchment. I was going to mail it to you, but suppose it got lost? I'm leaving for Singapore on the seven A.M. flight from Kennedy airport. I'm not coming back until I know Charles is in prison."

"The Raines Motel on Route 4. I'll be there right away. There won't be any traffic. I can make it in twenty minutes." Mariah pushed back the coverlet and in an instant her feet were on the carpet.

"I'm on the first floor in the rear area of the motel. It's room twenty-two—the number's on the door. Hurry! I've got to leave for Kennedy by four o'clock," Lillian said.

At three thirty, Mariah turned off the highway and drove past the quiet, shabby motel into the dimly lit parking area outside room 22. She opened her car door and a second later felt her head being slammed against the side of it. Waves of intense pain enveloped her and she passed out.

Minutes later she opened her eyes to almost total darkness. She tried to move her hands and legs but they were tightly tied. There was a gag stuffed into her mouth. Her head was throbbing. From somewhere near her, she could hear a whimpering sound. Where am I? Where am I? she thought frantically.

She could feel the movement of wheels beneath her. I'm in the trunk of a car, she realized. She felt something brush against her. My God, there's someone here with me. Then, straining to catch the words, she heard Lillian Stewart moaning, "He's crazy. He's crazy. I'm sorry, Mariah, I'm sorry."

74

At nine thirty on Friday morning Alvirah was sitting at the dinette table in her apartment, enjoying the cheese Danish that Willy, an early riser, had picked up for her in the coffee shop. "I know you only eat them once in a while, honey," he had said, "but you've been working hard and it will give you energy."

The phone rang. It was Betty Pierce. "I hope I'm not disturbing you," she said in a worried voice. "Mrs. Meehan, I mean Alvirah, is Mariah with you, or have you heard from her?"

"Not since about five o'clock last night," Alvirah said. "Isn't she there? I know she went into New York early yesterday. Have you tried her cell phone?"

"No, she's not. And she isn't answering that phone or the phone in her office."

"She could be on her way into the city again," Alvirah suggested. "I know that yesterday her cell phone was off almost all day."

"It's more than that," Betty said hurriedly. "Mariah is so neat. She never leaves clothes tossed around her room. Her nightgown is on the floor. The water glass on the night table was spilled and she didn't bother to wipe it up. The closet door was open. There are a couple of jackets hanging off the hangers, as if she just grabbed something and ran. The pearls her father gave her are on the vanity table. She *always* keeps them in the safe. I thought some emergency might have come up with her mother at the hospital and so I called over there. But Kathleen had a quiet night and is asleep. And they said they haven't seen or heard from Mariah today."

Alvirah's mind was working with feverish haste. "What about her car?" she asked.

"Her car is gone."

"Does it look as if there was any kind of struggle?"

"I can't say it does. It looks more like she left in a terrible hurry."

"What about the Scotts? Did you talk to them?"

"No. I know Mrs. Scott likes to sleep late."

"All right. I'll call Mr. Scott. I have his cell phone. If you hear from Mariah, call me at once, and I'll do the same for you."

"I will. But, Alvirah, I'm desperate with worry. Rory and Lillian seem to have both disappeared. Do you think there's any chance that—"

"Don't even begin to think like that, Betty. I'll talk to you later." Alvirah tried not to let the anxiety that was making her hand tremble show in her voice. As soon as she hung up, she dialed Lloyd's number. As she feared, he had not spoken to Mariah since yesterday afternoon.

"I've been in the office for an hour," Lloyd said. "Mariah's car wasn't in the driveway when I passed by her house. Of course, she might have put it in the garage."

"It's not in the garage," Alvirah said. "Lloyd, my hunches are good. You've got to call those detectives and get them to put a trace on Mariah's cell phone and rush Wally Gruber over to make that sketch. If he comes up with a face we can identify, we'll know where to look for Mariah."

If it's not too late, she thought.

As she put the phone down, Alvirah tried to banish that awful possibility from her mind.

75

He wasn't sure what to do. For the first time in his life, he felt a lack of control. Would the face in that sketch turn out to be a figment of that crook's imagination? Or would it bear a damning resemblance to what he saw in the mirror?

On the Internet, he had looked up the picture that had been in the newspapers of him and the others with Jonathan on that last dig. He had printed it out. If the sketch looks like me, I'll show this to them, he'd thought. I'll wave it in front of those detectives and say, "Look, this is where your sketch comes from." It would be his word against that of a convicted felon who was bargaining for a reduced sentence.

But once the prosecutor's office started to dig into his past, it might come out that Rory went to prison because she had stolen money from his aunt when she was her caregiver. Then, like a house of cards, his labyrinth of lies would fall apart. He had only visited his aunt once when Rory was working there, and Rory hadn't recognized him when she came to work at Jonathan's house. But I recognized her, he thought, and I used her when I needed her. She had to go along with me because I knew she had skipped parole, and she snapped at the money I dangled in front of her. She left Jonathan's gun in the flower bed that night. She left the door unlocked for me.

He had taken Mariah and Lillian from the parking lot at the

motel to his warehouse in the city. He had untied their hands and let them use the bathroom, then tied them up again. He left Lillian lying on the brocaded couch, whimpering. Across the room behind a row of lifesize Grecian statues, he had laid Mariah on a mattress on the floor. She had passed out again before he left. It had been a brilliant decision not to kill Lillian immediately. How else could he have convinced Mariah to come rushing out in the middle of the night? And long ago he had made it his business to be able to slip in and out of his apartment building without being seen. It really wasn't hard if you wore a cleaning crew uniform, pulled a cap down over your face, and had a phony ID around your neck.

He had gotten back home just before daybreak. Now he didn't know what to do except to act as if this was a normal day in his life. He was tired, but he did not go to bed and try to sleep. Instead, he showered and dressed, and had his usual breakfast of cereal, toast, and coffee.

He left his apartment shortly after nine and set about being visible in his normal routine. Trying to stay calm, he comforted himself with the realization that if that crook was lying about seeing anyone running out of the house, and if he had seen that picture in the newspaper, he could just as easily pick out one of the other three guys to describe to whoever was drawing the sketch.

Until he knew where this was going, he'd have to stay away from the warehouse. Mariah and Lillian, he thought sarcastically, I guess you'll get to live a little while longer. But if the sketch looks like me, and they tell me to come in and talk to them again, they still won't have enough at that point to arrest me. I'll only become what they call "a person of interest." They'll probably start following me, but that won't do them any good. I'm not going near the warehouse until I know where I stand.

Even if it takes weeks.

76

After speaking to Lloyd Scott, Detective Benet called Judge Brown at his chambers and received authorization to place a trace on Mariah's cell phone and to get records of the incoming and outgoing calls, both for that phone and the one at her parents' house.

"Judge, there's a strong probability that Mariah Lyons is missing," he explained. "I need a list of the last five days' calls so that I can see who she's been talking to, and I need access to her call log for the next five days so I can see who calls her."

His next call was to the designated contact at the telephone company who handled emergent judicial orders.

"I'll get right on it, sir," he was told.

Ten minutes later Simon had the location of the cell phone. "Detective Benet, we've got a hit from Route 4 East in Fort Lee, just before the bridge. It's coming from the immediate area around the Raines Motel."

Rita Rodriguez was watching Simon's expression and knew he had received bad news.

"We've got a major problem," he said. "The signal is coming from around the Raines Motel. That place is a total dump. We can be there in ten minutes. Let's go."

They raced down the highway with their lights flashing and were soon standing outside Mariah's car. The driver's door was slightly ajar. They could see a woman's shoulder bag on the passenger seat. As they opened the door carefully to preserve any fingerprints, the sound of a cell phone ringing came from inside the bag.

Simon reached for the phone and looked at the caller ID. It was Richard Callahan. Simon quickly scanned the log and saw that it was his fourth call in the last two hours. There were two others from the Lyons home, which he knew would have been from the housekeeper, and two more from Alvirah Meehan in the last hour.

Two days ago when Lillian Stewart disappeared, Richard Callahan claimed that he had been trying to reach her all day, Simon thought. He's covering his tracks again.

"Simon, look at this." Rita was shining her flashlight on the unmistakable signs of smeared blood on the rear door on the driver's side of the car. She pointed the flashlight to the ground. Drops of dried blood became visible on the cracked macadam of the parking lot.

Simon crouched down to examine the droplets closely. "I don't know what the hell she was doing here, but it looks like she was grabbed when she was getting out of the car. Rita, we've got to get that composite right away."

"The guys picking up Wally Gruber should be on their way back now," Rita said quickly. "I'll call and tell them to turn on the flashers and be there as soon as they can."

Almost beside himself with frustration, Simon barked, "Do it. I'll get the tech unit to come here and go over the car for prints." He paused. "And I'll have to let Lloyd Scott know what's going on."

Three missing women in five days, he thought grimly. All of them connected to Jonathan Lyons. And probably connected to that parchment.

His introspection was interrupted by Rita. "The guys with Gruber are already over the bridge. They'll be waiting for us at the office."

77

Her head hurt so much. Mariah tried to touch it but could not raise her hand that high. She opened her eyes. The light was dim, but she could see that she was in some kind of strange place. She lifted her head and looked around.

She was in a museum.

I'm dreaming. It has to be a nightmare. This can't be.

Then she remembered Lillian's call. I went rushing to meet her. He was waiting for me. He slammed my head against the car. Then I was in a car trunk and Lillian was there.

Bits and pieces about the ride came back to her. It was so bumpy. My head kept hitting against the floor. Lillian was next to me. She was tied up too.

Mariah recalled hearing the sound of a door opening, like a garage door going up. Then he opened the trunk and dragged Lillian out. She kept pleading, "Please don't hurt me. Please let me go."

Then he came back for me, she remembered. He picked me up and carried me to a lift. And then it went up. And then we were here in the museum. He took me into a bathroom and untied my hands. He said, "I'll let you have a few minutes in here." I tried to lock the door behind him, but there was no lock. I heard him laughing. He knew I was going to try to lock it. I tried to wash the crusted blood from my head and face, but then I started bleeding again. I pressed a towel against the gash and then he came back.

Mariah remembered how helpless she had felt when he retied her hands and legs and dragged her into this room and threw her down on a mattress on the floor. He didn't care at all that I was still bleeding, she thought. He wanted to hurt me.

Her head was throbbing but her thoughts were starting to come more clearly. He had held up what looked to be a large antique silver jewelry case and opened the lid. He reached inside and took something out. He held it over my head, she thought. It looked like one of those rolled-up scrolls that she had seen in her father's study.

"Look at it, Mariah," he demanded. "It is so unfortunate that your father would not sell this to me. If he had, he would be alive today and so would Rory. And neither would Lillian be here with us. But that was not meant to be. Now I want to honor what I know would be your father's fondest wish: that you touch it before you join him. I know how much you have missed him."

He brushed the parchment against her neck, taking care that it did not come into contact with any of the blood that was still oozing from her forehead.

And then he had laid it back into the silver chest, which he placed on the marble table next to her.

I don't remember what happened after that, Mariah thought. I must have passed out again. Why didn't he kill me right away? What is he waiting for?

She strained to raise her wrists and look at her watch. It was twenty minutes past eleven. When I was in the bathroom it was almost five o'clock, she thought. I've been unconscious for more than six hours. Is he still here? I don't see him.

Where is Lillian?

"Lillian," she called out, "Lillian."

For a moment there was no answer, but then a sudden terrified wail from near the center of the room made her cringe. "Mariah, he's going to kill us!" Lillian screamed. "He only held off killing me so that he could use me to trick you into coming to the motel. When he comes back, I know what's going to happen. I know what's going to happen."

The sound of Lillian's gasping sobs became a crescendo of terror that echoed throughout the cavernous room.

78

Wally Gruber did not know why the detective who was driving him to the New Jersey prosecutor's office suddenly stepped on the gas and turned on the flashers. "I'm in no hurry," he chided them. "I'm enjoying the ride. In fact I wouldn't mind if you wanted to stop for coffee on the way."

He was sitting in the backseat of the van, shackles covering his wrists and legs, and separated from the front area by a locked grille. There were two other detectives escorting him, one in the front passenger seat and the other sitting next to him in the secured section.

None of the three detectives answered him. Wally shrugged his shoulders. They're not too sociable today, he thought. So what? He closed his eyes, concentrating again on the face that might get him back on the street much sooner. He had made bets with some of his fellow inmates. In fact they had a pool going. The odds were up to four to one that he wasn't bluffing about seeing the killer of that professor.

They weren't in the parking lot of the courthouse long enough for him to get a decent breath of fresh air before he was in the elevator going up to the prosecutor's office. He was taken straight to a room where there was a guy sitting at a computer who stood up as they entered. "Mr. Gruber," he said, "I am Detective Howard Washington. I will be working with you to formulate the composite."

"Call me Wally, Howie," Gruber replied cheerfully.

Washington ignored the invitation. "Please sit down, Mr. Gruber. I will explain to you exactly how we're going to do this. I am informing you that this process will be videotaped. I will first take a detailed description from you of the person whom you have indicated you saw, then I will be using the computer to show you images of various head and facial parts, such as the forehead, eyes, nose, and chin, as well as head and facial hair."

"Don't stress over any facial hair, Howie. He didn't have any." Wally sat down next to Washington and leaned back in the chair. "I wouldn't mind a nice hot cup of coffee," he said. "No milk. Two sugars."

Simon Benet and Rita Rodriguez had just come into the room. Simon felt his blood boil as he listened to Wally's nonchalant comments. He felt Rita put a restraining hand on his arm. I'd love to deck this guy, he thought.

"I'm going to start with some very specific questions with regard to the person's physical appearance. I will be taking notes as you speak. I'm going to start with our initial checklist."

The questions began. "Male or female . . . color of skin . . . approximate age . . . approximate height and weight . . ."

When Detective Washington had completed the preliminary questions, he started putting up multiple images on the screen.

Wally began shaking his head, then said, "Hold it. That's the way the hair looked when he pulled the scarf down. You're hitting the nail on the head."

Simon Benet and Rita Rodriguez looked at each other. From Wally's description they already knew how the composite would come out. The question burning in both of their minds was, where and when had Gruber seen this face? Was it the night Jonathan Lyons was shot or was it from a picture in a newspaper after Lyons had died?

They waited until Wally Gruber, looking at the current composite on the screen, said to Detective Washington, "You did a good job, Howie. That's him."

Simon and Rita stared at the screen.

"It's as though Greg Pearson sat for the picture," Rita said as Simon nodded in agreement.

79

After she called Lloyd to tell him that Mariah might be missing, Alvirah rushed to shower and dress, leaving the half-eaten Danish on her plate. Her heart pounding with anxiety, she dressed in her lightweight running suit, swallowed her vitamins, and hastily put on some light makeup. Just as she was finishing, Lloyd phoned to say that Mariah's car had been found.

"I'm on my way to the prosecutor's office," he said tersely. "That guy Gruber should be there by now. If he's on the level, saving Mariah's life may depend on the description he gives to them."

"Lloyd, I have had my suspicions," Alvirah said. "And since yesterday I'm ninety-nine percent sure that I'm right. Albert West told the prosecutor's office that Charles Michaelson was trying to sell the parchment, but then I made Albert call his source, who admitted that the so-called tip came from an anonymous phone call. I think the person who made that phone call was trying to set Michaelson up. I just don't believe Michaelson or West is involved."

Warming up to her theory, Alvirah paced back and forth across the bedroom as she spoke. "That leaves Richard Callahan and Greg Pearson. My gut tells me Richard is not a killer. I knew he was holding back on something, and then I realized it's as plain as the nose on your face. He's so in love with Mariah that he's been willing to spend most of his own money to try to get that parchment back."

Hoping she was getting through to Lloyd, Alvirah said, "Lloyd, I can't be one hundred percent positive until we see that composite, but that leaves only Greg Pearson."

"Alvirah, hold on. I'm Kathleen's attorney. With the exception of Mariah, there's nobody who wants to get the real killer more than I do. So even if everything you surmise is true, I can tell you right now that no jury would ever convict Greg Pearson on evidence that consists primarily of Wally Gruber's identification. Pearson's attorney would annihilate him on cross-examination."

"I agree with you. I understand what you're saying. But he has to have a place where he's kept the parchment. He'd never be dumb enough to hide it in his apartment or office or a safe-deposit box. But if he thought that Gruber had identified somebody else and he was out of the woods, he might feel comfortable going to wherever that parchment is hidden."

Pleading her case to Lloyd, Alvirah tried to keep her voice from rising too much. "And you know, I think even the detectives are pretty convinced that Lillian had the parchment under her arm when she got on the subway. She had to be going somewhere to meet someone. I think it was Greg. Think about it. Rory could have let him in the house that night. She knew where Jonathan kept the gun. Rory could have easily left it out somewhere for him. She's an ex-con who skipped parole. Maybe Greg found out about her secret past and threatened to expose her if she didn't cooperate. And then he had to get rid of Rory because she was a danger to him."

"Alvirah, what you're saying makes sense, but why would he go after Mariah?" Lloyd said.

"Because he was crazy about her and could see that Mariah was crazy about Richard. I could always tell that he was jealous. He never took his eyes off her. Add that to his being terrified that he would be identified from that composite. I think all this probably sent him over the edge. My opinion is that the only way we have any hope of finding Mariah is to make Greg Pearson believe the composite shows someone else so he's sure he can come and go without anyone watching him."

Alvirah took a breath. Her voice passionate, she added, "I've got to talk to Simon Benet. If that sketch is of Greg, Simon has simply got to lead him into believing that he's in the clear. After that, Greg has to be followed around the clock."

"Alvirah, as much as you're helping, I don't think that Detective Benet will tell you about the results of the composite," Lloyd said. "But, as Kathleen's attorney, he *will* tell me. I will absolutely convey to him everything you have said, and I will call you back right after I speak to him."

"Lloyd, please make him understand that if Mariah is still alive, this may be her only chance to survive."

Willy had been making the bed and listening to Alvirah's side of the conversation. "Honey, it sounds to me like you got this whole thing figured out. I hope they'll listen to what you said. It sure makes sense to me. You know, I never said anything, but whenever we were with Greg at Jonathan's dinners, I could never quite figure out what made him tick. He always acted like the others were the ones who knew the most about that ancient stuff, but a couple of times he came out with a comment that said to me he knew a whole lot more than he let on."

Alvirah's face crumpled. "I keep thinking about poor Kathleen and how awful it would be for her if Mariah is gone. Even with the Alzheimer's, at some point it would sink in and it would kill her."

Willy was about to place the decorative pillows against the headboard. His forehead deeply lined, his warm blue eyes clouded with concern, he said, "Honey, I think you'd better start getting ready to hear some very bad news about Mariah."

"I won't believe that," Alvirah said forcefully. "Willy, I *can't* believe that."

Willy dropped the pillows and hurried to put his arms around her. "Hang on, sweetheart," he said. "Hang on."

The loud sound of the telephone ringing startled both of them. It was the doorman. "Willy, a Mr. Richard Callahan is here. He says he has to see you right away."

"Send him up, Tony," Willy said. "Thanks."

As they waited for Richard to come up, the phone rang yet again. It was Lloyd Scott. "Alvirah, you were right. I'm at the prosecutor's office and I've seen the composite. It's a dead ringer for Greg Pearson. I've been talking to Simon Benet. He agrees that at this point your suggestion is probably the best option they have. We know Pearson is in his office. Benet is going to make the call to him in about a half an hour, after he's sure the New York guys are in place to follow him."

80

At quarter of twelve, the phone in Greg's office rang. "Detective Simon Benet is on the line, sir," his secretary said.

His palms sweaty, his mind and body tingling with fear and apprehension, Greg picked up the phone. Was Benet going to ask him to come in for another talk?

"Good morning, Mr. Pearson," Benet said. "Sorry to disturb you."

"Not at all." He sounds pretty friendly, Greg thought.

"Mr. Benet, it's very important I get in touch with Professor Michaelson immediately. He's not answering his home phone or his cell phone and he's not at his office at the university. We're contacting all of his friends to see if we can locate him. By any chance have you spoken to him recently or has he otherwise mentioned any travel plans he may have?"

A gigantic wave of relief swept over Greg Pearson. That Gruber lowlife never saw me. He must have seen that picture of all of us that was in the newspapers and decided to pick out Charles. And probably Albert told Benet that Charles was shopping the parchment. My anonymous call to Desmond Rogers did the trick.

Once again, he felt fully in control, master of his universe. His voice cordial, he said, "I'm afraid I can't help you, Detective Benet. I haven't spoken to Charles since we were at dinner at Mariah's home on Tuesday evening. That was when you and Detective Rodriguez stopped by."

"Thank you, Mr. Pearson," Benet said. "If you do happen to hear from Professor Michaelson, I would appreciate it very much if you'd ask him to call me."

"Of course I will, Detective, although I must say that I think it most unlikely that Charles would contact me. Our mutual friendship with Jonathan Lyons and my going on his archaeological expeditions was pretty much the basis of our connection."

"I see. Well, I've already given you my card, but if you don't have it handy, perhaps you'd like to jot down my cell number now."

"Of course." Greg took out his pen, wrote the number, exchanged a pleasant good-bye with Benet, and put down the phone. He took a long deep breath, then got up.

Time to visit the ladies and say good-bye, he thought. Then he smiled.

Maybe I'll treat them to lunch first.

81

There are probably New York cops in plainclothes all over the place," Alvirah said. "I didn't ask for permission for us to follow Greg ourselves because I know I would have been told in no uncertain terms to stay out of it. But none of us can sit home at a time like this."

They were in the car on West 57th Street, stopped in a no-parking zone a few yards from the busy entrance to the Fisk Building, where Greg had his office on the tenth floor. Richard, his face and lips deadly pale, his expression agonized, was in the front seat with Willy. Alvirah was perched on the edge of the backseat behind Richard.

"Honey, one of those traffic cops is going to chase us away any minute," Willy said.

"If that happens, Richard can get out and keep an eye on that door," Alvirah replied. "We'll circle the block for as long as we have to. If Greg comes out and gets on the subway, Richard can follow him and stay in touch with us."

"Honey, if he spots Richard, he won't go to whatever hiding place he has."

"With that hooded sweatshirt of yours covering Richard's hair and with those dark glasses covering half of his face, unless Greg was two feet away from Richard, he wouldn't recognize him."

"If he gets on the subway, I'll make damn sure he doesn't see me," Richard said, his voice deadly calm.

"I keep going over and over this," Alvirah said. "If I hadn't lost Lillian the other day, Mariah might not be missing now. I'll never stop blaming myself because—*there he is!*"

Their eyes were riveted to the sight of Greg Pearson leaving the building. They watched as he walked the few steps to the corner and turned right on Broadway. Richard leapt out of the car. "He may be going into the subway," he said.

Willy started the car but by the time they reached the corner, the traffic light was red. "Oh, God, please don't let Richard lose him," Alvirah moaned.

When they were finally able to make the turn, they could see Richard's hooded figure turning onto 56th Street and heading west. "We can't follow him there," Willy said. "It's a one-way street. I'll have to turn on 55th and hope we can meet up with him."

Alvirah's phone rang. It was Richard. "I'm half a block behind him. He's still walking."

"Stay on the line," Alvirah ordered.

Willy drove slowly, going west on 55th Street, stopping and starting to stay even with Richard's pace.

"He's crossing Eighth Avenue . . . Ninth Avenue . . . Tenth Avenue . . . He's going into a luncheonette," Richard told them. "Hang on."

When Richard spoke again it was to report that Greg had come out of the luncheonette, carrying a brown paper bag. "It looks pretty heavy," he said, a hopeful note entering his voice. "There's a parking garage across the street. He's going into it."

"On that block he can only go east," Alvirah said. "We can turn right at Eleventh Avenue and come back up 56th Street. We'll pick you up there."

Three minutes later they were turning onto 56th Street. Richard was crouched down between two parked cars. As they watched, an older black sedan came up the ramp from inside the garage. There was no mistaking that it was Greg at the wheel. As he turned left onto the street, Richard darted back into the car.

"He's driving a different car!" Alvirah exclaimed.

Careful to keep several vehicles between them and the black sedan, they followed him down to lower Manhattan, then across town to the South Street area near the Williamsburg Bridge. Greg made a turn onto a shabby street with a row of boarded-up ware-houses. "Be careful. Don't get too close to him," Richard warned Willy.

Willy stopped the car. "He can't be going much further," he said. "This is a dead-end street. I know this area. When I was in high school I used to work part-time stacking cartons onto trucks. There was a loading area for all of those warehouses."

They watched as the black sedan traveled to the end of the street and then made a right turn. "He has to be going into one of those buildings," Willy said. "But it looks as if they're all shut down." He waited until Greg's car was out of sight, then followed him, stop-ping before they would become visible in the open area behind the buildings.

Richard got out of the car and looked around the corner to see where Greg was going. Then he raced back into the car, shouting, "Follow him, Willy. He's opening that large garage door. Don't let him lock us out."

Willy stepped on the gas. The car skidded as he made the sharp turn, then closed in on the sedan and tried to follow it into the garage.

The forty-foot-wide garage door was coming down. Alvirah shrieked as it hit the roof of their car and continued to grind lower. The doors flew open and they all managed to scramble out, just be-fore they would have been trapped inside the mangled frame.

Three feet from the ground, the garage door was finally stopped by the body of the crushed automobile. For a moment they stood in shocked silence. Then they heard the sound of feet pounding across the macadam. "Police!" someone yelled. "Stop!"

Richard was already on the ground, crawling into the warehouse through the space held open by the car.

"Stay back," one of the detectives warned Alvirah and Willy as they rushed to follow Richard. "I'm ordering you. Stay back."

82

He was upstairs, with the lift raised back up, again flush with the ceiling of the lower level, before they were able to stop him. How long would it take before they found the switch to bring the lift down again? Not long, he thought. I know it won't be long.

That detective was sharp enough to make me think that I was safe. But I'm not safe. I'm doomed. It is the end. I fell for their trap.

Furious, Greg flung aside the bag of sandwiches. He had only a dim light on in his private empire. He flipped on the overhead lights and looked around. Beautiful. Magnificent. Spectacular. Art. Antiquity. All worthy of the finest museums in the world. And he had gathered it here himself.

When he was nineteen, the lonely nerd, he had accomplished with a computer what Antonio Stradivari had accomplished with a violin. He had masterminded programming through unimaginable flights of fantasy. By the time he was twenty-five, he had quietly become a multimillionaire.

Six years ago, on a whim, I went on that dig and discovered the world that I belonged in, he thought. I listened and learned from Jonathan and Charles and Albert, and in the end I surpassed all of them with my expertise. I began to manipulate and divert shipments of priceless antiques without a single trace of where they had gone.

It was glorious when I touched that sacred parchment. When I told Jonathan about the extraordinary computer program that I had developed to authenticate antiquities, he let me examine it. The parchment is authentic. It's been handled by many people over the centuries, but there is a single DNA sample on it that is extraordinary. This unique DNA carries chromosomes with only the traits of a mother, who has to be the Virgin Mary. He had no human father.

This letter was written by the Christ. He wrote it to a friend, and two thousand years later I had to kill a man whom I loved as a friend because I had to have it.

Greg walked into the room that was full of his treasures. For once he did not pause and savor their beauty but looked first at Lillian. She was lying near the sofa, with its golden brocade and intricate carvings, where he always chose to sit.

Since Wednesday morning, when he had first brought her here and then decided to wait before he killed her, he had enjoyed his brief visits, sitting on this sofa with her feet on his lap and talking to her. He had relished explaining to her the history of one after another of his treasures. "I bought this artifact from a dealer in Cairo recently," he'd said about one artifact. "Their museum was looted during a civilian uprising."

Now he stood over Lillian. Her wide brown eyes were frantic with fear. "The police are surrounding me!" he shouted. "They're downstairs. They'll find a way to get up here."

"You're so greedy, Lily. If you had only given the parchment back to Mariah, you would have a clear conscience. But you didn't do that."

"Please . . . don't . . . no . . . no . . ."

As Greg slid a silken cord around Lillian's neck, he was sobbing. "I offered Mariah the love I never thought I would be capable of feeling for any human being. I worshipped the ground she walked on. And what did I get in return? She couldn't wait the other night to finish dinner and get rid of me. Now I'm going to get rid of her and rid of you."

83

This place is empty, but he can't have vanished into thin air," one of the New York detectives snapped. "This is the ground floor. There's got to be a way to get upstairs. I heard something, but I don't see anything." He flipped on the radio attached to his belt and called for backup cars to respond.

The second detective began thumping on the walls, hoping to hear a hollow sound from within.

Ignoring the orders of the police, Alvirah and Willy crawled past the wreckage of their car and into the garage. They had heard the detective bark his call for backup into the radio. It may be too late, Alvirah thought frantically. Greg has to know that he's trapped. Even if Mariah is still alive, we may not be able to get to her in time.

A minute passed . . . two minutes . . . three minutes. It was an eternity.

In desperation, Richard ran to the light switch and jiggled it. For a moment the room plunged into total darkness, then the lights came back on. "There's got to be a switch somewhere that will open something," he said bitterly. Alvirah hurried over to thump the area around the light switch herself. Then she looked down. "Richard, Richard!" She was pointing to the cover of an electrical socket just above the floor. "See . . . it's not embedded in the wall."

Richard dropped to the floor and tugged at the outlet. It snapped open. He pressed the button behind it. They heard a loud rumbling sound and as they watched, a huge portion of the ceiling at the far end of the room began to descend.

"That's the lift to get upstairs!" one of the detectives yelled as he raced over to it.

84

In the agonizing forty minutes since she had awakened, Mariah had summoned every ounce of her remaining strength to try to survive. She had managed to wiggle to her feet by leaning her back against the marble table where Greg had laid the silver chest containing the parchment. Inch by painful inch she had pushed her body upward, slipping and sliding back to the floor over and over again until she finally succeeded in standing on her feet. Her light jacket was shredded from being rubbed up and down against the ornate leg of the table, and her back was scraped and raw.

But now she was standing.

It was then that she had heard the rumble of the lift and knew that he had come back. She knew she had only one chance to try to save herself and Lillian.

It was impossible to free or even loosen the bindings around her hands and feet.

She heard Greg get off the lift. Because of the marble statues shielding her, she knew he could not see her. She heard him talking to Lillian, his voice rising with every word.

He was telling her that he had been followed. That the police were downstairs. But he shouted that they wouldn't find the way to get up here in time to save either one of us. Horrified, Mariah listened as he boasted that the parchment was genuine and then sobbed, "I loved Mariah . . ."

Lillian was begging for her life. "Please don't . . . please don't . . ."

Once again, Mariah heard the grinding of the lift. It had to be the police, but they would be too late by the time the lift went down and came back up again.

With her bound wrists she struggled to grasp the silver chest and managed to hold on to it. Her heart pounding, she inched her way past the statues the short distance to the couch, grateful that the heavy grinding of the lift would prevent Greg from hearing her approach.

He can't hear me, but if he looks up it will still be over for both of us, she thought as she shuffled quietly on the heavy carpet the last few steps to the couch.

While Greg wrapped the cord around Lillian's neck, Mariah raised the silver chest and with all her strength smashed it down on the back of his neck. With a startled grunt, Greg toppled over Lillian and slid to the floor.

For a long minute Mariah stood leaning on the couch to keep herself from falling. She was still fiercely holding the chest. Balancing it on the back of the couch, she opened the lid and took out the parchment. Touching it only with the tips of her fingers, swollen from the tight cords around her wrists and arms, she held the parchment to her lips.

That was the image that Richard saw as the lift stopped. Two detectives raced over and tackled Greg as he was struggling to his feet. A third detective rushed to Lillian and released the cord that had been tightening around her neck. "You're all right now," he said. "It's over. You're safe."

Mariah managed a weak smile as she watched Richard running

toward her. Instantly realizing that she was holding the sacred parchment, he gently slid it from her hands, set it down on a table, and enveloped her in his arms.

"I didn't think I'd ever see you again," he said, his voice breaking.

Mariah felt a sudden peace, a peace that was beyond understanding, fill her being. She had saved the parchment and by doing that she knew that she had at long last made her own peace with her beloved father.

Epilogue

Six months later, Mariah and Richard walked arm in arm through the empty rooms of her childhood home in Mahwah. These were the last few minutes that she would ever be here. She had thought in the beginning about staying, more for her mother's sake than hers, but as much as she had always loved this home, it would forever be the place where her father had been murdered. And it would forever be the place where, as Greg Pearson had confessed to the police, Rory had so treacherously left the gun outside and the door unlocked for him.

After the charges against Kathleen had been dismissed, Mariah had brought her mother home. As she had feared, it quickly became clear that this house was no longer a comfort to Kathleen but rather a constant reminder of the horror she had endured.

On Kathleen's first night back, Mariah had watched as her mother had gone straight into the closet in the study, where she curled up on the floor and sobbed. It was at that moment that she knew that Greg Pearson had not only robbed them of her father but had also robbed them of their home. It was time to leave it forever.

The movers had just loaded the last of the furniture and the carpets and the boxes of dishes and linens and books that she had kept for the roomy new apartment. Mariah was glad that her mother wasn't here to see this. She knew how painful it would be. Mom has adjusted better than I ever expected, she thought wistfully. The impact of the Alzheimer's had worsened and now Mariah had to comfort herself with the knowledge that her mother, whose memory had virtually slipped away, was content and safe. The nursing home where she now lived was in Manhattan, only two blocks from where Mariah and Richard would soon be living. In the six months since they'd moved Kathleen there, Mariah had been able to visit her almost every day.

"A penny for your thoughts?" Richard asked.

"I wouldn't know where to begin," she answered. "Maybe there just are no words."

"I know," he said gently. "I know."

Mariah thought with relief about how Greg Pearson had pleaded guilty to the murders of her father and Rory and to kidnapping her and Lillian. He would be sentenced to life without parole before judges in New Jersey and New York in the next two weeks.

As much as she dreaded seeing him again, she intended to go to both courtrooms and to speak about the wonderful human being that her father had been and the devastation that had been inflicted on her mother and her. After she was finished, she would know that she had done all she could for the two loving parents she had been so blessed to have. And Richard would be standing next to her.

He had been with her in the hospital that night as the doctors had cleaned and stitched the painful gash on her head, and he had barely left her side in the weeks thereafter. "And I'm never leaving again," he had told her.

Wally Gruber had received five-year sentences in New York and New Jersey, which he would serve concurrently. Peter Jones, the new county prosecutor, had sat down with Mariah and Lloyd and Lisa Scott, and they had given their approval to this reduction in his sentence, which otherwise would have been three times longer. "He didn't do anything out of the goodness of his heart, but he did save my mother from spending the rest of her life in a mental hospital," Mariah said.

"I'm glad he took my jewels and I'm glad he got them back," Lisa Scott declared.

After his sentencing in Hackensack, a cheerful Wally had left the courtroom beaming. "Piece of cake," he'd said loudly to his long-suffering lawyer, who knew that the judge had heard the comment and was not pleased.

In a plea agreement, also with Mariah's approval, Lillian had been sentenced to community service for trying to sell the rare stolen parchment. The judge had agreed that after her horrible ordeal, there was no real need for further punishment. The irony was that when Greg had planted the rumor that Charles was shopping the parchment, he had not been wrong.

Jonathan had showed it to Charles and told him that Lillian was holding it for safekeeping. Jonathan was horrified when Charles offered to sell it for him. After Jonathan's death, Charles called Lillian, offered to find a black market buyer for it, and split the profits.

After Mariah and Richard stepped out of the house for the last time, they walked to the curb where his car was parked and got inside. "It will be nice to be with your mom and dad tonight," she said. "I feel like they're already my family."

"They are, Mariah," Richard whispered. Smiling, he said, "And never forget: As proud as they were when I was in the seminary, I know they can't wait for us to give them grandchildren. And we will."

Alvirah and Willy were getting ready to go to Richard's parents' home for dinner. "Willy, it's been over six weeks since we've seen Mariah and Richard," Alvirah said as she reached into the closet for her coat and scarf.

"Not since we met them and Father Aiden and the Scotts for dinner at Neary's Restaurant," Willy agreed. "I've missed them."

"It has to be hard for her." Alvirah sighed. "Today was the last day she'll ever spend in her childhood home. That's got to be so tough. But I'm so glad that they're moving into that lovely apartment after the wedding. They can't help but be happy there."

When they arrived at the dinner they tightly embraced Richard and Mariah. In the few minutes that they allowed themselves to discuss the awful events they'd experienced, Alvirah told Mariah that, despite all of the tragedy, she had known when she touched the sacred parchment that she was holding something very special and wonderful.

"That's right, Alvirah," Mariah said, her voice barely above a whisper. "And what is also very special is that it is back in the Vatican Library where it belongs. And my dad can rest in peace."

ML   4/12